"We wanted to `chat with Kass and find out if Persephone was jealous of Marisol." Charlene put down her phone. "Could Persephone have stolen her clients?"

"And?" Jack prompted.

"We never got to ask," Avery said.

"*If* Marisol is dead, that would be a strong motive," Jack said. "From everything we've learned, the Santa Muerte shop was very lucrative."

"Money and passion," Avery said. "Rico was a dog and sleeping around. What are the chances that he'll stay faithful to Isabella?"

Charlene's mind circled Persephone. Could the witch have killed Marisol to get not only Rico, but Marisol's clients?

It made twisted sense, and Charlene really hoped that Marisol and the expensive statue were safely tucked away in the Bahamas. . . .

Books by Traci Wilton

MRS. MORRIS AND THE GHOST

MRS. MORRIS AND THE WITCH

MRS. MORRIS AND THE GHOST OF
CHRISTMAS PAST

MRS. MORRIS AND THE SORCERESS

MRS. MORRIS AND THE VAMPIRE

MRS. MORRIS AND THE POT OF GOLD

MRS. MORRIS AND THE WOLFMAN

MRS. MORRIS AND THE MERMAID

MRS. MORRIS AND THE VENOMOUS
VALENTINE

MRS. MORRIS AND THE DAY OF THE DEAD

And writing as Traci Hall
MURDER IN A SCOTTISH SHIRE

MURDER IN A SCOTTISH GARDEN

MURDER AT A SCOTTISH SOCIAL

MURDER AT A SCOTTISH WEDDING

MURDER AT A SCOTTISH CASTLE

MURDER AT A SCOTTISH CHRISTMAS

MURDER AT THE SCOTTISH GAMES

Published by Kensington Publishing Corp.

Mrs. Morris
and the
Day of The
Dead

TRACI WILTON

Kensington Publishing Corp.
kensingtonbooks.com

KENSINGTON BOOKS are published by

Kensington Publishing Corp.
900 Third Avenue
New York, NY 10022

All Kensington titles, imprints, and distributed lines are available at special quantity discounts for bulk purchases for sales promotion, premiums, fund-raising, educational, or institutional use.

Special book excerpts or customized printings can also be created to fit specific needs. For details, write or phone the office of the Kensington Sales Manager: Attn.: Sales Department. Kensington Publishing Corp., 900 Third Avenue, New York, NY 10022. Phone: 1-800-221-2647.

KENSINGTON and the KENSINGTON COZIES teapot logo Reg US Pat. & TM Off.

First Printing: September 2025
ISBN: 978-1-4967-4882-9

ISBN: 978-1-4967-4883-6 (ebook)

10 9 8 7 6 5 4 3 2 1

Printed in the United States of America

The authorized representative in the EU for product safety and compliance is eucomply OU, Parnu mnt 139b-14, Apt 123
Tallinn, Berlin 11317, hello@eucompliancepartner.com

I'd like to dedicate this book to my family and friends, grateful that most of us are readers and when things go sideways, we have an escape. Yes, nonfiction and audiobooks count!

ACKNOWLEDGMENTS

I'd like to thank Evan Marshall, my agent, and John Scognamiglio, my editor at Kensington, as well as the book production team. I'd like to thank Patrice Wilton, who started this Salem B-and-B series with me and then had the temerity to retire. I miss creating worlds with you but imagine you playing tennis and drinking margaritas in your spare time instead of being worried about page count.

While writing *Mrs. Morris and the Day of the Dead*, I pictured the readers that I've met and become friends with along this storytelling journey, and I hope this book resonates. The characters are very real to me, too. Thanks to Sheryl McGavin, and to my mother, Judi Potter. Thanks to my hubby, Christopher, who never complains about sandwiches again when I'm on deadline.

Mrs. Morris
and the
Day of The
Dead

CHAPTER 1

First week of October
Salem, MA

Charlene Morris hated to be late and yet that is exactly what she was—L A T E late. Her appointment with Kass Fortune at Fortune's Tea Shoppe had been at three, and it was now a quarter past the hour.

Her own fault for losing track of time posting photos on her Thursday blog for the B&B. Charlene grabbed a cardigan sweater from her bedroom and entered the living area of her two-room suite. The television played softly in the background, and her handsome spectral roommate, Dr. Jack Strathmore, sprawled on his favorite armchair. She patted the side pocket of her purse with an explosive sigh of frustration. "Have you seen my keys?"

"Here you are, my dear." Jack's captivating turquoise blue eyes twinkled as he floated the keys to her from the recesses of her love seat, where she must have dropped them when she'd tossed her purse last night after her dinner date with Sam.

Detective Sam Holden had an even fuller plate these days than usual, but he and Charlene did their best to meet once a week for at least a cup of coffee. To say her life was complicated was an understatement.

Jack had a wicked jealous streak. He loved Charlene though he realized he could never be with her in a romantic way. She loved Jack, too and credited him for easing her through her grief. He was her best friend.

Being careful with Jack's feelings meant keeping hers for Sam on the down-low. He knew they were dating and even empathized with their situation. Charlene had wanted slow and gotten a turtle's pace as Sam's parents had moved in with him in April after his mother's fall when she'd broken her hip.

"Thanks, Jack."

"Now, take a deep breath before you screech out of here like your tail is on fire as you tend to do," Jack instructed. "You need to arrive at Kass's in one piece . . . and then hurry home to share all the details." His low chuckle resonated around the room.

Jack was tied to this house as his death had occurred here and he couldn't leave the property, so he hungered for her stories. He liked Kass Fortune and thought her teas smelled wonderful, though he couldn't taste them. Charlene didn't have Kass over very often as she could sense ghosts, and they'd wanted to keep Jack's existence quiet.

Best laid plans, as Avery Shriver had been injured on the head in February and returned home from the hospital with the ability to clearly see Jack. The orphan had captured their hearts at sixteen and had her own room in the mansion on the very top floor. She was now nineteen and in her second year of college, studying to be a detective. Their silver Persian cat Silva could also see Jack.

"I wonder why Kass sounded so urgent." A teasing glint entered Jack's gaze. "Maybe she's had a premonition and wants to read your tea leaves."

"I'm not interested," Charlene replied firmly. Kass never pushed her psychic gifts on Charlene.

Her beloved soul mate, Jared, had been killed by a drunk driver over four years earlier. Would knowing his life might be cut short have changed anything? She didn't think so. They'd been so close that she'd unintentionally excluded anyone else from their duo. His death had gutted her.

Charlene had moved from Chicago three years prior to escape her sorrow and start over. She'd been more like Sam and hadn't believed in the paranormal or magic. She hadn't understood Salem's touristy vibe, or that it was known as Witch City for a reason. Now she counted not just Kass, but the Flint family, witches who traced their lineage to those days of old and the lying lasses who'd been hanged, among her dearest friends. The witch hunters hadn't been *all* wrong.

She hadn't believed in ghosts either, yet Jack was undeniable. He'd showed up in her living room, yanking on her heartstrings to help him find answers about his demise. They'd discovered that Jack had been murdered. She'd told Sam that her mansion was haunted, but he didn't change his mind. He saw nothing. Felt nothing. Though she knew differently, there was no way to prove it to the facts-only detective.

She'd probably make a mint if she opened her home to paranormal ghost hunters, but she preferred to offer an elegant oasis in the tourist town. Their B&B was lauded for her housekeeper Minnie Johnson's breakfasts and happy hours. She'd never regretted her choice.

Glancing into the small mirror on the wall by her desk, Charlene paused to take in her image. Hazel eyes lined in dark brown, brunette hair in a long ponytail, pale mouth. "I need lipstick!" Inching closer to her midforties every day, she noted the crow's feet and laugh lines. To fix, or not?

"You are beautiful," Jack assured her. "If you must, apply it when you get there. Hurry!"

He gave her a gentle air push toward the door.

Charlene smiled at Jack, pocketed her keys, and reached for the knob. Her phone hovered between her nose and the door.

"Almost forgot this," Jack said, tugging her ponytail.

"Thanks!" It was very handy to have a ghost as a best friend.

"You can call Kass on Bluetooth from the car. No speeding."

She waggled her fingers, not making any promises as she entered the kitchen.

"Going somewhere?" Minnie asked, eyeing Charlene's cardigan and purse. Her housekeeper had dyed blond hair, silver glasses, and a magic touch in the kitchen.

"Kass's. I'm late. Everything okay here? I hate to

leave you when we have a full house!" The guests were out on day trips and weren't expected back until five or later.

"I'm here if anybody returns early," Minnie said. "I have a spinach and artichoke dip, paired with chips, for happy hour just in case. I'll be prepping for the weekend."

"You're sure?"

Minnie made a shooing motion toward the front door. "I've got it. Say hello to Kass for me."

"I will."

As Charlene passed the dining table, a silver paw snaked out and grabbed her bootlace.

"Silva doesn't want you to go," Jack said.

Charlene bit back her response. After three years she was finally ahead in the game they played of Jack trying to verbally trip her up.

How had three years passed? She'd never believed she'd find happiness again and here she was, overflowing with it.

"Is Avery coming home this weekend?" Minnie asked.

"I think so. It's Seth's birthday."

Avery was dating Seth Gamble, who attended the community college in Salem where he was working toward a business degree. His mother, Dani Gamble, lived in a haunted house as well. Seth couldn't see ghosts, but his brother Stephen could.

"I'll make cake!" Minnie tapped her chin. "He likes orange the best, if I remember correctly."

"Love it. I bought him a gift certificate to Sea Level, if you'd like to sign the card." Since Seth would probably take Avery to the restaurant, it would be a present for her too.

"Perfect." Minnie nudged her down the hall. "Drive safe."

Stepping out of the house to the porch and the crisp autumn air, Charlene perused the gray sky with trepidation, hoping she wasn't in for a rain shower. She climbed into her car and started it, the Pilot's Check Engine light flickering. Probably time to get an oil change. Before she could call Kass, her phone rang, a picture of her friend on the screen.

"Kass!" Charlene said, "I'm on my way. I'm really sorry to be late."

"Don't speed," Kass said. "I was just making sure you didn't forget."

"Worse—I lost track of time. I swear, the older I get the more distracted I am." Recalling Jack's concern she asked, "Is everything okay?"

"No worries. See ya soon." Kass ended the call.

The phone rang and Charlene answered, thinking it would be Kass again.

"Charlene?" Nope. It was her mother. Her parents, Brenda and Michael Woodbridge, had bought a condo on the bay last month. They'd kept their home in Chicago as well, to see how they liked downsizing before making the move permanent.

"Mom!"

"Charlene—you sound out of breath. Is now a bad time?"

"It's fine!"

"I don't believe you," Brenda said.

"I'm in the car, on the way to visit a friend," Charlene said.

"Who? That wonderful man who owns the antique store? I was hoping we could pick up a lamp for the condo there."

"Archie Higgins at Vintage Treasures," Charlene supplied. "But no, not today. I'm on my way to Kass's."

"The tea lady!" her mom said. "You could have just told me that."

"Brenda, you're badgering our daughter."

"Thanks, Dad." Charlene was a grown woman in her forties and they still drove her nuts. Well, mostly her mother. But they had reconciled their relationship to one of forgiveness on Charlene's part and regret on her mother's.

"Sorry!" Mom chirped. "So, when might be a good time to go shopping?"

"Let me check my calendar—this month is the busiest time of year for Salem and the B-and-B."

"It's been an adventure," her mom said. "We love to sit on our balcony and watch the boats, don't we, Michael?"

"We do. It's as close as I want to get and a good compromise. I took Dramamine for motion sickness on our short two-day cruise and was still miserable."

"It was nice that you tried, honey," her mother said.

Charlene owed her mother's friend at church in Chicago a million thanks for setting Brenda down one enlightened day and telling her to shape up and not be so bitter. Probably in nicer, friendlier words, but the gist had brought about a changed lady.

"I'll check my schedule when I get back this afternoon," Charlene promised.

"Thanks! The Holdens, Daniel and June, are coming over for cards on Saturday night and I noticed last week that the corner was dark. A lamp would be perfect."

Daniel and June were Sam's parents, and the couples had taken to one another like celery and hummus.

"I can possibly squeeze in time Saturday right after breakfast when the guests leave for excursions," Charlene said.

"Perfect. I'm teaching June how to play mah-jongg while the guys talk history. Boring to us, but we still have fun."

June had been recuperating after hip surgery in April. Sam was the only one of his siblings to have an extra room, so he'd offered his home to his retired folks. Sam's mom was the life of the party, while Daniel was more reserved, but only a smidge. They had a condo on a golf course in Jupiter, Florida, but had liked Salem so much they'd put off their return until mid-October.

"I'm sure you do."

Charlene adored Sam's family, and though he'd been about to propose on Valentine's Day, the engagement ring had stayed in his pocket since. She accepted responsibility for that as her shock had been apparent.

Jared was her soul mate. Could a woman be lucky enough to have more than one big love? Including Jack, she had three.

"Talk to you later, Charlene," her mom said, pulling her to the present.

"Love you!" her dad chimed in.

"Love you both," Charlene said. Call over, she located a parking spot in a paid lot. There was no time to cruise around for a possibly free one on the street.

After parking, she hurried to the Pedestrian Mall across from the Peabody Essex Museum and the strip of quaint shops that ranged from tarot readers, witch supplies, a bakery, coffee, tea, several cafés and restaurants, a pub, tourists' stores, and a tall parking garage. One of the unsolved riddles in a popular historic town was the issue of where to put the influx of cars. There was only so much room before you hit the water, so up was often the only way to go.

Charlene passed a long bench that had the image of an attractive woman selling real estate printed on it. The photo trend was growing, something that appealed to her marketing background. Real estate, yacht sales, and dental care seemed to be the more popular choices, but she was considering an ad to improve her slower March and April months at the B&B.

Crossing the street, Charlene entered Kass's shop and stopped to take in the scents and sounds. No matter how many times she'd been inside, it was always a balm to her senses: lavender, citrus, sandalwood, cinnamon, and the focal point in the center was a large ceramic water fountain shaped like a goddess pouring tea into a cup. String music played through the speakers but melded with the soothing trickles. Kass had designed the fountain herself.

"Charlene!" Kass, six feet tall, thin, her hair in braids that swung at her hips, rounded the counter. Her eyes sparkled with welcome. Her embrace enveloped Charlene with lemongrass and mint.

"Hi!"

Several customers browsed tea towels and witch-shaped pots, but Kass also carried prettier accoutrements for a variety of tourist's desires. The back wall was all dried teas, and Kass was a genius at putting together blends. She had two college students on staff learning the tea business. Nate was helping a customer, while Sue priced porcelain teacups.

Charlene waved to Sue as Kass tugged her toward the long counter by the register that had four stools where clients could order tea and Kass would read their leaves when they were finished.

A stunning Hispanic woman with wavy chestnut hair to her midback rose and smiled. Her brows were thick over golden-brown eyes, her smile revealing twin dimples and white teeth set off by the perfect deep rose lipstick.

Lipstick!

Oh well, Charlene thought. Served her right for getting lost in her blog photos.

"Charlene, meet my old friend; not old, you know what I mean," Kass laughed, "Isabella Perez."

"So happy to meet you." Isabella exuded charm that suggested she had everything at her fingertips and was genuine in her joy.

Charlene immediately smiled back. "Charlene Morris. I apologize for being late. Thursday is blog day at the B-and-B. To my complete surprise, I've gained almost ten thousand followers since I opened."

Isabella grinned. "I'm one of those followers," she said. "I look forward to your weekly posts about the guests you've had and the places you've gone."

"You do?" Charlene shook her head, pleased. "That's really great to know. So often in marketing you aren't sure if you're reaching your audience or not." She placed her purse on the stool and shrugged out of her cardigan. Her jeans, brown leather boots, and brown plaid Henley was perfect attire on this fall day.

"Tea?" Kass asked. "Bella's is steeping."

Charlene glanced at the counter to see a timer shaped like a flower counting down and at twenty seconds.

"Oolong and lavender with a hint of vanilla," Bella said. She sat, and Charlene chose the seat next to her.

"Smells delicious," Charlene said.

"Charlene likes orange zest, honey, and cinnamon," Kass said. "Would you like a cup?"

"I hate to be predictable, but yes." Charlene laughed.

"You're a woman who knows what she wants," Kass demurred. She'd had Charlene's cup ready to go and added water from an electric kettle, setting the timer for five minutes just as Isabella's dinged.

"What are you having, Kass?" Charlene asked as Kass nudged the cup and saucer toward her old friend.

"Rosebud and hibiscus," Kass said.

Within five minutes they were chatting easily, including Charlene, who felt as if she had known Isabella—*Bella*—for ages.

"What's new in the neighborhood?" Bella asked, leaning her elbow on the counter, her chin in her hand.

Kass picked up her mug. "Hmm. You left two years ago for New York, right?"

"Yes." Some of the joy leaked from Bella's bubbling personality. "When Marisol disappeared."

"What a pretty name," Charlene said.

"My sister was beautiful." Bella's large brown eyes softened.

Charlene shifted to Kass for an explanation. Kass tilted her head, and her braids slid over her shoulder. "Marisol and Isabella owned a tarot shop."

"You read tarot cards?" Charlene asked Bella.

"No," Bella said. "*My* talent is in crystal healing. Marisol could read cards as well as use the pendulum."

"Her boyfriend designed the cards, didn't he? What was his name . . . ?" Kass asked.

Bella flushed. "Rico Flores. He is a very gifted artist."

"Didn't you espouse Santa Muerte?" Kass asked. "Your shop was dedicated to her worship."

"The Death Goddess." Bella nodded. "The practice is one of the fastest growing in the world. I still believe in her."

"I am at a loss," Charlene said with a shrug. "Santa . . ."

"Santa Muerte. The movement was started in Mexico City by a woman in Tepoli, Dona Queta. It's a very rough neighborhood. It had once been known for training athletes, but then drugs and gangs took over. Before her husband helped her build a shrine to Santa Muerte, the figure was hidden away—still prayed to, mind you, but Dona Queta changed that and brought Santa Muerte to the light of day. It's awful that she lost her husband to an organized hit. He and her brother were shot, but her brother pulled through."

"And she still believed in this . . . goddess?" Charlene couldn't imagine that, actually. The Death Goddess would have to go back into the closet.

"Yes. Her faith remained unwavering. Dona Queta was married to her love, Raymundo, for fifteen years." Bella sipped her tea. "She believes the message from Santa Muerte is one of love and acceptance for all. Her followers range from those not embraced by the Catholic religion to police officers—those who work after midnight in the dangerous areas."

"Well, a message of love can't be bad," Charlene said.

Kass offered a tray of fresh-baked cookies. "Vanilla and cinnamon."

"Yum!" Bella took one.

"What happened to Marisol?" Charlene asked. "If it's not prying . . ."

Bella broke off a piece of cookie. "No. She disappeared."

"Did you contact the police?" Charlene asked.

"Yes, but it didn't help. Rico warned me it would be a waste of time. I've never believed Marisol would just up and leave as the police suggested. We had a house and a business together here for ten years."

Kass reached over the counter to pat Bella's hand. She obviously knew the story. It must have happened around the time Charlene was moving from Chicago. If it had been in the news, Charlene had probably missed it.

"I filed a police report, but Rico was right—they didn't take Marisol's disappearance seriously. To them, she was twenty-eight, beautiful, and of sound mind." Bella's gaze clouded with emotion. "I'm the same age as she was when she vanished."

"I'm so sorry," Charlene said.

"Me too, Bella," Kass seconded.

"I felt pulled to come back to Salem." Bella placed her hand to her heart. "In here."

"How long are you visiting?" Kass asked.

"I drove in from the City for a few days. I'm staying at the Hawthorne. The hotel has a view of me and Marisol's old house. Our tarot shop is a cupcake bar now, can you believe it?" Bella shook her head. "I see Persephone is still in business. She was probably very happy when we moved away."

"What does Persephone do?" Charlene asked. She liked to know all the local business owners.

"She offers a full-service psychic reading that includes tarot cards and crystals," Kass said softly. "We're friends. Not like you and me and Marisol were, but . . . I missed you, too, when you left."

"I was so torn up that I didn't give how you must be feeling as much consideration as I should have," Bella said. "I'm sorry, Kass. Marisol was my everything. She raised me after our mother died. It was her brave choices that landed us in Salem with Santa Muerte."

"Where were you from?" Charlene asked.

"New Orleans. Mom was also a gifted psychic." Bella blew out a slow breath. For as bubbly and joyful as she'd been, sorrow now engulfed her.

Charlene empathized with the awful process of

grief. The only thing that eased the pain was time. "Is there anything I can do?"

Bella nodded, taking Charlene by surprise. The question had been just to be polite.

Kass appeared interested too. At Charlene's arched brow, Kass explained, "Bella just dropped in and asked if I knew you and could set up a meeting—I assumed about the B-and-B."

"You're right, Kass." Bella shifted on the stool and focused on Charlene. "October thirty-first through November second is when we celebrate the Day of the Dead."

Charlene sipped her tea. The scent of orange zest was as bright as the citrus note on her tongue. "The Day of the Dead?"

"It's becoming more popular," Kass confirmed. "There will be a parade this year and everything."

A Day of the Dead parade? "Just when I thought I knew everything about Halloween," Charlene joked.

"This period of time is when the veil is the thinnest between worlds." Bella's voice was hypnotic.

Kass gasped, jumping ahead. "Oh! Do you think it will work?"

"I want to bring my sister through," Bella said. "If Marisol is dead, I want to know. I want to know what happened to her. If she isn't dead . . . then where is she? I need answers." Tears gathered at her long lashes.

"I don't blame you," Charlene said. When Jared died, she'd known he'd been in a car accident. There was closure. If Avery just went missing, she'd move heaven and earth to find her.

"Thanks to your blog," Bella smiled at Charlene, "I

knew when you had a cancellation for Halloween and kept calling until I was able to book a suite, my favorite with the view of your oak tree."

"Well done!" Kass said. "Persistence pays off."

"You're booked for *this* Halloween?" Charlene said. Minnie sometimes took the reservations, and Isabella Perez wasn't ringing any bells.

"Yep. Me and Rico. I'm not leaving Salem until we have answers." Bella looked at Kass. "Will you help me?"

"You know it!" Kass gestured to Charlene. "Charlene will too. Once she has her teeth sunk into a mystery, she doesn't let go."

Charlene had been called downright nosy, so she didn't take offense. "Thanks?"

"And her boyfriend is a detective in Salem," Kass continued.

"That's true." Charlene raised her palm. "Why don't you want to be at the Hawthorne?"

"Marisol always said that your bed-and-breakfast was haunted." Bella batted her lashes at Charlene. "Is it?"

Charlene reached for a cookie and took a bite, chewing to buy time. A half-truth would be the most authentic-sounding. "Sometimes it feels like it, but it's turned out to be an open window or door."

Bella sighed. "Marisol felt masculine energy. Not that we were ever inside, but she'd drive by sometimes."

"The only guys around are the guests," Charlene said. "Even our cat is female."

"And Sam and Seth," Kass said, studying Charlene.

"Are you sure you haven't felt anything suspicious or spooky?"

"Kass!" Charlene placed her cookie on a napkin.

"Sorry," Kass said.

"It's okay," Bella said sweetly to Charlene. "Not everybody is that in tune with the other side of the veil. What day will the parade be, Kass?"

"The local coven is organizing it on November first, but at midnight through November second," Kass said. "It's going to be a lot of fun."

"What does Sister Elizabeth Abbott think of the festivities? She was horrid to Marisol and me for the ten years we were in that location, handing out religious pamphlets." Bella blinked up at the ceiling. "Santa Muerte includes all faiths. We never put down another religion."

"Sister Abbott still crusades like it's sixteen ninety-nine," Kass half-jested. "The tourists usually dismiss her fanaticism as part of the tours, which just makes her even madder. You should talk to Persephone about it."

"We weren't close," Bella says. "I think Marisol and Persephone fought over silly things like guys. Persephone and Rico might have dated a few times, until Rico met Marisol. He fell head over heels in love with her."

Charlene took another bite of her cookie, glad that the conversation had turned away from her mansion being haunted. Jack had very, very masculine energy.

Marisol was the real deal. She'd need to warn Jack about their guests coming at the end of the month and the purpose of reaching Bella's dead sister. *If* she was dead.

Just then, the tea shop door opened. A man of medium height in a security guard uniform entered. A cap covered brown hair.

"Brian," Kass said. Her voice was too polite, which warned Charlene she didn't care for him.

Bella whirled on her stool. "Brian Preston?"

"Isabella Perez," the security guard replied with heat. "I thought I saw Marisol."

"Just me," Bella said. She flipped her long brown hair.

"You look similar." Brian stepped closer to them, passing the ceramic goddess. He pulled a key chain from his pocket with a circular disc on white enamel. Was that an owl? Could be a cat or a bird. "How is your sister?"

"Fine," Bella said.

Charlene kept her mouth shut.

"Well, tell her I said hi," Brian said.

"Will do." The hatred in Bella's eyes should have melted the security guard, but he'd already turned around, so Bella's glare hit his back. Each emotion the young woman felt seemed amplified yet authentic.

"Bye, Brian," Kass called. She waited until the door shut behind him to say, "Idiot."

"What is that all about?" Charlene asked.

"Brian wouldn't leave my sister alone," Bella said. "We complained to the cops, who told us in a smarmy way that his job was to watch out for us. To keep us safe. Marisol hated him. That was one good thing about when she and Rico got together . . . Brian had to back off."

Kass hugged her mug to her chest. "Brian's transferred that stalker behavior to Persephone. I told her she should file a complaint, but she won't. She's got her protection spells."

"Marisol used them too." Bella drained her tea and passed the mug to Kass. "Can you see what happened to my sister?"

After several minutes, Kass shook her head sadly and replaced the cup on the saucer with a click. "I'm sorry. It's too murky for me to decipher." Charlene shuddered as her friend proclaimed, "We will have to wait until the veil thins."

CHAPTER 2

Friday, October 29th

In the kitchen at the B&B, Charlene stacked orange paper napkins next to the tray of silverware. She wore a black silk top over skinny black jeans, black boots, spider earrings, and a long silver chain with a blinking silver-and-white eyeball that told the time: 3:45. "It feels so festive!"

"This is going to be our best Halloween yet," Minnie declared.

Charlene wholeheartedly agreed. Her housekeeper had on a bright orange half-apron wrapped around her ample middle and leggings with skeletons on them.

"I never thought I'd see the day when Charlene Morris would tell the time from a digital eyeball," Jack drawled. "I love it." He maintained his doctorly decorum in khakis and a turquoise blue oxford that matched his eyes.

Charlene grinned. She'd gone all in on the décor and

fun. It would be an epic Halloween weekend, starting with today and most of the guests staying through Wednesday, so they could participate in the Day of the Dead celebrations downtown. Extending the holiday was great for local businesses.

Minnie opened the oven and pulled out a tray of jalapeño poppers wrapped in a crust like a mummy. The pumpkin-shaped cheese puffs, reminiscent of a hand pie, were tempting Charlene for a tiny nibble.

"I bet Avery will love the poppers," Charlene said. "But you did some that aren't as spicy for my boring palate?"

Minnie laughed. "The mummies with red bows are spicy. Try one of the regular poppers." She put an appetizer on a napkin and handed it to Charlene.

Charlene set it aside as it was still steaming. She'd learned that burning the roof of her mouth because she was impatient ruined the taste.

"Avery is here," Jack said. "Early. She must be excited for Halloween too."

"I'll go see if anybody is down yet," Charlene said, taking the mummy on the napkin with her as she walked down the hall to the foyer. She broke off a piece of pastry and blew. Nobody was in the living room, which they'd decorated with fall colors. The sideboard had paper plates and trivets ready for the hot trays of food on one side and space for room temperature items on the other.

Avery hadn't come in yet. She might be on the phone with Seth.

All the guests had RSVP'd for their happy hour at four. They didn't have any kids this year and she didn't hear anybody moving around upstairs. They must be unpacking and, hopefully, enjoying their gift baskets. Each room they prepared for their guests had wine from Flint's Vineyard, tea from Kass's tea shop, and assorted cookies and pastries baked by Minnie.

Charlene bit into the now cooled popper and walked back into the kitchen, narrowly avoiding Silva's outstretched paw from her spot beneath the dining chair.

"You can't have any of this, Silva. Jalapeños might be up there with chocolate on the bad-for-animals list." Charlene gave Minnie a half-hug of appreciation. "Delicious."

"Jalapeños contain capsaicin," Jack said. "Which can cause vomiting." At Charlene's impressed expression, he gestured to her suite and the computer he sometimes used. "I looked it up."

"Our diva cat has already had shredded chicken," Minnie said, shaking her oven mitt at Silva as the cat hovered over her dish like she hadn't been fed in years.

Nobody fell for her ruse.

"What are you and Will doing tonight?" Charlene asked.

"We've got the grands, so probably scary movies. Cinema Salem has a lineup of the older features tonight, eighties slashers tomorrow, and Sunday, *Hocus Pocus*—the original and the sequel. I think they might have one theater dedicated to showing all the seasons of *Bewitched*."

"That would be fun." The statue of Elizbeth Montgomery, the star of *Bewitched*, which had eight episodes filmed in season seven in Salem and the

Hawthorne Hotel, was a Salem landmark in Lappin Park, at the end of Essex Street Pedestrian Mall.

"I've seen them all," Minnie said. "Elizabeth's a lovely actress. People who worked with her at the hotel said she was very kind. As we've learned with celebrities, that matters."

Part of *Hocus Pocus* had also been filmed in Salem. The front door opened, stopping conversation as Avery walked in. "Hey guys!" She entered the long hall before reaching the kitchen and tossed her backpack and purse on the dining room chair.

Silva greeted Avery with loud, complaining meows.

Avery, trained, went to the jar in the pantry and pulled out a fish-shaped treat. "Are you guys starving her?"

Everyone laughed as Silva accepted the treat and then returned to her bowl to stare into the empty depths.

"Silva missed her calling as a cat actress," Jack said. "She could be the next Binx."

"Right?" Avery answered. The teen took off her army green canvas jacket and dropped it on top of the backpack. She wore a flannel shirt in browns over jeans and leather half boots. Her hair, light brown, had been styled short after her injury in February, revealing the delicate spider tattoo on her nape.

"Beg pardon?" Minnie said. Luckily, her back was turned as she transferred jalapeño mummies and cheese pumpkins to serving dishes to bring to the living room.

Charlene shook her head at Jack, who laughed like

he was the funniest man in the world. He did have his moments. Avery would need to be careful answering their resident ghost, or develop a habit of talking to herself.

"I was saying that everything looks amazing," Charlene said.

"And it does." Avery lifted Charlene's digital eyeball clock for the time. "Sweet. Five minutes until happy hour. How are the guests?"

"We haven't gotten to know anyone just yet, but we have repeat clientele, and a woman who wants to contact her sister on the Day of the Dead to see if she is deceased."

"Cool." Avery grinned. "What's the plan for after happy hour?"

"Very loose ones with Sam, but you know how it is—you?" Part of dating a police officer, even a detective, meant that the best-laid plans often went awry.

"Seth and I want to get dinner. Why not double date?"

Charlene coughed and Avery handed her some water.

"It would be fun." Minnie headed out of the kitchen with a steaming cauldron of apple cider.

"And that way if Sam blows you off, you still have someone to eat with," Avery said in a practical tone.

"If he blows me off it's because he has an emergency. I imagine there will be a lot of those this weekend." Charlene shrugged without bias. Sam excelled at being an officer and she loved that Sam kept Salem safe.

"Still, think about it." Avery washed up at the kitchen sink.

"Okay." Charlene handed Avery a paper towel. "Kevin has a shindig tonight at Brews and Broomsticks. Tomorrow, Sharon at Cod and Capers is hosting a Halloween Eve party. The fall festival downtown has events through Monday. Sunday is the epic Halloween party at the Hawthorne. We'll wind up our weekend on Sunday at midnight for the Day of the Day parade to honor the spirits of those who have gone on."

"Not me," Jack said. "You ladies are stuck with me now."

"Hardly stuck." Avery threw the wadded towel in the trash.

Minnie returned and picked up the tray of napkins and silverware just as Charlene's eyeball watch dinged with spooky music. "Four o'clock."

"Here they come," Avery said with big round eyes. Indeed, it sounded like a herd of elephants clambering down the stairs, across the foyer, and into the living room. Minnie would supervise the sideboard, and Charlene would pour drinks from the custom bar she'd had made from Parker Murdock, a local wood artisan.

"Avery, hon, can you be in charge of the cauldron? It's spiced cider. If people want it loaded with a kick, I bought individual fireball whiskey shots to add into it."

"Yep."

The trio brought the supplies into the other room. It wasn't a super chilly October, so Charlene hadn't lit the fire, but it still gave off a scent of cinnamon from the basket of pine cones inside the grate.

Jack appeared by the mantel.

"Welcome, everyone." Charlene stood by the bar in the front corner of the room and counted heads.

Everyone was there except for Isabella and Rico, who she had yet to meet.

"On the first day of your stay, I like to introduce myself and have everyone say a little something about themselves to break the ice. We're going to be best friends for the next five days or more, and it helps to know a bit about one another." Charlene patted the bar. "And then we can have drinks."

Everyone applauded. Charlene missed not having the younger kids around, but she had Avery, and the pang wasn't as sharp.

"A reward," one of the women said with a chuckle.

"You got it! I'll be fast. I'm Charlene Morris. I run this bed-and-breakfast with Minnie Johnson, our acclaimed chef," Minnie bowed and blushed, "and Avery Shriver, who is going to college to be a police detective." Avery fluttered her fingers. Charlene noticed the two college kids, Leo Northern and Patrick Quick, nod and smile. Avery was cute, yes, but off limits, as she was dating Seth Gamble. "If you need anything, just let us know."

More applause sounded.

"In your gift baskets, you have drinks and snacks as well as a map of Salem and coupons for discounts at businesses that we have vetted. I highly recommend Brews and Broomsticks for a drink and live music. For the sake of time," Charlene patted the bar, "and thirst, I'll wrap up." She pointed to a couple in their sixties. "Go!"

"It's like speed dating," one of the guys said.

"It's been forty years since I've dated," the older man with graying hair and a bald spot said. "I'm Timothy Cranston, and this is my wife, Dotty."

The short, round, dyed fire-engine redheaded woman next to him tipped her chin. "We are retired teachers and Salem at Halloween is a bucket list item for us. We waited two years to come, and the reviews for the weekend breakfast have us salivating."

"Welcome!" Charlene's gaze went to the couple with twin mohawks in pink and blue. "And welcome back."

"We're so excited to be here! Spence Mahoney." The skinny guy with the blue mohawk patted his hand over his chest and squeezed the woman's shoulder next to him. "And this is my wife, Darla. When we were here last year, we got engaged. Now, we're hitched." They wore matching besotted grins and showed their ring fingers with tattoos.

"I remember them from last year," Jack said. "The music they played was atrocious. Punk rock." He shivered. "I think he's a musician."

Charlene would ask them about that later, but for now drinks were waiting. "Congratulations!" She turned to the couple who were decked out head-to-toe in black and Jack Skellington gear.

"That's the most romantic story," the woman dressed like Sally the doll in *The Nightmare Before Christmas* said. "I'm Juleen, and this is my husband, Marty. We're the Drakes." She waved at the Mahoneys.

Charlene heard Isabella and Rico crossing the foyer as they neared the living room. She smiled at Leo, who promptly said, "I'm stoked to be here for Halloween in Salem! Leo Northern." He turned to Avery. "You gotta tell us the hot spots."

"Sure," Avery said.

"I'm Patrick Quick. Why don't you show us, if you're free later?" His blond hair was shaggy cute.

"Smooth," Jack said disapprovingly.

"I'm too busy studying to party," Avery said. "I'll check with my boyfriend. He might be able to hook you up."

Nicely played, Charlene thought. Jack nodded.

"Sorry to be late!" Isabella said as she entered the living room with a man of Hispanic descent. "Isabella Perez. This is Rico Flores. We're so happy to be here in Salem with you all." A hint of Louisiana slipped through the last two words, making them one.

"And that's drinks, right?" Leo said, rubbing his hands together.

"You got it—cider, unspiked, is in the cauldron by Avery. If you want to add fireball whiskey, we've got individual shots to give it a kick." Charlene patted the bar. "I've got white wine, red wine, sangria, and an assortment of waters and sodas." She gestured toward Minnie by the food. "The mummies are jalapeño poppers, the ones with the red bows are spicy and the pumpkins are cheese pasties. Go!"

Everyone laughed and split off in the direction of their choice.

"I'd like a white wine, please," Isabella said. "We drove from the City, and traffic can be such a bear. And then we had a lot to unpack upstairs. The room is gorgeous. I apologize if we interrupted anything."

"Not at all." Charlene gave her a generous pour of the Flint's pinot grigio. She smiled at the man next to her. He was in his thirties and had lines around his eyes and mouth, as if he spent a lot of time in the sun or maybe was a smoker. These days everybody seemed to vape. He had a thin mustache and dark hair and eyes. He was maybe the same height as Charlene but taller than Isabella, who wore boots with heels and was still six inches shorter.

"This is Rico," Isabella said.

"Nice to meet you." Charlene didn't ask any questions about Marisol as it didn't seem the time. "What would you like to drink?"

"Tequila. On the rocks," Rico said.

"Not a problem." Charlene reached under the bar for her hard liquor bottles. "Gold or silver?"

Rico chuckled. "*Blanco*, por favor. Silver is best for sipping. Nice place, Charlene."

"Thanks." She poured a hefty shot of silver tequila over ice. "Oh, I didn't cut any lime. I'm not sure we have any."

"It's fine," Isabella said when Rico hesitated. "We hardly expect full bar service at this amazing bed-and-breakfast."

"It used to be a home, *sí*?" Rico glanced around the room, his gaze passing right over Jack without a blip of awareness.

"Yes," Charlene said.

"A doctor named Jack Strathmore lived here." Isabella sipped her wine. "He was very kind to Marisol and me when we were teenagers from New Orleans. We didn't know anybody or have health insurance.

Marisol cut her arm and needed stitches, so we were in the emergency room, scared. He helped us with no charge."

Jack studied Isabella closer. "I'm glad she has that positive memory. I've seen so many patients that I don't recognize her."

"I heard he was murdered," Rico said.

Jack's manifested body flickered at the bold statement.

"Where did you hear that?" Charlene kept her tone light. The story had been in the papers, but the way he said it seemed abrasive.

"Not now, Rico," Isabella said. "Let's get some food in you before you start drinking, eh? You can be so pushy."

Rico scowled like a petulant child but allowed himself to be tugged toward the appetizers.

Charlene and Jack exchanged a glance.

Leo and Patrick were chatting up Avery as she poured hot cider and offered them individual fireball shots.

"We really want to see a ghost," Leo was saying loudly. "I was here as a kid with my parents, searching for the Lady in White at the Old Burying Point Cemetery."

"Did you say Lady in White?" Juleen asked Leo. "Have you seen her?"

"No. We want to, though," Leo said.

Darla, with her cute pink mohawk, joined their little group with excitement. "When me and Spence were here last year, we totally got orbs in that old cemetery."

"Sweet!" Patrick said.

Avery and Charlene looked at each other. They had their own ghost right here that nobody, thank heaven, seemed to pick up on.

Minnie handed Charlene a plate with some chips shaped like headstones and bloodred salsa. "Here. Before it's all gone. I used tomatoes from my garden."

"Thank you. You know I couldn't do this without you, Minnie, right? These people could be your fan club. We need to do a Charlene's B-and-B cookbook."

Minnie's cheeks turned rosy. "I have some ideas. We can circle back to it later. I'm not opposed."

Her housekeeper had some sway in her walk as she returned to the sideboard.

"Hey, when you know you're good, you know," Jack said. "I give the idea two thumbs-up."

It would be nice around Christmas as an additional sales funnel . . .

"Charlene?" Timothy said. "This is only our first day in Salem and we're already over the moon. Thank you so much for the welcoming gift basket."

Dotty sipped a hot cider sans whiskey. "It's a dream come true to be here. We used to teach the kids about Plymouth Rock and the witch hunts. How do you feel about the fact that innocent women were killed here? The church? Or witches?"

Charlene wasn't sure what tack to take. "Well . . ."

Timothy elbowed his wife. "Dotty, give Charlene a minute." He leaned toward Charlene. "She'll talk your ear off."

Dotty shrugged. "I do like to talk. People are so interesting. I would love to meet a witch, for real. And get a tarot reading. I want to do it all while we're here."

Charlene laughed at her enthusiasm. "I can help you. Tomorrow I was going to suggest an outing to Flint's Vineyard around one. Brandy and the Flint family are genuine witches who can trace their lineage back for centuries. Tomorrow evening there will be a lot going on downtown, and Kass Fortune is a very good tea leaf reader. Persephone Lowell is offering tarot card readings."

Dotty leaned into her husband with excitement. "I want to see the vineyard too. Yes to everything, Charlene."

Timothy sipped his deep red wine. "This is delicious."

"It's where I get my house wine," Charlene said. "Brandy makes it special for me—that's the cabernet."

"I'll be sure to buy some tomorrow. Not that I'm a wine connoisseur or anything, I just know what tastes good," Timothy said.

"Do you have suggestions for tonight?" Dotty asked.

"Brews and Broomsticks will have pub fare and live music. Tomorrow night Cod and Capers down by the wharf is having a Halloween set menu. There will be all kinds of parties, as well as the festival downtown."

"Thanks again," Timothy said. "Come on, hon, let's get some more poppers." The couple walked off.

"Nice folks," Jack said.

Charlene nodded, in total agreement.

She smiled at her guests, making her way toward Avery and the caldron of cider to see if it needed to be refilled. "How's it going over here?"

"Fine. About out of cider, though—and shots," Avery said.

Leo and Patrick were on their second cider with a shot and laughing by the fireplace. They were the youngest of the crew.

"Should I get some more whiskey?" Charlene asked.

"No. Let's help our guests not to overdo. They're both just twenty-one, so barely legal." Avery gave an amused shake of her head.

"You sure you don't want to meet up with them?" Charlene teased.

"Funny." Avery kept a straight face. "I'm surrounded by guys just like that in Boston too. Good thing they grow up. Makes me very grateful for Seth."

"Maybe the brisk fall air when they go outside will sober them up." Charlene loved this time of year, from the changing weather to the vibrant colors of the leaves.

"I'm not too worried. So, Isabella is gorgeous," Avery said quietly. "And Rico is her dead sister's boyfriend?"

"Yes." Charlene searched the room for them, locating the pair in close conversation.

Avery's nose curled.

"What?" Charlene was curious what Avery would say as the teen was incredibly observant.

"Charlene?" Spence called.

"Yes?" She turned, wondering what Avery had been about to share.

"I overheard you say that Brews and Broomsticks

was having music." Spence sipped his beer. "Is that the place where the cool guy with the broomstick tattoo works?"

"Yes, Kevin Hughes. You have a good memory, Spence."

"He knew so much about the ghost scene in Salem. Me and Darla want to book a tour with him," Spence said. "Can we do that for Halloween night?"

"You're probably bored with it, Charlene," Darla said. "But you'd be welcome to join us."

"Let me call him and see what I can set up." Kevin's tours never failed to entertain. "Be right back."

Charlene pulled her phone from her pocket and passed through the happy, mingling guests to the foyer. Silva watched, curled up on the second-to-last step of the grand staircase.

Scrolling until she found Kevin's name, she sent a text about his Saturday night tour plans.

The answer was immediate. She sighed. Kevin was booked. There were more dots. He could do a tour Halloween evening at ten. He and Amy had plans, but she had caught a cold and was backing out for the weekend.

She immediately sent a get well to Amy text while also accepting the Halloween slot.

Charlene turned to go into the room and ask who wanted to be part of the tour when her attention snagged on Isabella and Rico's close proximity to each other.

It occurred to her that they had one room. Saving money? Times were tight. She could have offered a rollaway.

Maybe Minnie already had and she was reading something into what was sure to have an innocent explanation.

Rico caressed Isabella's hip in a very familiar manner that was not sisterly at all. He pinched lightly, and Isabella leaned closer to him.

Charlene stifled a gasp and brought her hand to her mouth.

Isabella turned with Rico at her side.

"Let me explain," Isabella said.

CHAPTER 3

"You don't owe me an explanation!" Charlene said, her face red.

Jack manifested behind Isabella and Rico. "What's going on, Charlene?"

Charlene had no answers, even if she could reply to Jack. Isabella hadn't even hinted that she was sleeping with her missing sister's boyfriend.

"I . . ." Isabella grabbed Rico by the hand and dragged him from the living room to the foyer and Charlene. Her face was pale, showing embarrassment, but Rico shrugged her off.

"We have nothing to apologize for." Rico turned on Isabella. "I'm sick of this. Either you love me or you don't. I'm tired of being your dirty secret."

Isabella bowed her head. "I do love you." She looked at Charlene, exuding confusion but sincerity. "It wasn't intentional. We comforted each other in our grief over Marisol's disappearance. The next thing I knew, we were in love."

Charlene kept silent—not judging, just unpacking everything Isabella had unloaded. It would have been nice if Isabella had mentioned this at Kass's tea shop.

Was this why the couple had moved away from Salem so quickly after Marisol's absence? "Does Kass know about you two being a couple?"

Isabella shook her head. "She wouldn't understand."

Rico grew angry, deepening the lines around his mouth. "Ashamed of me?"

"No!" Isabella placed her hand to his heart. "We can tell her at dinner when we meet her and her boyfriend."

Charlene took a step around the pair but hated to leave Isabella if Rico had a temper. "I'm sorry for my reaction. It's really none of my business."

"You got that right," Rico said.

Jack sent a chilled blast of air toward Rico, who shivered. "Watch yourself."

"Let me explain." Isabella's humble demeanor drew Charlene closer. "I want to. I . . . Rico and I are in love, but I don't want to get married without my sister's blessing. It's why it's so important that we reach her this weekend with our *ofrenda*."

"I don't understand," Charlene said.

"An *ofrenda* is an altar." Isabella's eyes glittered, but she didn't cry. "We worship Santa Muerte and appeal to her with five different talismans that are supposed to invoke the spirit of Marisol."

"If she is dead," Charlene clarified.

"Don't get us started on that again," Rico declared theatrically. "If we find out that Marisol bailed because things were getting . . ." He broke off.

"Getting what?" Isabella said. "Serious? Marisol didn't want to marry—it wasn't personal to you, Rico. Our mother had bad luck with men and warned us against it. Said we would lose our power through the Death Goddess by splitting our loyalty between a husband and Santa Muerte."

"You couldn't be married?" Charlene asked. Would that stop Rico and Isabella, if it was in fact why Marisol might have bolted?

"It was frowned upon. I'm willing to risk it, with Rico." Isabella's narrow shoulders raised. "You can have lovers. Passion is encouraged—but love and loyalty is for Santa Muerte first."

"The Death Goddess demands a heavy price," Rico said. "In exchange for protection and miracles." He showed Charlene a tattoo on his inner arm of a tall skeleton with a scythe and a flowered crown around the skull. His shirt had three-quarter sleeves, and various tattoos peeked out at his collar and other arm.

Isabella's long-sleeved peasant top covered her arms, but that didn't mean she wasn't also tattooed. Tattoos were so popular right now, but as Charlene aged, she could clearly imagine the way an original design might distort with sagging skin.

Minnie left the living room with an empty tortilla chip bowl. "Everything okay?" she asked, taking note of Charlene in intense conversation with Rico and Isabella.

"Yes. I'll be right in." Charlene looked at a miserable Isabella, wanting to reassure the young woman that everything would be fine. She'd offered to help her locate Marisol and she would follow through. "I have plans for this evening, but tomorrow after breakfast we can get together and discuss the Marisol situation. How does that sound?"

"Wonderful. Thank you." Isabella clasped Charlene's wrist. "You understand why it's so important? I must know, one way or the other, what happened to my sister. We can't move forward."

Rico jammed a hand into his front denim pocket. "I am not waiting forever, Bella."

"Hush." Isabella frowned at Rico.

"Convince me," Rico teased, lowering his voice. Isabella blushed and allowed him to usher her toward the stairs, his arm around her hip.

"These two have secrets," Jack said.

Secrets were never good things when it came to relationships.

Minnie returned with a full bowl of chips, and Charlene glanced over her shoulder as Isabella, giggling, reached the landing with Rico. *Not her business.* She followed her housekeeper into the room of happy people in full pre-Halloween cheer.

"Charlene, you ready for a glass of cider?" Avery asked.

"No, thanks. I'll stick with my white wine. Where is it?" Charlene reached the sideboard as Avery gave Charlene her glass.

"I rescued it. What was going on with Isabella and Rico?"

"I'll tell you later." Charlene sipped and smiled as

Timothy gestured for her to join him and Dotty by the sofa. Though older than the others by twenty years or more, they were entertaining and had the guests laughing.

Before Charlene had moved, her phone dinged. She placed her wine on the sideboard and pulled her phone from her back pocket to read a text from Kevin, wanting to know how many takers for Halloween night's special tour of the graveyard.

Charlene pocketed her phone and clapped until everyone faced her. "Hello, my friends—Spence had a good idea, and we lucked out as Kevin Hughes has a tour available on Halloween night at ten if we wanted to go on a ghost hunt."

Cheers erupted.

Charlene laughed at the unbridled enthusiasm. "A show of hands, please!" Timothy and Dotty, Spence and Darla, Avery, and Marty and Juleen. Leo, and Patrick.

"And maybe Seth too," Avery said.

Charlene texted Kevin back, **Possibly 13.**

My favorite number. Coming by tonight for music?

No, but expect some of my guests. Thank you! For you, anything.

"What has that smile on your face?" Jack demanded. He manifested near her, reminding her of his jealous streak.

Charlene didn't answer, but Avery peeked at Charlene's phone.

"Kevin's a good friend to have," Avery said. "Once

I'm twenty-one I'll be able to enjoy the music at Brews and Broomsticks."

"Time will pass before you know it," Jack said.

Charlene nodded.

"I wish our other friend could come out with us," Avery said, tilting her head toward Jack.

"I do too, Avery." Jack's hair and clothing brightened into crisp detail and then flickered. It required energy for him to manifest his physical body. "If it wasn't for you both, this existence would get tedious. Seeing things through your eyes helps." He looked toward the threshold of the living room. "Our secret lovers have returned."

Avery flipped her short shag. "That's what I wanted to talk to you about. Rico was way flirty with Isabella, and I thought he'd been with Missing Marisol."

Jack chuckled at the nickname. "What if Marisol decided she was just done with Rico? He thinks very highly of himself. If Marisol wouldn't marry him, it could be a reason for her to leave."

"I suppose. Isabella shared that she and Rico fell in love by accident." Charlene kept her smile in place. "Here they come."

"Charlene, Avery, thank you again for making us so welcome." Isabella's lipstick was perfect, as if she'd just reapplied it. Rico preened like Silva after a dish of cream. "Is it possible to get a plate for snacks?"

"Sure!" Normally folks drifted off to dinner reservations or parties by six and it was only five.

Avery gave them each a plate. Isabella chose a jalapeño popper and a cheesy pumpkin as well as some chips and salsa. Rico went for the poppers with the red ties.

"Gracias," Rico said.

"You're welcome." There was nothing Charlene liked more than making her houseguests happy. "Would you care to join us for a paranormal tour at ten with Kevin Hughes on Halloween night?"

Rico nodded at Isabella with a shrug.

Isabella swallowed her bite of chip. "We must be back here with the *ofrenda* set up at midnight on Halloween. You promised you would help, and Kass did too."

"I will," Charlene said. "We can be here even if the others aren't finished with the tour yet."

"Thank you." Isabella's emotive golden-brown eyes welled. "I miss my sister so much. I want to know one way or the other. Nobody has been able to say. It's like Kass's reading for me—the answers are murky."

"I hope we find clarity," Charlene said. "What are your plans for this evening?"

"We'll be at Kass's for dinner, to meet her boyfriend, Franco," Isabella said. "She's invited Persephone, so we might be home early." Her nose scrunched as she averted her gaze from Rico.

"Don't be jealous, Bella." Rico's expression suggested that perhaps Isabella needed to be on guard against her boyfriend's wandering eye; he had been her sister's lover, and Persephone's too.

Isabella lowered her lashes. "Just behave, Rico. That's not too much to ask, surely?"

"I'm just teasing," Rico said. "I can't help it if the ladies love me."

"Franco is very cool." Avery's observation broke the awkward moment. "He's all about the movies."

"Movies?" Rico shrugged. "We don't really spend a lot of time doing that."

"What do you do for entertainment?" Charlene asked.

"Rico likes to play poker," Isabella said. "With his friends. I like to read."

"Boring," Rico said.

"Mind-expanding," Avery countered. "What do you enjoy, Isabella? Fantasy? Romance? Thrillers?"

"I can't read thrillers," Isabella confessed. "Too scary for me, especially when Rico isn't home until the wee hours. I'm a baby."

"*My* baby," Rico said.

"I like romantic comedies," Isabella told Avery before smiling at Rico.

"And I get to be her hero, *si*?"

"*Sí*." They shared a kiss.

"I'm feeling nauseous," Jack said. "This guy is too smooth. What does Isabella see in him?"

Charlene cleared her throat before she lost her composure at Jack's commentary. "Avery, honey, should we get more jalapeño poppers from the kitchen? Excuse us." She tucked her hand at Avery's elbow and moved the teen away from the oblivious couple.

Jack gave a deep, unrepentant laugh. Avery's lips twitched as she tried to keep it together.

Darla and Spence stepped in front of them with happy expressions. "Thank you," Darla said. "For setting up the tour. And also for tonight. We're taxiing to Brews and Broomsticks, with Dotty, Timothy, Juleen, and Marty. Leo and Patrick are walking downtown to the Pirate Bar but know where we'll be if they want to catch up with us later."

"That was very sweet of you guys to keep everyone together!"

"We had an amazing time here last year," Spence said. "Everyone was so welcoming that we want to do that for others too."

"Anytime you want to come back, say the word." Charlene gave Darla a hug, then Spence, her heart full.

Avery moved off to give Leo and Patrick directions and also a backup hangout spot if the Pirate Bar didn't work out, recommended by Seth.

Juleen and Marty joined Charlene. "Thank you for tonight. We're gonna grab our coats. This place rocks," Juleen enthused. She looked behind her for Dotty and Timothy. "It's a small world. Dotty was a teacher at my brother's elementary school in Brooklyn. Crazy!"

"I love it," Charlene said.

Dotty and Timothy thanked Charlene profusely, leaving Isabella and Rico. They finished their drinks and placed the empties on the table.

"Thanks. See you in the morning for our meeting," Isabella said.

"Don't forget," Rico warned with an arched brow.

Isabella smacked his arm. "Don't be rude. We should Uber to Kass's. I don't want to drive, and my heels are way too cute to be functional."

"Have fun," Charlene said to the couple, then turned to Minnie and Avery as they all started to clean up the dishes and sideboard.

By six, they were finished.

"Well done, team!" Charlene wiped her brow with exaggeration. "We *are* pretty good at this."

"On that note, I'll go pick up my grandkids. They're all taller than me now. Take after Will. See you in the morning." Minnie waved and left.

Avery ran her backpack upstairs to her private room on the third floor. Jack and Charlene caught up in the kitchen about the party—their wonderful guests, and the mystery of Rico and Isabella.

"Rico didn't sense me at all," Jack said.

"Isabella never mentioned whether Rico had talent in that direction. She is a crystal healer. Marisol was the one with the psychic ability. Kass agreed that she was very gifted."

"Kass knew them all ten years ago?" Jack had been standing by the sink but reappeared by Silva's dish as she meowed mournfully that it was empty. Trying to distract her, Jack levitated her bowl, and the cat scurried backward, deciding to take shelter beneath the kitchen table.

"Yes. Marisol and Isabella would've been teenagers, fresh from New Orleans." Salem had always been a magnet for witchy folks—some who wanted to capitalize on the subject and others who belonged to actual covens. "I'm having a hard time imagining dinner at Kass's tonight." Kass's boyfriend was tall, thin, and quiet. Rico was the opposite. And Persephone?

"Drama!" Charlene rested her hip against the kitchen counter.

"Isabella might be gifted with crystals, but she didn't notice me either."

Avery returned in time to hear Jack's statement. "That's good, right? You don't want random people to see you. Not even Kass."

"Charlene was concerned about paranormal investigators at one point. When she first moved into my home." Jack jiggled the eyeball necklace from his spot by the fridge. "She wanted elegant and now look at her."

Charlene smacked the eyeball to her chest and out of Jack's spectral grip. "That's one of Kevin's side hustles, so yes, I was concerned. Kevin is sensitive to psychic activity, but he hasn't so much as felt Jack's chill though he's been here plenty of times. Kass sees ghosts everywhere for sure, so Jack stays out of sight when she's here."

"But Kass is so cool!" Avery said.

"That she is." Charlene focused on Jack to try to read his emotions. "You said things would be tedious without us. I don't want a bored ghost, Dr. Jack. Would you like to meet Kass?"

"No, I don't want to meet Kass." Jack's denial lacked the ring of truth, causing Charlene to doubt his words. Before he'd been able to interact with Avery, he'd considered running an online doctor's practice.

It was the perfect time in history for an identity to be created that would allow Jack to use his medical knowledge and help others. For some reason that he hadn't shared, he'd never pursued it. Maybe she would press.

Avery sat forward and clasped her hands before her at the table, as if ready to launch into a debate. "It would be interesting to find out if Kass could see you, for real. I had no talent for it until my head hit the mantel. If not for you, Jack, I would have been very seriously injured or, worse, dead. Charlene hadn't had any paranormal talents until she saw you."

"You needed my assistance with your death so were quite persistent, which meant a physical manifestation. I don't see the little girl ghost at Seth's house."

"I do," Avery said. "She's not clear, and I can sense other spirits, but none as visible as Jack. This is a miracle, yes, but there's a part of me that wonders if we can teach others how to hone that skill." She touched the place on her head that she'd hit.

"With questions like that, have you thought about being a doctor?" Jack asked.

"No way. Too much school." Avery shuddered. Her phone beeped and she read the screen. "Seth's off work and ready for a break from school too. His mom is having a party at her house tonight, so he doesn't want to hang out there. We know Seth isn't able to see Jack, or the ghost at his house, but can hear the fridge opening. I'm telling you, it's so strange how it's different for everyone. And Sam never has picked up on Jack?"

"No," Charlene said.

Avery switched subjects. "Have you talked to Sam about double-dating with me and Seth?"

"Let me check in with him." Charlene grabbed a can

of fizzy water and poured it over ice, walking to the foyer to make the call. She and Sam were due for some alone time because his parents had just left for Florida two weeks before. She'd been over for romantic lunches, breakfasts, and dinners whenever he could get away that melded with when she could get away.

"Hello," Sam rumbled in his sexy voice.

"Hi, Sam," Charlene answered, the pit of her stomach clenching in response.

"Any chance we can grab dinner at my place?"

"About that . . . Avery and Seth want to double-date."

"What?"

"I think it's sweet."

"Charlene." Sam exhaled. "Whose idea was it?"

"Avery's." Charlene lowered her voice. "I've got two hours free after the winery tomorrow and before the festival where we can catch up. This is important."

Even though it was her fault for her overreaction to his almost-proposal at Valentine's Day—she'd been shocked by the ring in his pocket, plain and simple— she hadn't realized their relationship would take an even slower path because he'd kindly offered his house to his parents to help with his mother's recovery. Charlene couldn't have Sam sleep over at her place because of Jack. She told Sam it was because of the guests and Avery, but there was no way she would hurt Jack by having Sam stay overnight.

"Where should we go for dinner?" Sam acquiesced as he adored Avery and was growing to like Seth. "It's packed out there. People are crazy. Halloween is a free-for-all in this city, always has been, and the fact that it's on a weekend means things are over-the-top. Folks are already in costume and it's only Friday."

"I think it's fun," Charlene said.

"Unless you're trying to get a table somewhere," Sam rumbled.

"Good point."

"Well, how about pizza? My place okay?" Sam suggested. "It'll make Rover happy to have company."

Charlene loved Sam's Irish setter and thought this to be the perfect solution. "It's great. What can we bring?"

"Whatever you all want to drink. I've got water and water. I can make coffee and there might be some tea bags left over from when Mom and Dad were here."

Laughing, Charlene said, "Understood."

"I'll wait to order pizza until you get here." Sam's voice changed and dropped several octaves to a husky promise. "And you and I will catch up tomorrow, one-on-one."

"That sounds terrific to me too." Charlene turned back toward the kitchen, where Jack and Avery were discussing her forensics classes. "See you in a bit, Sam."

Avery turned from her casual slouch, elbow propped on the table. "Well?"

"We're going to Sam's place for pizza." This would be the first time they'd have dinner family style.

"Seth too?" Avery's brow arched. This was an invitation into the detective's private lair, and Sam was slow to share Avery with her boyfriend.

"Yes, Seth too."

"Cool! Let me text Seth real quick." Avery straightened and grabbed her cell phone, thumbs moving at hyperspeed across the screen. "Done."

Charlene opened the fridge and grabbed unsweetened iced tea and a variety of fizzy waters. Pizza would be great. Drinks, check. She knew her suggestion of a salad would fall on deaf ears.

"Dessert! What should we bring?" Charlene asked.

"Halloween candy?" Avery suggested. "We have two big bags."

"Minnie made chocolate cupcakes," Jack said.

"That's a much better idea." Charlene went into the pantry, and sure enough, there were a dozen chocolate cupcakes with orange sprinkles.

"Are they for a special occasion?" Avery asked.

Jack shrugged. "I just noticed they were made. You know how Minnie loves to bake and be prepared for our guests."

"True." Still, Charlene sent Minnie a text to ask if she could take the cupcakes to Sam's.

The answer was an immediate thumbs-up, with a big hello to the detective from Minnie, who had a small crush on Sam.

"That's a yes." Charlene put the cupcakes into a plastic to-go container. She scanned the shelves and grabbed the chewy dog bone for Rover she'd bought, just in case the dog needed a treat too.

"Can we pick up Seth on the way to Sam's?" Avery asked.

"Yes—Sam has limited parking, so good idea," Charlene said. Sam's three-bedroom rancher had space for two vehicles in the drive and zero street parking.

"Cool! Jack, what will you do tonight?" Avery asked.

Jack manifested very strongly for them as he stood by the kitchen sink, touching his forefinger to his temple. "I'm studying up on Santa Muerte, so I'll know what the heck Isabella is talking about tomorrow night. Don't worry, ladies. I'll share the notes."

CHAPTER 4

Charlene swung by Seth's. Avery was in the front holding the cupcakes, with the beverages at her feet. Rover's dog bone was on the back seat.

The Gamble home was decorated to the max and even had an inflatable Jack Skellington hanging over the roof. Orange and black lights rimmed the windows, and pumpkin yard stakes adorned the lawn. Twenty vehicles crowded the driveway and street, leaving no place to park, so she pulled in behind a giant truck and honked.

Seth darted out in jeans and a heavy flannel, running across the grass. For the brief moment the door was open, the thumping beat of music had escaped.

"Mom says hi." Seth got in and shut the door. "We are welcome to hang out here later. It's all her friends, so you know, that's a big no for me." He ruffled his light brown curls. "My brother is staying over at a friend's house too."

"That's very nice of her," Charlene said. "Love the decorations."

"Thanks," Seth said. "She's dating this guy who was one of her cleaning clients, and it's cool but weird."

Charlene thought very highly of Dani Gamble, raising two boys on her own terms. Now Stephen was in high school, and she was ready to unwind a little. Couldn't blame her. It was commendable even that she'd waited and put the boys first for so long.

Avery sent him a teasing smile. "You're worried you might catch them kissing?"

Seth sank back with a groan. "Avery!"

"She's walked in on us kissing plenty of times, just saying, maybe cut her some slack." Avery faced forward and balanced the cupcakes on her lap.

"I know logically what you're saying is the right response, but she's my mom, and I need time." Seth clicked on his seat belt. "Can we talk about something else, please? Like, how did we get the invite to Detective Sam's for dinner?"

"Avery thought it would be fun to double-date, but Sam pointed out that the restaurants are really crowded, so he suggested pizza." Charlene looked at Seth. "Okay?"

"I love pizza. I could eat it for every meal," Seth said. "What will we talk about? I don't know him that well."

"You know Rover," Avery said. "When Sam brought his dog to Charlene's?"

"Yeah. Cool dog. Irish setter. Our dog is a mutt."

Within minutes they'd arrived at Sam's house on the

outskirts of Salem. The rancher had a fenced yard and an attached garage.

There were no decorations at his place, but the porch light was on, so that was good.

Piling out, Charlene took a moment to orient herself. Here she was, with two teenagers, about to have dinner with her boyfriend, in Salem.

What would Jared think? Her nose stung. He'd been everything to her, and then he was gone so suddenly that it had wrenched her heart from her body. She hadn't thought she'd live through it.

She'd made a desperate bid for her sanity, buying the bed-and-breakfast to start over. And now she was in love with another man.

A wonderful man.

If Sam offered her the ring again, she would say yes, without hesitation.

The front door opened and Sam was knocked to the side as Rover slid by with a cheerful bark. The fence went around the entire yard, with a gate to keep the dog safe.

While Charlene and Rover had bonded, the pup and Silva remained wary. Her cat would hiss and arch her back but still wanted to be in the same room to play with Rover's tail. The dog was tolerant.

Sam crossed the brick path and opened the silver gate for them. His hair was still damp around the edges, as if he'd just showered. He didn't like cologne but smelled of shampoo and shaving lotion, from where he'd shaved his beard and trimmed his glorious mustache. Not a hint of silver dared make an appearance in his chestnut hair. He wore jeans, a dark brown Henley, and boots.

Avery and Seth went first, and Charlene followed them. Sam gave her a firm kiss. He was six foot six to her five eight and made her feel petite. "Welcome."

"Hi." Charlene's lips tingled; Sam's mustache was soft and perfectly ticklish.

Seth and Avery burst into laughter.

"Can't get away from it. Romance is in the air." Avery pulled Seth back and kissed him. "It's a good thing."

"Did I miss something?" Sam shut the gate. He tucked his thumb into his jeans pocket, his expression confused.

"No biggie." Seth kneeled and patted Rover on the head, giving the dog a full body rub. "Hey, girl."

"Come on in." Sam led the way, climbing the two brick steps to his front door. He opened it, and a waft of warm air invited them in. His house was cozy, with leather couches and wooden accents from the floor to the table.

"This is nice," Seth said.

"Very masculine." Avery had been here once before. "I like it, though."

"Mom did her best to lighten it up with throw pillows," Sam said. "Which are in the spare bedroom now she and Dad are in Florida."

"How is she feeling?" Charlene asked.

"Fine. She's back to golfing eighteen holes, which makes Dad happy. They like their life in the sunshine state, but I was getting worried that they might adapt to

Witch City." Sam gestured toward the armchair in the living room, where the TV was on. "Toss your jackets there if you'd like. Can I get anybody anything, or should we order?"

Charlene followed Sam into the kitchen. "Minnie made chocolate cupcakes." She pulled the container from the bag and retrieved the bone for Rover. The pup gently took it from her. "Good girl."

"Treats for everyone," Sam said, caressing her hip when the kids weren't looking. "The menu for the pizza place is on the table there if you want to check it out. I always order the thick crust with everything."

"Sounds great," Seth and Avery said.

"That was easy." Sam stepped around Charlene to the landline. "Garlic knots okay? Figure I'd ask because of the kissing question." He winked at Charlene.

Avery slung her arm around Seth's shoulders. "Fine with me. I have no problem with garlic kisses."

"These garlic knots are lethal," Sam promised. "But delicious."

Sam ordered the food, and Charlene brought cups, ice, and plates to the dining table.

"What would you like to drink?" Charlene asked the kids.

Seth perused the choices—lemon, mango, or lime fizzy water, or unsweetened iced tea. "This looks good." He picked lime and a cup of ice, pouring it over with a fizz, as promised.

Avery chose mango, and Charlene went for unsweetened iced tea. "Sam?"

"I'll have what you're having," Sam said. "Pizza will

be here in forty-five minutes because of the holiday. Should we have dessert first? I'm starving."

Avery, about to argue, stopped after counting the cupcakes. "There's a dozen. We can have one now, like an appetizer, and still have one for dessert."

"Deal!" Seth said. "I like how you roll, Sam."

They each lifted a chocolatey cupcake. Charlene gently nudged her hip against Sam's. "I didn't think you'd be the kind to go for dessert first. You're usually a by-the-book kind of man."

"Second that," Avery said. "But I love it. People are so complex."

Sam leaned against the counter in the kitchen, facing the dining area. "That we are. Human nature has always fascinated me."

"Me too," Seth said. "I'm taking a psychology course for my business degree that's got me thinking of changing direction."

"Really?" Charlene asked. "To be a psychologist?"

Seth ducked his head. "I'm probably not smart enough."

"That's not true." Avery licked a chocolate crumb from her lower lip.

"What would that entail?" Charlene asked.

"Not sure," Seth said. "Haven't even talked to Mom about it yet, but it's been on my mind since the start of the school year. First year of college is mostly prerequisite stuff, so it would be a solid time to change."

"If you're serious, you should definitely make an appointment with your guidance counselor." Avery traded her cupcake for her phone and scrolled. "You can be a social work counselor with a master's degree. Your doctorate would be longer."

Seth gave a noncommittal shrug. "Sam, what's the strangest case you've ever worked on? People are nuts and you see them at their worst. I don't know if I can handle that twenty-four seven."

"Yeah! Good question." Avery put her phone in her back pocket. "We want all the details, please."

"Be careful, Detective. What you say could guide Seth's career." Charlene sipped her iced tea and exchanged a small smile with Sam. She loved that this felt like a family.

"It could take all night," Sam quipped.

"Pizza won't be here for another forty minutes," Seth said.

Chuckling, Sam gestured to the dining area. "Let's sit down. I have a story to share from when I first arrived in Salem as a police officer. I wasn't even a detective yet. A long time ago." He shook his finger at Avery. "And this is not the way to do things. Got it?"

Avery nodded.

Charlene, enchanted by Sam's charisma, sat to his right. She could easily imagine him as a twentysomething newbie. Had he sported that luxurious mustache then?

Avery was opposite her and Seth took the other end of the square table. Rover put her head on Seth's knee. They all focused on Sam.

Sam wrapped a napkin around the base of his cup of iced tea to collect the condensation. "I'd moved from New York and didn't really have a clue about Witch

City. I thought it was a joke that the police uniform emblems had a witch on the patch."

"Oh man." Avery winced. "Not a joke but a point of pride in Salem. What happened?"

"I almost quit the force. This might be a lesson for you both when it comes to your careers." Sam sipped his iced tea, his manner calm, cool, and collected.

"Quit?" Avery said.

Seth watched Sam intently, petting Rover's head in his lap.

"I can't imagine that," Charlene admitted. Once Sam made up his mind about something, he was steadfast. "Why did you leave New York?"

"It started with a girl," Sam drawled.

"Now that I believe." Avery twirled a ring around her slender finger. "It obvi didn't work out."

"Are you going to let me tell the story or what?" Sam smoothed his mustache.

"I'm working on my interrogation skills," Avery said.

"It starts with listening." Sam tapped both ears.

Avery made the motion of zipping her lips.

Charlene smiled but of course wondered what sort of girl would bring Sam to Salem. She'd be pretty and smart and . . .

Avery kicked Charlene under the table to get her attention, the teen rolling her eyes at her, knowing darn good and well where her mind had gone.

She took a drink of tea, studying Sam over the rim. She swallowed down with it the tiny bit of jealousy that he had ever loved another.

"April in Salem is gray and rainy," Sam said. "Same as New York. Fewer people, which I thought would be a step up from the crowded city I'd worked in for the past five years. I had an agreement with my old chief that if I hated it here within thirty days, I could go back with the same benefits. I was tempted right away when I realized that they took the Witch City theme seriously. I thought the witchy emblems were demeaning."

Charlene put herself in his position—young, in love, and feeling like he'd made a mistake. She cringed for him.

"As you know, the Wicca religion is a recognized doctrine here in Salem. That's fine with me—I have no problem with people's beliefs. If that person breaks the law, then I'll get judgy." Sam shifted on his chair. "I had never met a witch or warlock practitioner before. Several of my coworkers, male and female, worshipped the Wiccan faith."

"We know lots of good people who are Wiccan," Charlene said, mentally running down the list of her friends.

"My circle has expanded to include several as well," Sam said, "but at the time I was quite sure that *my* faith was the only true one. Also something I've grown out of. Living in Salem forces one to expand their narrow way of thinking."

"True that," Seth said.

Charlene couldn't agree more. She braced herself for what Sam was about to share. She'd never heard this early history of his before.

"I had one foot out the door from the first day," Sam

said with a self-deprecating expression. "I can't imagine anything worse than an arrogant young police officer who thinks he knows everything. I guess I shouldn't have been surprised when after my first week I started to get threatening notes in my locker."

"What?" Avery asked.

"Old-school handwritten notes demanding that I leave Salem and go back to the City." Sam sat back and placed his elbow on his crooked knee. "This was before everyone had such ready access to cell phones. Told you—the dark ages."

Charlene laughed softly.

"What did you do?" Avery leaned her forearm on the table.

"I tossed the first two notes," Sam said. "I could barely read the name. I wasn't sure if it was male or female. I showed it to a fellow coworker to try to get to the bottom of who was sending them." His eyes twinkled. "He tried to tell me that the notes were from a ghost."

Charlene straightened. It took all she had not to look at Avery. Seth's expression also turned very serious.

"Did you believe him?" Seth asked.

Sam drank his tea and looked at them like they were the crazy ones. "No. Ghosts aren't real."

Silence hovered over the table. The three of them knew differently.

"What happened next?" Charlene asked.

"I thought I was losing my mind . . . the person was getting into my head. The reason that this position in Salem had opened up in the first place was because one of the officers had been killed in the line of duty," Sam said.

"Oh no," Avery said. "That's so sad."

"The signature on the notes was the same as the officer who had died, William Dotson. I kept the next one, only to find it in a pile of ash on my desk in the morning." Sam's eyes narrowed.

"Did you tell your boss?" Charlene asked.

"I didn't believe it was a ghost, but I was starting to wonder if I should just pack up my gun and go. Tammy and I were fighting," Sam said. "I blamed her for making me give up my job in the City."

Charlene reached over to pat Sam's broad shoulder. Tammy.

Tammy sounded cute and . . . not the point.

"The next day another note appeared in my locker, demanding that I quit or I'd be dead within the month. Killed." Sam looked around at each of them. "Signed by a dead man."

"And?" Seth said.

"I showed it to my sergeant," Sam admitted with a cringe. "Blamed the Wiccan coworker who had muttered more than once that I should go home if I didn't like Salem or the police force."

Charlene covered her mouth with trembling fingers. Poor Sam.

"When I came back the next morning, the note had burned to ash on his desk too." Sam pulled his mustache. "Sarge asked to see me, asked if I'd been the one to do it, but of course I wasn't. Unfortunately, he had me on video coming into the station the night before."

Seth expelled a breath. "No way."

"I don't understand," Avery murmured.

"I was being set up," Sam said. "It wasn't a ghost, it wasn't me, so it was up to me to find the responsible party. I was glad that they had someone on camera, because it meant it was a real person and not a ghost, like I'd said all along."

"What did you do?" Avery asked.

"In our line of work, Avery, it is our job to look beyond the simple answer. My coworker was Wiccan, but he wasn't the only one who was upset that I'd gotten the position. There was another coworker, your run-of-the-mill Christian, who had blamed the Wiccans while we'd have coffee in the morning."

"The plot thickens," Charlene said.

"I did a stakeout that night, and right after our shift change at the department at two a.m., a man in black with a black ski mask punched in the code to the back door. He knew how to get in but didn't want to be seen. I tackled him and uncovered a skinny little runt. Booked him right then for breaking in. Turned out to be a known burglar in the Salem area who'd been hired by my Christian *friend* to scare me off so I'd go back to New York."

"I can't believe that!" Charlene said.

"You caught him," Avery said with admiration.

"That I did." All these years later, Sam still sounded proud.

"What happened to the guy who set you up?" Seth asked.

"He was fired."

"Motive?" Avery asked.

Sam chuckled. "He wanted his friend to get the job I'd gotten, plain and simple." He looked at Seth. "I don't know if that's crazy enough for you, but I thought I was losing my mind."

"It is pretty wacked," Seth said. "But not a sociopath, true. Maybe I'll stick with business."

"It sounds like you're restless," Avery said. "Maybe you should still go talk to your guidance counselor. You could get advice on your options."

"That's a good idea," Charlene said.

"Yeah, I think so too," Sam said.

"My mom always says to trust but verify," Seth said, petting Rover. The pup must have sensed a fellow dog lover. The Gambles' dog was an adorable black-and-white mutt that weighed about fifty pounds to Rover's seventy.

"As a detective, we never trust," Sam said. "Always verify."

Charlene looked at Avery to see what she thought about that, but the teen was nodding in agreement.

"You're right," Avery said. "That had to be terrible."

Sam scooted his chair back a bit from the table. "They had me doubting my own senses when I know damn well and good there is no such thing as ghosts. And I was right."

There was no room in his statement for discussion, but at least Charlene better understood why Sam felt the way he did. If he hadn't been tricked, perhaps he wouldn't be so closed-minded now. "Why did you stay in Salem? Tammy?"

"Tammy and I split up within a year," Sam said. "I stayed because of the integrity in the rest of the police department. Once I got out of my own way." He reached for Charlene's fingers. "They were decent officers who cared about doing the right thing when it came to . . . we can call him Fred. They let me know he hadn't been a team player, and his impulsive actions had played a part in the death of the man I'd replaced."

"Brutal," Avery said. "You have to trust your team."

Sam and Avery bumped their knuckles together.

A knock sounded on the door. Rover raced to answer it before Sam.

"Pizza!" Avery jumped up.

Charlene couldn't believe it when, an hour later, they'd demolished two large pizzas. Nobody could move, so instead of playing cards as they'd talked about, they watched a movie in Sam's comfy living room.

An action film that had them all on the edge of their seats. Charlene and Sam held hands, hip to hip on the couch. Avery and Seth snuggled on the love seat.

Rover sat next to Charlene.

This moment was bliss, and she was grateful for it. She couldn't worry too much about what tomorrow might bring.

Charlene dropped Seth at his house after the movie, the party at his mother's still in full swing at midnight. She and Avery drove home.

"So, Sam will never understand about Jack," Avery said as they turned down the driveway to the large mansion.

"No." Charlene tightened her grip on the steering wheel, grateful for the heater. Traffic was steady despite the late hour.

"I get it now," Avery said, "why you haven't tried harder to tell him."

"What would you have done if I'd told you the B-and-B was haunted by a very attractive doctor?" Charlene slowed for a red light.

"Before the head injury, I would have had my doubts."

"Exactly." The thick clouds blocked the moon. The light turned green, and Charlene carefully pressed on the gas.

"I'm glad I hit my head so that I can see Jack, and the little girl in Seth's house. There is so much more to this world, but you don't know what you don't know. And we can't go around bopping people on the head, hoping it might work."

"We'd get in trouble," Charlene agreed with a laugh, turning on Crown Pointe Road and driving toward the bed-and-breakfast.

Once they arrived and Charlene parked the car, Avery said, "Maybe we should write a manual."

They got out of the car and went inside. The B-and-B was empty—her guests out and Jack not answering their soft hello.

"The manual would have to warn people that the rules of play are subject to change," Charlene said. "Night, honey."

"Night!" Avery, after giving Charlene a hug, raced up the stairs and out of sight.

Charlene entered her suite to find the TV on low, Silva curled up on the love seat, and her afghan folded neatly on the arm. No Jack. She didn't know where he went when he wasn't with her, and he had a hard time explaining it.

A manual on ghosts would have more questions than answers.

"Night, Jack," Charlene whispered before heading to her bedroom.

CHAPTER 5

Saturday morning Jack was waiting for Charlene in her living room suite when she ambled out of her bedroom in flannel pajamas and bedhead.

He tried to hide a smile at her dishabille and smoothed down her hair, which was alive with static electricity. "Why don't you go back to sleep? I hope I didn't wake you by turning up the TV."

Charlene shook her head and yawned. "That would be the nightmares induced by too much garlic on the most delicious rolls. Silva was as big as this house and grinning like the Cheshire cat."

"It was also a late night for a lot of our guests," Jack said. "They came in around two. It will be interesting to see who gets up for breakfast and who skips it."

"Nobody will skip Minnie's breakfast. She's got a cult following." Charlene collapsed on the love seat. "How was the research on Santa Muerte?"

Jack raised the volume of the TV even more so they could talk without being noticed by Minnie in the kitchen. "Perfect segue about a cult and following, only Minnie's omelets shouldn't put her in danger, like those who Santa Muerte is supposed to protect."

"I should hope not, Jack!" Charlene reached for the afghan on the arm of the love seat and snugged it over her lap. "Where were you last night?"

Jack shrugged. "Resting. Here, there . . . ruminating on religion. It makes people manic. Is a difference of opinion worth the heartache? War?"

Charlene brushed her hair from her face to study Jack. "Sounds serious."

"I *know* there is more beyond this earth and yet I wonder if God cares one bit about religion. I am beginning to suspect not. And then what does that mean? As a doctor, I believed in my two hands. My brain." Jack dropped to his knees next to Charlene. "And now here I am a ghost, a dead man, and I'm having an existential crisis. What is it all for?"

"Oh, Jack!" She quickly patted his icy shoulder wishing she could hug him.

He sat back on his heels, his eyes filled with angst. "What is the damned point, Charlene?"

Charlene didn't care that her fingers stung but continued to pat his shoulder as she held his gaze. "Love. Connection. And here I was just going to ask you to give the high points of Santa Muerte before breakfast, but this is much more important." She was at a loss as to what to say or how to comfort him.

Jack stood, not fully manifesting his figure. It was always disconcerting to see the TV through his body.

"*Love*." Jack lifted his arms out from his sides. "Santa Muerte is a folk saint that has come out of the closet so to speak, spreading words of acceptance. Her origins are Mexican. She is seen as a giver of miracles, and an escort to the afterlife. She has a globe, and a scythe, and wears a robe. She represents the inevitability of death."

"We don't need to talk about her. Let's talk about you—"

Jack seemed to grow bigger in size. "Santa Muerte is always a skeleton but has many other nicknames such as the Bony Lady or the Death Goddess. The Catholic Church officially doesn't approve of her, but that just makes her devotees even more zealous. She lovingly assists her followers through the transition of death."

Charlene understood better about why Jack had gone into a tailspin though she didn't have answers for him to ease his mind. "Faith. Believing without proof. We know there is more."

On an exhale, Jack resumed his usual form. "I'm proof."

"Yes," Charlene agreed. "I can't see Isabella worshipping something evil, can you?"

Jack shrugged. "Santa Muerte, according to her followers, is not evil, but delivers a message of love for all. And yet, someone killed Dona Queta's husband."

"A test of her faith?" Charlene blinked, her head beginning to clear. She allowed Jack to skip away from a conversation about his emotional crisis, but no way was the subject over. "I think I'd better lay off the garlic today. I can't afford any more bad dreams." She stood. "Showering. Coffee. Thank you."

Jack gave a sad chuckle and disappeared. He was

her best friend, yet her boyfriend couldn't see him and demanded proof of Jack's existence. How could she do that when Sam wasn't even open to the possibility? She'd tried when she'd first moved here to tell Sam the mansion was haunted, but he didn't believe in the paranormal all around them. Now, it was simpler to avoid a confrontation. She couldn't prove Jack's existence just by willing Sam to see him. It hurt to keep this secret, but it was for the best.

By ten Charlene was on coffee number three, with cream turning the brew an au lait color, just the way she liked it, and the leisurely breakfast with her guests drawing to a close.

"Raise your hands if you want to come with me to Flint's Vineyard. We'll leave at twelve thirty and be there by one. Once there, the Flints will offer a tour of the grapevines and then a lunch of small plates." Charlene scanned the room. Everyone was accounted for except the college kids, Patrick and Leo, who had grabbed food and gone back to bed, not interested in the field trip.

"I can't eat another bite," Darla said. Her pink mohawk was straight and perky. Spence's blue spikes listed to the side as if he'd had a long night dancing at Brews and Broomsticks.

"You might work up an appetite while walking the gorgeous grounds. It's really impressive, even in the fall," Charlene said. Her stomach was full as well, but she always had room for shrimp wrapped in grape leaves that Evelyn Flint made for tapas. "My favorite time to visit is spring, when the grapevines are green and budding."

"There is a season for everything," Dotty said wisely.

"So right, my dear." Timothy patted his wife's hand. "We are a yes for the vineyard. Will they ship the wine that we might buy?"

"Absolutely," Charlene said. She and Brandy had a wonderful business partnership that had turned into an unexpected but welcome friendship.

They were on the board of new businesses together, and Brandy truly cared about Salem's future, probably because she could trace her lineage back to the 1600s. The next century mattered too.

"I'd like to go," Juleen said. "Marty?"

"Yeah, count me in." Marty and Juleen wore matching black T-shirts with skeleton faces on the front.

"Isabella?" Charlene asked.

Isabella glanced at Rico, who was nursing a cup of coffee. "Hair of the dog," he grumbled. "Maybe. Real witches are nothing impressive to me."

"I would like to go and absorb some vibrant earth energy," Isabella said.

"What do you mean?" Juleen's makeup was neutral, her brown hair pulled back in a clip. She sported an orange I LOVE HALLOWEEN pin.

"Here we go." Rico eyed the ceiling as if very put upon.

Isabella ignored Rico and smiled at Juleen. After a drink of her cranberry juice, Isabella tugged a small leather pouch from under her shirt and opened it, spilling stones to the table. "My sister could read tarot cards and auras and psychic energy, like our mother, but my gift is in healing with crystals. Earth energy is very grounding, which helps me during a cleansing ritual."

"Bet she needs constant recharging with Rico at her side," Jack said.

Avery spluttered her water. Everyone looked at her in alarm. "Sorry," the teen mumbled.

Charlene happened to agree with Jack.

"I don't understand . . . so, like if I have a headache," Juleen said, "you could heal it with one of those rocks?"

"Yes." Isabella's nod was confident.

"That's sweet. Can I learn how to do that?" Juleen asked. "My mom sometimes gets migraines that lay her out for days."

"I don't know," Isabella said. "It was a gift I was born with."

"That's very, very cool," Spence said. "And I have a splitting headache. Don't judge, ya'll. I had a lot of fun last night."

Isabella laughed softly. "We honor Santa Muerte, and in our practice we absolutely do not judge. Would you like me to help you with your headache?"

"Is it rude to ask you?" Spence exuded misery. "I can pay."

"Fifty bucks," Rico said, all of a sudden not minding so much.

"Sure," Spence said. "I have cash in my room."

"All right." Isabella studied the crystals and stones on the table and then looked at Spence. She closed her eyes and let her palm hover over the pile, humming, before choosing a reddish-orange stone. "Carnelian." She opened her eyes and lifted it, showing her palm to everyone. "Yep."

"It's pretty," Darla said hesitantly. "But how can that take away a headache? I'm very curious!"

"It's a detox stone, so it should help relieve the effects of overimbibing." Isabella stood. "Let's go into the living room, Spence, where you can lay down. We will need about twenty minutes."

"We had plans with Charlene," Rico said sharply.

Isabella glanced at Charlene. "I . . ."

"It's fine," Charlene said. "We aren't leaving for the vineyard until twelve thirty. For those who are interested, meet me in the foyer then."

"I'm in no rush to get up from this table," Marty said. "This is the best kind of vacation. No deadlines, no laptops."

"What do you do for the daily grind?" Avery asked.

"I'm a computer tech. Juleen is an office manager. We work our forty hours a week each and live for the weekends. Halloween is our jam."

"We are working hard now to retire at sixty and travel," Juleen said. "Dotty and Timothy were giving us some pointers."

"You both are doing much better than we were in our forties. We had kids and didn't make a lot, so we had to put in the time." Timothy shrugged. "You are leagues ahead of us."

"We loved teaching," Dotty said. "It wasn't anything we hated, like in your situation, and we had summers to travel. We hit all the national parks. Our kids say those are some of their best memories."

Isabella and Spence went into the other room. Rico drank his coffee, eyes at half-mast.

Avery gestured to the stones. "I recognize some of them, like rose quartz and amethyst." She reached for a purple rock, but Rico put his hand over hers.

"You can't touch another healer's stones," Rico warned. "You could pick up their energy, which isn't good. You could also transfer your energy to her, also *no bueno*."

"Oh! I didn't mean to," Avery said. She sat back and folded her hands on the table before her.

"You didn't know," Rico said. "I didn't have a clue about those things until Marisol and I hooked up. It was a crash course in weird. Any of you ever date a psychic?"

A chorus of *nos* rounded the table.

"You can't get away with nada." Rico finished his coffee and set the cup down with a thunk.

"Who is Marisol?" Dotty asked.

"My e . . . Isabella's sister," Rico said. "She vanished from Salem two years ago."

"That's so sad," Juleen said.

"Yeah." Rico centered his mug on a napkin. "We had a business together. Everything went downhill with her gone."

Jack disappeared and reappeared with updates on Spence's headache. "I don't see anything magical, but his face is definitely relaxing. Isabella put the stone in the center of his forehead and then to each temple."

Charlene thought that sounded very intriguing. Crystal magic. Why not? She'd learned that a lot of things were possible if you opened yourself up to them.

Spence and Isabella returned in ten minutes, and you could tell just by looking at him that the pain was gone. "This is so cool. Thank you, Isabella."

"You're welcome." Isabella shook out her hands before gathering the crystals and rocks. "I will need to ground myself at the vineyard. When I used to live here, I would take the crystals to the beach or one of the parks. Nature is a powerful asset not enough of us tap into."

"Shall we get to why we are here in the first place?" Rico stood. "You should come to our room, Charlene. That might be the most private for our conversation."

"Sure." Charlene finished her last sip of coffee and rose, scooting her chair backward.

"See you up there," Jack said.

"Can we hang out for a while?" Timothy asked.

"There is no rush at all," Charlene said with a smile at her guests. "We aren't leaving for another two hours."

Charlene nodded at Avery, who would visit and help Minnie with the dishes while she went upstairs to see what she could do for Isabella and Rico, and Marisol.

Rico left the dining room first, leaving Charlene and Isabella to follow. The crystal healer was peppered with questions about her gift, which slowed them by the threshold.

"It's very intuitive, and something I was born with," Isabella said shyly. "Compared to my sister and our mother, this is nothing at all."

Charlene helped Isabella escape by gently nudging her forward. At last, they reached the foyer and climbed the stairs to the blue suite. Isabella opened the door. Charlene was surprised that though Isabella had requested the room with the view of the oak tree, the blinds were closed, the dim room lit by candlelight.

"This is strange," Jack announced.

"Check this out," Rico said proudly. "We have the beginnings of the *ofrenda* to entice Marisol from the other side."

"The shrine," Charlene said, glancing at Isabella as she stepped toward the desk that they'd cleared off to put a cardboard box on. One side had been cut out, reminding her of a diorama she'd once made in school.

"Or altar, if you prefer," Isabella said.

"When does it need to be finished?" Charlene asked.

Rico said, "The *ofrenda* is usually assembled on the thirtieth or thirty-first of October and left up until November second."

"Only in the Santa Muerte faith?"

"No," Isabella explained. "*Ofrendas* are used in many religions, even by Catholics. *Dia de los Muertos* is a time to honor those gone before us." She pointed to the partially assembled cardboard box. "These are some of the things Marisol likes."

There was a glass of water and a plastic statue of a white Santa Muerte that was an inch tall. A stack of tarot cards splayed with Santa Muerte on the backs. A velvet bag. Tequila.

"We have Marisol's preferred brand of tequila *blanco*," Rico said. "The four elements must be represented: earth, water, air, and fire. We have salt, water, and a central candle. We'll use paper to represent wind, but you could use a feather instead. We need to get

Mexican cigarettes. Babe, I've got a call into Jonas. He's here in Salem."

"He is? What a nice surprise!" Isabella sighed. "Inside the velvet bag is her favorite charm bracelet that I made for her protection, with Santa Muerte symbols." She touched the stack of cards. "Her tarot cards she used for tarot readings, designed by Rico. Aren't they beautiful? We need to buy crawfish, Louisiana style, and grits from home."

"If your friend doesn't come through with the crawfish, we can ask around at some local restaurants," Charlene said.

"Marisol's connection to New Orleans is important to honor," Isabella said. "I feel like we have one chance to reach her, and I don't want to take shortcuts."

Charlene nodded. "Do you have prayers or a ceremony to do once you have the shri—altar, put together?"

"Yes. We will try tomorrow on the thirty-first at midnight, but the veil will be the thinnest the evening of November first, through the second." Isabella lifted the velvet bag. "We talked to Kass last night about joining us on the first if Marisol doesn't reach us. I believe that the more powerful witches we have, the better to attract and pull Marisol through."

"*If* Marisol is dead," Charlene reminded her. "Wouldn't you rather her be alive somewhere?"

"No." Rico shoved away from the desk with his arms crossed, his eyes narrowed. "That would mean she'd stiffed me and stole our statue of Santa Muerte. Taking it ruined our livelihood."

"Stiffed you?" Charlene noted the plastic statue of

Santa Muerte on the *ofrenda* and didn't understand the value.

"Our store sold Santa Muerte items that had to be stocked. I fronted the money with the expectation of making it back." Rico rubbed his thumb and finger together. "Business."

"Don't like this guy," Jack said.

"Rico, please. You chipped in some of the money. We sold all the merchandise in New York. There is nothing left to complain about." Isabella pressed her fingers to her brow. "Marisol told you we didn't need all of that extra stock in the first place."

"Had to sell at a deep discount so we didn't get stuck with it. Our business failed with her gone," Rico said. "Marisol had all the magic and earned so much more than you with her tarot card readings. She'd better be dead or I will hunt her down myself."

Isabella paled and placed her hands on her hips, showing spunk for once. "How dare you! Marisol loved you, and she loved me, and our lives together. If you don't believe that, Rico Flores, then go."

Contrite, Rico crossed the room in an instant to gather Isabella in his arms. "I do believe that—you know I do. I'm broken that she's gone." He rested his forehead against Isabella's. "I just want answers."

"Now that I believe," Jack said.

"I'll see you guys downstairs, okay?" Charlene asked. "We have today to get what you need for the shrine."

"*Ofrenda*," Rico said.

Charlene backed out of the room as they held each other. Love. It could be a real pain.

"Twelve thirty in the foyer." Charlene left them to commiserate in each other's arms. Or whatever they were doing behind closed doors. It seemed strange to have such passion when concerned for your missing sister.

Charlene went downstairs and joined Minnie in the kitchen as she cleaned the dishes and wrapped up leftovers.

"I'll bake some more cupcakes today," Minnie said. "How were they?"

"Beyond amazing. We had them for appetizers and dessert." Charlene explained that Sam had been surprisingly okay with dessert before dinner.

"And how was Sam?" Minnie asked with a twinkle in her eye. She adored the detective, and he adored her right back. It was sweet.

Recalling the way the conversation had gone, Charlene shook her head. "Stubborn as ever. Do you believe in ghosts, Minnie?"

"Yes, I do."

"Interesting," Jack said. "And yet she's never seen me. She's felt my cold essence sometimes, though."

Minnie was open to more than met the eye. "Well, Sam doesn't and refuses to even consider the idea. If he can't touch it, it's not real."

"And what brought this up?" Minnie turned and smiled, putting her hands in her apron pockets. "Does it matter? Will and I don't agree on everything either."

"She has a point," Jack said.

Charlene blew out a breath. "I suppose you're right."

"Did you and Jared agree on everything?" Minnie asked.

The question about her husband just out of the blue didn't sting as much as it might have three years ago. Time lessened the pain of grief, though it remained a scar. Charlene couldn't remember a single argument. If something had been important to the other, they usually compromised. "Not everything, but there was never an argument."

Minnie brought the ingredients from the pantry for chocolate cupcakes. Flour, cocoa powder. Salt. Sugar. Baking powder and baking soda. Such simple ingredients that in her housekeeper's hands became delicious.

"I don't mind a little disagreement every once in a while," Minnie said sassily. "It leads to making up."

Charlene burst out laughing and Jack, the coward, vanished from the kitchen.

CHAPTER 6

Charlene had rented a Mercedes passenger van for the weekend in the event her guests all wanted to go somewhere together. She was very close to saving the money to buy one for the business but, for now, this suited her.

Renting meant she didn't have to pay for damage during freak storms or vandalism, although she did have to fork out extra for a higher insurance premium.

Avery rode with Charlene in the front. Dotty, Timothy, Juleen, Marty, Darla, Spence (headache-free), Isabella, and, surprisingly, Rico. He was in a better mood, at least, and not so growly. Leo and Patrick were sleeping, so they'd be ready for tonight's round of parties.

Turning from the front passenger seat, Avery called out to the folks in the back, "Music?"

"Sure!" Marty enthused from the center row of seats. "Anything nineties works for me."

"Classic choice," Spence agreed.

Charlene felt old when what was her high school music was deemed classic.

Avery hooked up her phone to Spotify and had an alternative music station on in minutes. She chose a volume that was more geared to the back, so it didn't pop Charlene's eardrums.

"Thank you," Charlene said.

"Not a problem. Happy to be your copilot anytime." Avery's dark denim jeans and jacket were cute as well as comfortable for walking around outside. Her nod to the Halloween holiday were black cat accessories from a headband, to earrings, to a necklace.

Because they'd be having lunch and drinks, something Charlene had coordinated already with the Flints, Minnie, Charlene, and the guests had decided to skip happy hour at the B and B. Which meant she had two hours in her day to take Sam up on his offer of some *them* time.

Charlene couldn't wait. She'd changed from jeans to a rust-colored dress with a high collar and boots that she thought made her look pretty and Sam had mentioned was one of his favorites.

"What's the plan today since we're skipping happy hour?" The folks in the back were singing along to Fall Out Boy. "I thought I'd find Seth and hang out for a while. Can you believe he might change his business degree? I mean, he's a good listener and everything, but it would be more school for sure." Avery scrunched her nose. "And money."

Charlene glanced toward Avery at the stop sign at the bottom of Crown Pointe Road. "Seems like Seth went for a business degree because it was a practical choice and nothing else was calling to him, but now his interest has been teased by psychology."

"Yeah." Avery tapped her fingers to her knee in time to the beat. "I worry because he already works so hard. He'll need to take out student loans, which won't make his mom happy. I think Dani wants Seth and Stephen to take over her cleaning business."

All of a sudden, Seth's uncertainty made more sense. "The best thing is for Seth to be open with Dani and make sure they're on the same page."

"I know." Avery shrugged. "Seth knows that, too, but he's not there yet. Life shouldn't be so hard when we aren't even twenty."

"You are both very smart—you especially, hon. Does Seth want the business? Does Stephen?"

"Seth thought he would, but now he's not sure. Maybe Stephen is interested?"

"It's wonderful that Dani has built a business that is sustainable. Everyone wants their house to be clean," Charlene said. "Have you met her boyfriend yet?"

"Nope. And I can't talk to Seth about it," Avery shared. "He goes into protective son mode, and I didn't even realize he had the protection switch. He's never overbearing with me."

"It's different when it's your parent. I can guarantee that I would have died if Mom and Dad started kissing in front of me." At the thought, Charlene's cheeks turned red.

Avery laughed. "Kissing is a good thing."

When Charlene thought of Sam and his kisses, she totally agreed.

They arrived at Flint's Vineyard. The turnoff had a

sign with the Flint's logo of red and white grapes in a heart shape. Smart branding, and Charlene had her marketing degree, so she approved. It was memorable and told what they sold: both red and white wine.

Charlene followed the curving road, passed the mansion that had housed the Flint family for centuries, and arrived at the gift shop beyond it. The Flints had added a courtyard with heat lamps and sheets of weather-resistant shade cloth to keep off sun or rain. It was a space to entertain while showcasing the wine and the vineyard.

Parking the van, Charlene unlocked the doors. Brandy, Serenity, and Evelyn all came out of the gift shop to greet them. Three generations of beautiful and powerful witches. Evelyn's hair was snowy white and styled in a chin-length bob, her eyes green and sharp. Brandy, hair a rich, deep auburn, intelligent green eyes, and a flawless complexion, and Serenity, the youngest, with lighter red hair, ivory skin, and those same bewitching green eyes.

Rico and Isabella exited the van first. "Serenity!" Isabella said. "It's been a long time. How have you been? Do you remember Rico Flores?"

"Hi!" The young women hugged. "I do—Marisol's boyfriend. Nice to see you both again."

"Oh!" Dotty said with sudden understanding of Isabella and Rico's relationship. And Marisol's too.

Rico scowled. "Hola," he said to Serenity, moving aside.

Serenity looked uncertain, but Isabella shook her head. "It's fine."

Charlene leapt into the fray of introductions to

smooth over the awkward moment. "We've been bragging about your wine and what a lovely setup you have here."

Brandy stepped forward with a friendly smile. "Thank you. I'm Brandy, this is my mother, Evelyn, and my daughter, Serenity. Welcome!"

"I want to order a case of red," Timothy said right away.

"Well, you are my favorite guest so far," Brandy teased.

"I'll order two," Martin said.

Juleen smacked his arm, knowing it was all in fun. Brandy was beautiful and had a power that collected men like bees to honey.

"We have a special treat for you all today." Evelyn rubbed her hands together. "We are creating a new white wine blend and would love your feedback."

"Sure, twist my arm to sample wine," Juleen said with a grin.

"Mine too." Darla patted her husband's shoulder. "How you feelin', Spence?"

Spence tapped his temple. "Totally ready to sample wine!"

"What happened?" Evelyn asked.

"Well, Spence was so excited to be here in Salem that he didn't pace himself last night at Brews and Broomsticks." Darla pointed at Isabella. "But Isabella used her crystals to heal him. Completely blasted the headache. I am a believer."

"I am, I am, I am too," Spence crooned.

Brandy turned to Isabella with a smile. "How come

I didn't know you're a crystal healer? Your mother was from New Orleans . . ."

"You had a shop with your sister, didn't you, downtown?" Evelyn asked. "Marisol read tarot cards. You were followers of Santa Muerte."

"Yes, you're correct." Isabella brought her bag of crystals from her pocket and shook them. "I'm hoping to gather positive earth energy today while I'm here."

"We still follow Santa Muerte," Rico said, patting his tattoo of the Bony Lady. His stylish leather jacket was slung over his shoulder, his forearms visible in his T-shirt. "Hope that's not a problem here."

"Of course not," Brandy said. "And how is Marisol?"

"Mom," Serenity warned.

"She is missing." Isabella raised her chin. Charlene had to give the young woman credit; it would be very hard to come back to a town with your missing sister's boyfriend without some pushback. They all knew Marisol with Rico and had to have questions.

Brandy's brow lifted.

"It's why we left two years ago," Isabella continued. "But I don't want to monopolize your time right here. I would love a moment to chat privately, if you can."

Evelyn wore a concerned expression as she left the group to go into the gift shop. Everyone had light jackets, and the sky had hints of blue behind the gray clouds. The air was crisp. Fall weather was Charlene's favorite. One just had to dress for it, and there were so many cute options to choose from.

Brandy swept her arm to the rolling hills of barren

grapevines. Evergreens and oaks dotted the landscape. "If you'd like to hike around the property, please do. We have paths marked, so we'd appreciate it if you'd stay on them. Ignore our dogs—they're big but friendly. Give us about thirty minutes and then meet over there under the canopy." She gestured to the covered outdoor area. "We'll have our wine tasting and food too."

Her guests split off into small groups to wander. Avery went with Juleen and Darla. Brandy grabbed Charlene's wrist so she didn't leave; Isabella and Rico also remained.

"Is now a good time?" Isabella held Brandy's gaze without flinching from possible censure. "Charlene is helping Rico and me, so you can speak freely in front of her."

Brandy and Serenity exchanged a look and then Brandy nodded. "Let's go inside the gift shop."

The space had a long counter with barstools. Evelyn was behind it wearing an apron over her jeans and sweater in autumn colors.

"I'm sorry about Marisol's disappearance," Serenity said. "When you left I'd assumed you'd found her but decided to start over in New York."

Charlene pegged Serenity, Marisol, and Isabella to be around the same age. Young witches of Salem. Evelyn and Brandy had been aware of their shop and what they sold but hadn't been in the same social circle.

"Marisol is a gifted psychic," Evelyn said. "She had a real talent for reading tarot cards. And you inherited crystal healing. I knew of your mother in New Orleans.

She was a powerful witch, so it is no surprise her daughters would be too."

"I remember your mother," Brandy said. "She was the only woman who ever made me wish I had black hair. So lovely. She credited Santa Muerte for all her success in New Orleans. Her shop in the French Quarter was famous."

"Mom was amazing." The tip of Isabella's nose reddened with emotion. "I miss her very much. Marisol too."

"You sold Santa Muerte merchandise and were ahead of your time in your worship. She's only grown in popularity since then. The Bony Lady, the Death Goddess. It's admirable how she's appealed to the masses," Brandy said. "She isn't Catholic or the Divine Feminine we worship in our Wiccan creed, but unique."

"We have no argument against her." Evelyn touched the silver pendant with the phases of the moon on a long chain around her neck. "It's simply not our personal belief. We honor the Triple Moon Goddess."

"Santa Muerte doesn't disregard other faiths," Isabella said with assurance. "She is the protector of those who might not be welcome elsewhere. She welcomes all."

"Santa Muerte is the granter of miracles," Rico inserted. "She gives one's true desire, for a price."

Isabella bowed her head and then raised it. "Marisol and I kept the Santa Muerte statue we inherited from our mother in a place of honor at the counter in our tarot shop. Believers could offer her a token and get their prayer heard." A tear slipped down her cheek. "I feel like I've been praying nonstop for two years. I am ready for answers, even if they break me. I can't continue like this."

Brandy looked at Serenity, who gave a minute shrug.

Eveyln kept her expression neutral and went to the back room, returning shortly with two bottles of wine. One red, one white. She opened both.

"I remember you calling around and asking if we'd seen Marisol. A month later you were just gone," Serenity said. "Your shop was boarded up. You didn't call or text."

Isabella brushed a tear from her cheek. "I couldn't talk about Marisol without breaking down. Rico and I . . . we comforted each other." She clasped his hand and dragged him next to her. "We fell in love. There is nothing wrong in what happened."

"Of course not!" Serenity said.

Rico puffed up and glowered but didn't meet the witches' gaze. Charlene's intuition kicked into gear that he had to know more about Marisol's disappearance than he was letting on.

Isabella released Rico's hand. "I'm sorry I didn't let you know what was happening, but I was so hurt that I wanted to hide."

"Sister Abbott praised God that you'd been sent to the Devil as you deserved." Serenity rolled her eyes. "We didn't have details, so we couldn't defend you. There is nothing to apologize for. I'm sorry I didn't try harder to stay in touch."

Isabella gave Serenity a tremulous smile. "Sister Abbott has had it in for me and Marisol since we moved from New Orleans. Kass also shared that she wished I'd reached out before now."

Serenity clasped Isabella's hand.

Charlene sensed that they would mend their broken friendship.

"We left in a hurry," Rico said. "Marisol's absence made it hard to be here. She was gifted with her tarot and psychic readings. Her clients brought in a lot of money, much more than Isabella's crystals. We really couldn't afford the place without her."

"She must have had wealthy clients," Brandy said. "That was a prime location."

"People always want to know the future, don't they?" Rico shrugged. "The merchandise in the shop was gravy. Her Santa Muerte tarot cards were designed by me. I created others that we sold at the store."

"You designed the tarot cards?" Brandy asked.

"*Si*. I did." Rico lifted his gaze.

"Each card was a version of Santa Muerte, if I recall correctly," Serenity said. "And you hand-painted Marisol's personal set."

"That is correct," Rico said.

"A psychic's tarot deck should be unique to the practitioner," Brandy said with approval. "Did you study art?"

"No." Rico bared his forearm to show the tattoo of Santa Muerte. "I was a tattoo artist."

"From Salem?" Brandy asked.

Charlene wondered if her friend would offer to help him in the art world as she favored those who were just starting out if she thought they had talent.

Rico arched his brow. "What is it to you?"

And with that attitude, Charlene knew he would blow any chance of her benefaction. Too bad for him; Brandy was very, very wealthy and connected.

"Rico!" Isabella scolded. "I apologize—he didn't sleep well last night. Rico was born in Mexico City and moved to the United States as a child."

"My apologies if the questions were too personal." Brandy's lips twitched, as if she was trying not to smile.

"Can you tell us about Marisol's disappearance?" Evelyn asked. She poured three glasses of white wine with an inch of liquid in each and set them in a row on the counter.

Rico stepped back. "Isabella thought the three of you might help us, being powerful brujas, but I don't think I want your assistance after all."

"What?" Isabella exclaimed. "You begged to come to Salem with me, Rico. Don't ruin things right now."

"Help with what?" Serenity asked.

Rico kept his back to them as he perused the bottles on the shelves and knickknacks like key chains and magnets with the Flint logo.

Isabella blew out an exasperated breath and then focused on the Flints. "I want to contact Marisol, if she is on the other side. To find out . . . what happened. We need answers."

Rico reappeared at Isabella's side and clasped her hand in a possessive manner. "I want to get married. Isabella wants Marisol's blessing before we do."

"What are the chances that she simply left town?" Evelyn asked in a gentle tone.

"I don't think Marisol did that." Isabella placed her

hand on her heart. "We were very close. We shared a house, a bank account, a business."

"What does Sam say?" Brandy asked, her gaze going from Isabella to Charlene.

"Sam?" Rico released Isabella's hand in a dramatic fashion. He made the name sound like a bad word as he was instantly jealous.

The man was something else.

"Charlene's boyfriend," Brandy explained.

"The detective," Isabella said, no doubt remembering the tea with Kass, when they'd offered to help her find Marisol. "We haven't talked to him about it."

"What did the police say two years ago?" Serenity asked.

"We filed a police report when it happened," Isabella shrugged, "but they didn't take it seriously. They believed that Rico and Marisol must have argued and my sister left Salem in a huff."

"With the Santa Muerte statue," Rico said. "But Marisol wouldn't leave us stranded like that. Our business's success is tied to our worship of the Bony Lady."

"Did you argue?" Charlene asked.

"Yes." Rico transferred his leather jacket to his other shoulder. "Lovers argue."

"Over what?" Serenity asked.

Isabella nodded at Rico with encouragement. "It's okay. We need to find answers, which means being honest with everyone—no secrets."

"Fine." Rico perused the bottles of wine on the counter as he confessed, "I was having an affair with Persephone."

Charlene winced.

"Not cool," Serenity said.

"Don't cast your judgment on me." Rico's eyes narrowed. "Marisol wasn't faithful either. It was her nature to mess around, as well as mine."

"Then why argue if it was something you were both all right with?" Charlene was so old-fashioned that she could never be in an open relationship. Boring monogamy for her, please.

Rico stuffed his hand into his front denim pocket. "Persephone had feelings for me. She loved me, which was dangerous. It wasn't casual on her part, which meant that she could hurt Marisol through me."

"What lovers did Marisol have?" Isabella demanded, sounding shocked by the accusation.

"Brian Preston, for one." Rico rocked back on his heels. "There was a reason he was so enchanted with her. I told her that if she wanted me to stop seeing Persephone, she had to stop hooking up with Brian. That's what we were arguing about."

Brian Preston, the security guard who had followed Isabella into Kass's tea shop? Charlene was very confused.

"I don't understand," Isabella said.

"There is immense power exchanged in certain sexual rituals," Rico said. "Santa Muerte is a greedy saint. She wants everything, and she will give you everything, but it will cost you."

Isabella stared at Rico as if he had two heads.

"I hate to interrupt," Evelyn said. "But our guests will want their wine samples and appetizers in five minutes." They hadn't gotten to the tasting of what Evelyn had set out for them on the counter. "Charlene?"

Charlene moved around Isabella and Rico, accepting the wine. She sipped it, noting the crisp pear taste. Was this the new blend? "It's delicious."

Rico and Isabella scowled at each other, clearly uninterested in the wine.

"Thank you." Evelyn poured the last two together and drank it down in one swallow.

Brandy gave a delicate sniff, but snagged the inch of red before her mother quaffed that one too.

"Will you help me search for my sister?" Isabella asked, looking at Serenity, Evelyn, and Brandy.

"When?" Serenity asked.

"Tonight, and tomorrow. Possibly Monday too. I need to locate Marisol," Isabella said, her voice breaking on her sister's name. "As you know, the veil is the thinnest at these times."

"Sweetheart," Brandy said. "I would like to help you find peace with this situation, but we already have commitments with our coven. This is an important time of year in our Wiccan faith." She finished her wine and put it down by the rest of the empties.

"That's true," Evelyn seconded, her brow furrowed.

Serenity, appearing miserable, nodded. "Samhain is a big deal. I could possibly get away for an hour or two, but I couldn't stay all night, and not for all three days."

"Fine." Rico pushed away from the counter. "We will do it without your magical powers."

He left the gift shop.

"Latin temperament," Isabella said, dismissing Rico's temper tantrum. "He gets worse when he's under stress. I understand that you have commitments, but it was worth a chance to ask you. Can you think of anyone who might be able to help?"

"Detective Sam Holden can look into her disappearance from the physical proof angle," Brandy said.

"Charlene, will you contact him for me?" Isabella tilted her head.

"Sure!"

Brandy tapped her long nails on the counter. "Isabella, doll. I hate to say this, given the history we just learned between Rico and Persephone, but she and Kass are the strongest of our local witches."

"Besides us." Evelyn gathered the glasses.

Isabella cringed. "I was afraid you would say that."

CHAPTER 7

Charlene brought her van of very, very happy guests back to the B&B at five o' clock. They were full, tipsy, and enchanted by the Flint witches.

She was not quite as ecstatic because poor Sam had to reschedule their date for some one-on-one time because something had come up at the station. Honestly, the fact that they hadn't been interrupted last night by the Salem Police Department had been a miracle.

He was on for breakfast at the B&B in the morning, though.

Her mother, as if sensing there was an opening in the void of Charlene's schedule, had texted to see if Charlene could drop off some of Brandy's white wine because she knew Charlene had just visited.

Before unlocking the doors of the van, Charlene turned down the music and said, "Here's the plan for those who want to stick together." She waited until her guests looked her way. Isabella and Rico, Timothy and

Dotty, Marty and Juleen, and Spence and Darla all the way in the back.

As a savvy businesswoman who had learned how hectic Halloween in Salem could be, she'd prepaid for parking in the garage downtown to guarantee a space. "This van will leave here at six thirty. There will be a festival at the Pedestrian Mall with various activities, from food trucks to bobbing for apples. I highly recommend Kass Fortune's Tea Shoppe."

"I want to do that!" Dotty clapped her hands.

Charlene smiled at the older woman's enthusiasm. "We will reconvene at midnight at the parking garage, and I will drive us home. I am your designated driver so that you can relax and unwind. You don't have to stay with me, but this will be a crazy night—not as crazy as tomorrow, but still wild, so look out for one another. For now, you have an hour and a half to rest, change, or whatever."

Charlene unlocked the doors, and they all spilled out in a wave of giggles and chuckles.

Charlene and Avery exchanged grins before exiting.

"I'm going to meet Seth for his meal break because he has to work tonight," Avery said. "I'll catch up with you guys downtown."

"Text me and I'll tell you where we end up." Charlene stepped toward the porch. The guests grouped together around the front door. Silva's fur was puffed for warmth as she balanced on the railing. No sign of Jack.

"What are you up to?" Avery pulled her keys from her pocket. She had her own car, which Charlene's parents had bought for her as a graduation gift to help with college transportation. Nothing fancy, but reliable.

"I'm going to deliver a few bottles of white wine to my mother."

"You are a good daughter, Charlene." Avery smiled. "Want me to do it for you? I'll be in that area."

"It's two miles out of the way." Charlene shook her head. "But thank you. That was very sweet. Besides, I know Mom really wants the dirt on our guests. I made the mistake of sharing about Isabella's missing sister, so she'll want an update."

"Charlene?" Dotty called from the porch. "I forgot the code again."

"On that note . . . see you later, sweetie," Charlene said. Avery waved and went to her car while Charlene climbed the steps to the porch.

The security system had been updated at the bed-and-breakfast and was up to Jack and Sam's standards. There were security cameras around the property and the house. Because her business was also her home, she'd decided on the code lock so that it could be changed after each round of guests.

Charlene had the master key that would override the code system if necessary, but that meant digging through the side pocket in search of them as she'd just dropped them inside her large purse.

Silva reached out for Darla's scarf as the young woman stood before her and tugged it loose. Spence saw the cat and laughed. "Careful, Darla. You almost lost your scarf."

Darla whirled and scratched Silva under the chin. "She has good taste, right, kitty? It's cashmere."

Silva purred and tilted her head so Darla had better access.

Jack appeared in an instant. "You're home!" he said while Minnie unlocked the door from the other side.

"Hello?" Minnie had orange icing on her cheek. "Oh, forget the code? I do it all the time." She widened the door. "Hey, Charlene. Sounds like everyone had fun."

"They did. We did." The guests filed past Charlene and Minnie over the threshold of the open door. "I won't be here long. I'm running some wine to Mom, but I'll be back by six thirty to take our crew downtown."

"Wonderful—let me make them a quick tray of treats. My skulls are still cooling so they aren't ready yet, but the eyeballs are done," Minnie said with a straight face. "The extra chocolate cupcakes too."

"Skulls? Eyeballs?" Charlene said, following Minnie across the foyer.

"Dessert! I thought it might be fun to have a sugar skull cookie decorating contest because it is Halloween. Winner could get a Starbucks gift card for ten bucks. I always have those on hand because they're a nice way to tip people."

"You're a genius," Charlene said. "I'm in. Let me run to the bathroom real quick and I'll take some of the eyeballs to Mom." She burst out laughing. "It's so funny to say out loud!"

As soon as she was in her private living room suite,

Jack adjusted the volume of the TV a bit. "How was Brandy's?"

"Good—hey, I found out that Marisol and Rico had an argument before she disappeared. What if he . . . you know." Charlene arched her brows at Jack. "Killed her?"

Jack's body shimmered with alarm. "I remember a documentary I watched recently that said a high percentage of victims know their killer. Boy next door, lovers thwarted. Jealousy." He manifested fully. "I really hope Marisol is alive."

"Me too—Isabella asked me to contact Sam. I've invited him over for a casual breakfast tomorrow." Charlene looked at her image in the mirror, reached into her purse, and applied a lip tint with sunscreen—important despite the lack of sunshine. Who knew your lips could age? This getting older wasn't for the faint of heart.

"Casual breakfast. Just conversation that you are so good at," Jack enthused. "Sam should be taking notes."

Her phone dinged. Her mother, wanting to know her ETA. "I wish I could stay here and talk with you, but Brenda Woodbridge wants her white wine, which is a cover for the fact that she wants to gossip about the guests—Isabella in particular."

"You're onto her." Jack chuckled. "But you've got to admit, all of those mysteries she reads makes her pretty good at patching clues together."

"You have a point." Charlene adjusted the strap of her purse over her shoulder and put her hand on the doorknob. "Will you see what you can find out about the disappearance of Marisol Perez? I'll be back at six thirty to take the guests downtown."

"I'm on it!"

"Thanks. Bye!" She bit her tongue before she said *Jack* aloud and left the suite for the kitchen.

Minnie had a reusable plastic container for the sweet treats in a cardboard box with three bottles of white wine from the wine cellar in the basement. "Tell your parents I said hello."

"I will." Charlene gave Minnie a hug. "Thank you so much—I'll be back shortly."

"The guests will be okay if you're a few minutes late. Don't speed, all right?" Minnie shook her finger at Charlene.

Charlene made no promises as she left, driving her trusty Pilot rather than the Mercedes rental van. As she drove down Crown Pointe Road and reached the main street that would lead to the wharf and her parents' condo, she was amazed by the number of people already in costume though Halloween wasn't until tomorrow. Salem natives loved to party. Of course, there would be a full weekend of dress up for those who were into it.

She planned to borrow Avery's cat ears and had bought a tail for tomorrow, but that was the extent of her dressing up. As the driver for their guests, it was more important that she be comfortable, so her black jeans would have to do.

Avery had an Agatha Christie costume put together and had convinced Seth to dress up like Hercule Poirot. He had to work tomorrow evening, but they planned on going to a bonfire on the beach with their friends at two in the morning.

Not driving more than four miles over the limit, Charlene arrived at her parents' condo in fifteen minutes. The white building was modern and had a view of the bay, the docks full of expensive pleasure boats. A bench with Benjamin Fiske's very handsome face greeted her as she exited by the sidewalk. According to the dozens of benches around Salem, he was the number one salesman for the yacht club. He also had several commercials with his business phone number in the tune of a sailor's jig that she immediately began to hum. It was brilliant marketing, if you could afford it.

She'd need to call for pricing.

Charlene entered the lobby and pressed the elevator button for the tenth floor, setting the box Minnie had packed so expertly on one hip.

Once there, she stepped out to a tiled hallway and turned to the right: 1011. Her parents had a Halloween carpet before their door. She was still knocking when the door opened, and her mom pulled her inside.

"Charlene!" Her mom hugged her like she hadn't seen her just last week.

"Daughter," her dad greeted her with a doting smile.

There were worse things than having loving parents, even überloving ones. Charlene hugged them with one arm and carried the box of goodies into the condo with the other.

She perused the two-bedroom with an appreciative eye and noted all the homey touches that made it welcoming. A braided rag rug in ivory and chocolate, the lamp they'd gotten at Archie's Vintage Treasures, the fisherman's knit afghan over the ivory leather couch.

"Great job in here, guys." Pictures of the three of them adorned the sideboard table in matching silver frames. The front window overlooked the bay with a lovely view. She could see the lighthouse.

Making her way to the kitchen, Charlene put the wine and treats on their round table.

"What's that?" her dad asked. He loved his sweets.

"Minnie sends her love in the form of dessert," Charlene teased.

"I'll put the electric kettle on," Mom said.

"I can't stay." Her parents both looked at her expectantly and she read the time on the kitchen clock. Five thirty. "For more than thirty minutes," she said. "I'm taking the guests downtown for the festival. Have you guys been?"

"We're planning to go tomorrow. Maybe we can meet for a coffee?" Her mom narrowed her eyes at Charlene and then smiled. "You look beautiful. Not as tired. Salem agrees with you."

Charlene's knees buckled at the sincere compliment. "Thanks, Mom. It does."

So did her life here with Jack, and Avery, Minnie, Silva, and Sam. Would her parents understand her feelings for the detective? They were well aware of how deeply she'd loved Jared.

"I can't believe it's been three years since I moved." Charlene took off her light jacket and slung it over the back of the kitchen chair, hanging her purse on the arm.

"Time passes so fast," her mom said.

Dad got out three mugs and removed the top from the dessert container. He laughed so hard he had to suck in a breath. "That looks like a real eyeball. Minnie is an artist."

"I'm talking her into a Charlene's cookbook." The yellow pudding was in a tiny pastry cup with a black dot in the center and chocolate wisps for lashes.

"This needs to be included." Dad picked it up and put it in his mouth with a sigh of delight. "Brenda. Don't touch those—they're awful."

Her mom smirked. "Uh-huh. That's fine. I'll try a mini cupcake." She took a bite. "Devil's food!"

Dad brought out a tin of tea from Kass's shop, each in individual muslin bags. "We have your favorite, hon, orange spice."

They chatted seamlessly about Halloween, the costumes, the scandal of Isabella and Rico's love affair. Jack was right about her mom, who seconded his opinion. "People are usually killed by someone they knew or loved. If Rico and Marisol were arguing, what if he did it?"

Her dad frowned. "I don't like it—what if you are in danger?"

"We have security cameras all over the property. We'll be fine." They didn't know about Jack and, like Sam, preferred their facts tangible. Then again, they were Catholic, so not everything was visible. Sam didn't discuss religion with her. "And Marisol very well could have taken off."

"I hope she is alive," her mom said, sounding doubtful.

It was ten after six by the time she finally got out of there, and traffic was so thick that what normally took fifteen minutes dragged to twenty-five.

Charlene hurried inside the B&B. Silva meowed, chiding, from the gallery. Her guests were ready in their coats.

"Give me just a second!" Charlene ran down the hall, through the kitchen to her suite. Jack waited for her, but she raced into her room and slammed the door, changing into something warmer than the dress she'd had on for Sam.

Done, she opened her bedroom door and hopped into one boot, then the next. "How's it going?"

Jack shook his head. "You should take a breath." He smoothed her hair off her cheek.

Her heart warmed. "You were right about Mom. Did you discover anything regarding Marisol's disappearance?"

"Not a thing, and that is unusual *if* Isabella filed a police report, which I didn't find. The building they rented, with their joint business, was leased to Marisol and Isabella Perez. Rico wasn't on the paperwork anywhere."

"I think he came into the picture later, after the girls were established," Charlene said. "I'll find out when."

"Okay—it took me that long just to uncover that little bit of information." Jack shrugged. "Sorry it's not more."

Charlene grabbed her purse and jacket. "You're the best. Do you think Rico is a danger to any of us?"

"I'll research him next. Be careful."

Charlene blew him a kiss and raced from her suite, down the hall, and greeted her guests in the foyer. "Who is ready to party?"

Dotty, though the oldest, cheered the loudest. "I want to get my tarot cards read, and have a psychic reading, and the tea leaves . . ."

"All of the things," Juleen teased kindly. She and Marty had dressed in black, of course, though Juleen had painted her face white and doll-like. "We're making headway through Dotty's list and it's not even Halloween yet."

"My Dotty has always had a joy for life." Timothy smoothed Dotty's coat collar. "I love it about her."

Dotty took his hand. "And I love your sense of adventure. Other men would say *why*, and you say, why *not*?"

The last part was echoed by the other couples in the room, so it was a thing she must have said often before. Darla had also painted her face, but Spence didn't have any makeup on. It was Halloween weekend and there were no rules.

Charlene waved to Minnie and Jack, then opened the door. "Let's go!"

She climbed in, missing Avery in the passenger seat. She started the van, made sure everyone was buckled in, and hit the gas.

Darla and Juleen were having a spirited discussion on best Halloween movie ever. Juleen, of course, voted for *The Nightmare Before Christmas*, and Darla insisted it was *Child's Play*.

Charlene wouldn't have chosen either but was a fan

of *The Stand*. It had a slow, steady, creepy, end-of-the-world pace that she loved.

By ten minutes after seven, Charlene was carefully driving through the horde of people that reminded her of the *Walking Dead* zombies. Some folks were even dressed like zombies, which made it stranger.

"This is madness." Spence's tone was excited. He and Darla were way in the back again and his voice echoed toward her.

Leo and Patrick had chosen to walk and would meet them somewhere around Kass's. As Charlene neared the parking garage, she saw Brian Preston in his security guard uniform, monitoring the flow of traffic in and out of the cement building.

The tickets were automated, so there wasn't any need to check them in. Charlene drove by Brian with a polite smile that he ignored. Isabella and Rico, behind Charlene, tensed.

Isabella pointed Brian out and Rico swore in Spanish. Charlene parked on the first floor in the space she'd purchased. "Is everything okay?" If there was danger, she would call 911.

"I'm not sure!" Isabella's words trembled. "Now that I know Brian and Marisol were hooking up, something I cannot fathom, it makes me wonder if he'd actually been stalking her. Was that a ruse by Marisol for whatever reason? Maybe I should talk to him and ask if he's seen her. Remember how he'd thought I was Marisol a few weeks ago?"

"No, Bella," Rico said. "He's a creep. I don't trust him."

"What should we do?" Charlene thought Brian was too intense.

"I don't think Brian saw me," Isabella said, sinking back into Rico. "Let's avoid him."

Charlene turned off the engine and unlocked the van. Juleen opened the side door and slid it back. Marty hopped out after her and helped everyone else, while Isabella, Rico, and Charlene remained in the car.

Charlene dug through her bag for a pashmina. "Here. You can cover your hair. Should I drive you back to the B-and-B?"

"No. It's okay. Why should *I* have to be afraid? What if he . . . *argued* with Marisol?" Isabella shuddered. "We have to talk with him, but not here, where he can blow me off."

"A private conversation." Rico pounded a fist into his opposite palm. "Good idea."

"No fighting," Charlene murmured. "If there is a problem, find me, or go to the Salem police station, which is just a mile away. Give or take."

"We are not going to the police. I have a way to handle things myself." Rico's eyes turned cold, and for once she considered him dangerous rather than full of himself.

"Let's stick together," Charlene suggested.

"Don't worry. We won't confront him yet," Rico said. "I have plans to meet with Jonas to get the things for Marisol's *ofrenda*."

"Should Isabella stay with me?" Charlene had to protect the young lady who only wanted to find her sister.

"I'll be fine, Charlene. Uncle Jonas is family. We will have a nice visit." Isabella wrapped the pashmina around her hair and face. "Thank you. If we don't see you tonight, we will catch up over breakfast."

"Oh—good, because Sam is going to stop by if he can," Charlene said quietly to Isabella as Rico was out of the car. How did one suggest that they should be on guard from their boyfriend?

Isabella slipped out, and she and Rico were gone in the shadows without Brian being the wiser.

Charlene locked the van and pocketed her keys. Juleen, Marty, Dotty, Timothy, Spence, and Darla were waiting for her with wide, expectant smiles.

She had to put her worry behind her and focus on the positive. Her guests deserved her full attention. "Who wants to get their tarot cards read?" The ladies raised their hands. "Okay. Shall I take the women to Persephone's across the street and see if she has any openings? The guys can grab food or a drink or something."

"I'm okay waiting," Timothy said. Marty and Spence nodded that they didn't mind hanging around either.

"That makes things a little easier." She pointed across the street to a brick building with a neon sign that blinked TAROT and PSYCHIC.

They crossed the street, caught in the wave of festivalgoers. Most were dressed in costumes, but there were some who were in jeans and jackets. On the corner next to Persephone's was a bar with a skull and crossbones over the door that had smoke seeping beneath it.

Charlene paused to sniff. Not fire, but cigarette smoke.

Dotty headed toward Persephone's place. She whirled, her expression crestfallen. "Oh, darn it."

"What is it?" Charlene sighed as she read the sign that read, "Closed."

CHAPTER 8

Charlene patted Dotty's shoulder. "There is more than one tarot card reader in Salem. Why don't we go to Kass's and those who want them can get tea leaf readings? She will absolutely know some good backup tarot card readers."

Dotty pulled herself together. "Sorry. I was just so excited. Serenity at the winery said that Persephone was really good, like, the best."

"We can wait or ask Kass if she knows another. Her tea shop is down here at the end, so we can walk five blocks on one side and then come back on the other," Charlene said. "The middle of the mall will be packed with outdoor food trucks and stalls for things to buy. It's meant for foot traffic."

Spence smelled the air. "Bratwurst!"

Darla giggled. "How can you be hungry?"

Spence patted his flat tummy. "I'm a growing boy. All the work we do in the band keeps me skinny."

"I'd love to hear you play sometime," Juleen said. "I think it's cool that you guys perform together."

"You sing?" Charlene asked Darla, thinking she'd be an adorable front woman. She wore a leather jacket with silver buttons and tight jeans with black motorcycle boots. Her outfit matched her husband's. They weren't playing punk rockers for Halloween but lived the lifestyle every day.

"No," Darla said. "I'm on drums. Spence sings and plays guitar. He's the best front man ever."

"We have our first single being released in December." Spence spoke proudly and put his arm around his wife. "She's amazing on the sticks."

"Send me the information and I'll buy it," Charlene said. *And not play it where Jack can hear it*, she thought with a chuckle.

They walked down the street, hopping into touristy shops that appealed. Everyone bought something, from a witch's globe—Juleen—to dish towels—Darla and Dotty.

As it turned out, there were TAROT READER signs in a lot of shop windows, but Dotty wanted Persephone and so would wait. Kass and Persephone were friends, so maybe she could pull some strings.

"I have cash," Dotty said.

"Sh!" Darla said. "You are too nice a lady to be mugged."

They arrived at Kass's, and Charlene checked the time on her phone. Nine already. Avery had texted that she was hanging out at the theater with Seth and wouldn't meet them after all. It was slasher day at the movies.

Charlene shuddered. Not her type of horror. She opened the door to Kass's tea shop, and her six guests wandered in.

"This is the best!" Juleen exclaimed. "Charlene, will you take me and Marty's picture with the goddess and the teapot? Nobody would believe us if we told them this was here."

"Sure! Kass Fortune designed the fountain herself."

Charlene took the goth couple's picture as they wore huge grins and handed the phone back.

Kass, her hair out of braids, so perfectly crimped, came around the counter. "Is that Charlene Morris I hear?"

"Yes, ma'am!" Charlene urged her flock forward.

"And she's psychic?" Dotty murmured.

"The real deal—I'll let her tell you about her special type of gifts." Charlene nodded at Kass. "We have several takers for your tea leaf reading, if you don't mind."

Suddenly the guys were into it too, so all six raised their hands.

"Come on over and have a seat at the counter. I'll tell you my spiel and then have my intern help you pick a tea blend." Kass rubbed her hands together. "You drink it and then I try to decipher messages from the arrangement of your tea leaves."

"I didn't know that was a thing for real," Marty said.

"We are learning a lot this trip, like with the crystals too," Juleen said.

"Crystals?" Kass asked.

"Isabella got rid of Spence's headache with the red-orange rock," Darla said.

"Carnelian." Kass nodded. "Good for detoxing."

"That's what Isabella said." Darla tapped her chin. "I don't understand the whole psychic thing . . . you'd think that if you had one talent, you should be able to do them all. Isabella said her sister was a good tarot card reader, but her gift is crystals."

"It is interesting how paranormal abilities work . . . so much of it is being intuitive to understand what you can do. I can see ghosts, but not always. There are a lot of ghosts in Salem. I can read tea leaves, but I can't see auras or divine the future with a pendulum. No cards for me either. I love crystals and rocks; they remind me of nature. Maybe I could learn to use them, but I don't know." Kass scrunched her nose. "That sounded very confusing."

Darla laughed. "I get it. Bottom line? You aren't sure."

Juleen asked, "Does it matter what type of tea we choose? Like, if I want to know how many kids I'll have, do I have to drink, I don't know, lemongrass?"

Marty choked. "Uh, Jules, we are not having kids, so let's save the magic for something you really want to know."

Kass chuckled. "It doesn't really work like that, with a yes or no answer. It's an overall feeling I get as I read the shapes of the leaves in the cup."

"I'm open to whatever," Spence said. "I mean, we have a single, so no matter what we are on the road to success, right, Darla?"

"Right." Darla slipped her hand into Spence's.

Kass waved to Nate as Sue was helping a customer with a teapot selection. Nate was twenty, dark-skinned, with a pierced nose and a friendly manner.

"Hey!" Nate called in a general greeting.

"Nate, will you help select the teas for their readings? Charlene, do you mind going in the back for mugs and more timers?"

"Not at all." Charlene went around the counter and ducked behind a curtain where Kass kept her mugs, the timers, and the saucers. Spoons, sugars, and honey. There were some biscotti she'd baked as well, but Charlene didn't want to bring it out if Kass had it for some other purpose.

Charlene arranged everything on the counter and brought out two extra stools so they could all have a seat. She preferred to observe from a standing position.

"And I was really hoping you could get me an appointment with Persephone," Dotty said, charming her way to Kass's heart.

"Sure. I know she was at the booth in the middle of the mall earlier but had to leave for an important client," Kass said. "Guy's a regular, so he calls the shots. Persephone should be done by ten. I'll text her to see what she can do." She put her hand on Dotty's shoulder. "She's expensive, though. Is that all right?"

Dotty nodded and whispered, "I have cash."

At the end of the tea readings, everyone was very pleased with Kass and what she saw for them in their leaves. Darla and Spence were going to be famous with their band, Timothy would travel. Dotty had married her soul mate. Marty was a savvy investor and would be able to retire by sixty if that was what he truly wanted. Juleen had Kass puzzled. "I see books around you. Do you like to read?"

"Yes. Love it."

"It's all she does," Marty said.

"Is it?" Kass questioned.

"What do you mean?" Marty asked, looking from Kass to Juleen.

"I see, yes, I see a pen. Like, a writer. Do you want to be a writer? Fiction?"

Juleen's eyes were so wide that Charlene got worried for her. "How can you know that? I haven't told anyone."

"Obviously!" Marty said, sounding hurt.

"Don't be upset, Marty, honey, I just . . . I see these stories in my head and I know I can write just as well as some of the authors of the books I've read." Juleen pursed her lips. "I . . . I want to write Gothic romance."

Kass applauded, and so did the rest of their group. "You should follow your dreams." She let her warm gaze touch each of them. "This time on earth is short. Be happy, be kind, and dream."

"Can I buy some tea to take home? I never want to forget this day," Juleen said.

Marty was slowly coming around to the fact that his wife wanted to be an author. Romance. He seemed very pleased about it as he said, "Can we practice the kissing scenes?"

Juleen blushed.

Kass laughed. "Nate, will you get Juleen a tin to go?"

They all wanted some, as it turned out, and nobody complained about the prices for the handcrafted tea blends.

Kass read a text and looked for Dotty. "Persephone's

running late with her client, but she can see you at ten thirty. It takes an hour."

"Juleen and I wanted readings too," Darla said. "Maybe tomorrow?"

Kass fired off another message. "If you want the whole experience, she will need to get some rest, so tomorrow at noon and one. An hour is three hundred per person, cash only. Yes?"

Dotty nodded. "I have enough for tonight."

"We can go to the bank tomorrow and get some money," Spence told Darla. "I think you should do it. We're gonna be famous." He winked.

"Yes, for me too. Oh, wow. I'm so glad you wanted to do all these things, Dotty." Juleen slung an arm around the older woman's shoulders, grinning from ear to ear.

"Where is Isabella?" Kass asked Charlene as they headed toward the door. They were going to get food on the way to the van but had time to spare. She was hungry, too, as the small snacks from Brandy's had worn off.

"She and Rico were meeting with an Uncle Jonas who was bringing Marisol's favorite things for the *ofrenda* shrine from New Orleans," Charlene said.

"I didn't think Bella had any family left." Kass sighed but let it go. "Well, it's probably an affectionate title. I really hope we find out what happened with Marisol."

"What do you think of Rico?" Charlene whispered.

"He's kind of a jerk . . . oh, what do I think of Rico, as in could he be behind Marisol's disappearance?" Kass exhaled and flexed her hands. "I don't know. I hope Marisol has the Santa Muerte hidden away somewhere and will decide to come home."

"Did Isabella talk to you about tomorrow night to help with the magic?"

"She did, but I am celebrating with my coven," Kass said. "I'll try my best for Monday night, if needed." She lowered her voice. "Bella texted Persephone, and I think Persephone is willing to do it. Maybe to get back at Rico?"

"Who was Rico with first? Persephone or Marisol?"

"I don't know. We should find out . . ." Kass said. "You are so *good* at conversation, you should do it."

"Hey now," Charlene said.

"It's important," Kass said. "We have to help Isabella."

"I'll try." Charlene had nobody to blame but herself and her own curiosity.

They reached the door where her guests were waiting for her with bags of goodies one could only find in Salem.

"Let's talk tomorrow," Kass said. "This long weekend is a wonderful thing for our cash registers. Anytime you want a tea reading, Charlene, it's on the house with all the business you've brought me."

Before Charlene could answer, Kass was walking toward Nate and the back counter. Sue rang up a customer with three teapots.

Charlene exited into the cool fall evening air and read the time on her phone. How had it gotten to be a quarter past ten? No wonder her stomach was rumbling.

"Why don't you guys grab food and drinks, and I'll

walk with Dotty and Timothy to meet Persephone, okay? The van will leave at midnight, and we can gather there. If you don't want to catch a ride, just text me."

Charlene waited for nods and then went with Dotty and Timothy down five blocks to the opposite side of downtown. Music was blaring out of the Skull and Crossbones bar next door.

"I was hoping for a drink and a bite to eat," Timothy said, "but that is a bit too loud."

Charlene pointed to a quieter establishment.

On the other side of the building was a darker pub with a captain's wheel above it. Timothy peeked inside. "Clean too. The window has a view of the tarot place, so we can see when Dotty's finished with the reading."

"I can text you too," Dotty said. She held up her phone.

"True. All right." Timothy nodded.

"Do you want me to go inside with you, Dotty?" Charlene asked.

"No, of course not. Persephone Lowell is the best." Dotty grinned. "I won't be in any danger."

Charlene knocked on the front door and Persephone, in a turban that mostly covered mermaid pink hair and a caftan, answered. "Dotty Cranston?"

"Yes." Dotty was so excited she giggled.

"Come in." Persephone stepped back and waved her arm invitingly.

"We'll be next door," Charlene said.

"Okay!" Dotty said. "Bye!"

As Charlene turned, she saw a man with a stylish wool coat with the collar pulled up and a knit cap leave

Persephone's by a side door—a discreet entryway if you didn't want to be seen.

Of course this made Charlene even more curious, but the figure, after winking at Charlene, hurried the other way. Kass shared that Persephone had high-end clients, as had Marisol. Enough to afford the expensive rent of these old buildings. The man had looked very familiar to her, but she couldn't place it just yet.

"That's fine. Kass said that Serenity Flint recommended me? How sweet." Persephone pulled Dotty in and closed the door, leaving Charlene and Timothy on the sidewalk.

"What a day!" Timothy walked the few paces to the next building and opened the door of the pub for Charlene. "After you."

"Thanks!" Charlene went inside to the hostess stand. The interior was dim and smelled like fish and chips.

"How many?" a woman as old as literal dirt asked.

"Two," Timothy said.

The woman passed over menus, her hands afflicted with gnarled arthritic knuckles. "We have a limited selection this late, but the cheeseburger is always good. We have amber on draft for three dollars."

"Sounds great to me," Timothy said. "Charlene?"

Her stomach rumbled. "The cheeseburger, but an ice water, please."

"I know you drink," Timothy said when the hostess ambled off toward the kitchen with surprising speed. Several tables were full, and the room held the din of low conversations. "You don't like beer?"

"Not while I'm driving the rental van. I wouldn't

feel right if something happened." Charlene smiled. "When I get home, I'll have a nice glass of red to unwind."

Timothy laughed, and they went to a booth on the left. Charlene shrugged out of her jacket and put her purse on the bench.

"I'll be right back." Charlene needed the restroom and wanted to wash up. Timothy had his phone on the table and a view of the window and the building next door. If Persephone made three hundred bucks an hour for an eight-hour day . . . no way could she have that full of a schedule on a consistent basis. How else might she make money? Salem's historic district wasn't cheap.

Walking into the dim recesses of the pub, she heard Rico shouting in Spanish. He didn't handle his booze well.

Was Isabella all right?

Embarrassing or not, Charlene wouldn't let Rico hurt Isabella.

Trying to be discreet, Charlene peered around the massive shoulders of a man who was red in the face with fury—not Rico. He was around fifty, Charlene surmised. Dark brown hair mixed with gray and a full bushy beard. Blue eyes.

"Uncle Jonas," Isabella said. "Rico. Please calm down."

Was this man actually her uncle? He had a Louisiana accent, so it might be someone from her past in New Orleans.

"Calm down? Issie, darlin', I'm willing to welcome you back to Salem with open arms, even though you left me in the lurch two years ago with all of the Santa

Muerte merch. I miss you and love you and your sister like you were kin." Jonas picked up a packet of cigarettes, and Charlene noticed the Louisiana-style grits and a bottle of Mexican tequila, silver. For Marisol's *ofrenda*? "I hope to God she isn't dead. For the gold Santa Muerte statue and Marisol to both be gone?" The man growled low in his chest. "She could live like a queen anywhere. I'm not sure how I feel about it." He tapped the table with impatience. "Well? Would you come back?"

Isabella shrugged with confusion. "I don't know."

Rico slammed his hand to the table, sloshing his glass of tequila. "We made a lot of money here. I don't hate the idea of reopening the shop."

Isabella raised her head as if coming to a decision. "I don't want to come back. I want to find information about my sister. I am not leaving Salem until I know one way or the other what happened to Marisol." Isabella glanced over toward where Charlene was blatantly eavesdropping. "Charlene? What are you doing here?"

CHAPTER 9

"I thought I recognized your voice, Isabella," Charlene said, trying to play off her snooping. It was true, anyway, but she should have made her presence known. "Timothy and I are grabbing a burger while Dotty gets her tarot cards read with Persephone next door."

Jonas started to get to his feet. "Who the hell are you?"

Charlene understood his anger and spoke in a very reassuring manner. "I'm Charlene Morris. I own a bed-and-breakfast on Crown Pointe Road." She didn't add that Isabella and Rico were staying with her there, just in case Isabella hadn't mentioned it. This meeting smacked of secrecy. Gold statue? This was the first inkling she'd had that it might have been valuable. The one on the *ofrenda* had been white plastic.

"Sit down, Uncle Jonas," Isabella said. "Charlene, this is Jonas McCarthy." She checked the time on her phone. "We're going to finish up here and we'll meet you at the van. I'm glad you haven't left. Thanks again for all you did to arrange our evening." She turned her attention to Jonas and the items on the table.

Dismissed, Charlene hurried to the restroom to wash up, and when she returned, the trio were talking in much lower tones.

When she reached the booth where Timothy waited, their burgers were just coming from the back of the restaurant. Her stomach rumbled. The delicious appetizers at the winery seemed a million years ago.

"I wonder if Persephone has a different business going on in the back of her tarot shop," Timothy remarked after they'd each eaten a few bites. He was on his second amber draft.

"Why do you say that?" Charlene glanced out the window, and though the streetlamps provided some illumination, it was still dark.

"Since I've been sitting here, I've counted three different people coming and going." Timothy took another bite of burger.

Charlene turned to study the space, squinting, but of course the covered entryway remained empty. "A lot of these old buildings have been split into apartments."

She'd have to ask Kass about it. At eleven thirty, Timothy's phone went off with a message from Dotty asking if they were still at the pub. She was hungry.

"Will you order Dotty a cheeseburger and beer? I'll go get her," Timothy said. "She's a fast eater if the waitress has a problem."

The hostess watched him go and returned to their

table. "Can we get another cheeseburger and draft, please?" Charlene asked. "Timothy's wife is joining us."

The neon lights at Persephone's place that read TAROT went off, leaving the corner dark and shadowy.

"You bet," the older woman said.

Timothy and Dotty entered, hand in hand. Dotty enthused over her reading and said that she and Timothy were real soul mates and this was their third lifetime together.

All before she scooted onto the bench of the booth. Timothy, grinning, sat down after her. "Of course we are, hon."

"What was it like?" Charlene had never had her cards read for the same reason she hadn't had a tea leaf reading. She didn't want to know.

"Very, very cool. The only thing Persephone was missing was a crystal ball." Dotty's cheeseburger arrived along with her draft by eleven forty.

"Anything else?" the waitress asked.

"The bill is fine," Timothy said.

"Have you ever had your cards read?" Dotty asked their waitress, who unbent enough to smile at Dotty's enthusiasm.

"Sure, when I was younger. Now, I know what the future will hold and I'm in no rush to meet my Maker." She shuffled off.

"Well!" Dotty said with a perplexed expression.

"Eat your fries, dear," Timothy said. "And as your soul mate, I feel like I should have one, you know, just to test it out for you."

"They were great." Charlene preferred skinny fries such as these compared to the wedges.

Dotty nudged her plate a little toward Timothy, happy to share.

At five till midnight, they were gearing up to go when Charlene happened to look out the window to see Brian Preston, in his guard uniform, come out of the side entry. He was heading away from the parking garage.

Did he know that Isabella and Rico were in the Captain's Wheel? Did he know Jonas? It seemed clear that he knew Persephone. Kass had mentioned that Brian had transferred his stalking attentions from Marisol to Persephone.

Isabella, carrying the items for Marisol in a box that read FISKE'S WHARF, walked past them to the hostess stand. Once there, she turned and saw Charlene, Dotty, and Timothy. "Oh, hey," she said.

Jonas and Rico, arms slung around each other's shoulders to show that they were friends again, joined Isabella by the podium.

Rico took the box from Isabella. Jonas focused his attention to where Isabella was looking and gave Charlene an apologetic smile.

"Sorry about that." Jonas jerked his thumb to the back table. "I didn't realize that you and Isabella knew each other."

"It's okay," Charlene said. "I shouldn't have startled you." She wasn't sorry for making sure Isabella was all right. Her sister was missing, possibly having been murdered. Rico had argued with Marisol before her disappearance.

"You headed back to the boat, Uncle Jonas?" Isabella asked.

"Yeah." Jonas adjusted the buttons on his navy-blue canvas coat. "I'll be in town for the next few days, though, just to see how the *ofrenda* works out. You can find me at the harbor." He looked at Isabella. "Don't leave town without letting me know."

Isabella nodded, her cheeks red with embarrassment that Charlene didn't understand. "Promise."

Jonas left, the old door screeching closed behind him. Dotty and Timothy got out of the booth, as did Charlene.

"He lives on a boat?" Dotty's eyes sparkled. "I've always thought that would be very interesting. Like a sailboat?"

"No—nothing so glamorous for Uncle Jonas." Isabella laughed. "He has a sturdy vessel meant for the ocean that is bare bones for transferring merchandise. Not even a flushing toilet."

"Whew. I was getting worried that Dotty might be off on another adventurous tangent," Timothy said with a chuckle.

"We've had several lifetimes together," Dotty informed Isabella and Rico.

"That's really lovely," Isabella said with complete acceptance.

"One woman only for multiple lifetimes?" Rico gave a little headshake and adjusted the weight of the box in his arms.

"You can be such a jerk, Rico." Isabella tipped up her nose. "Maybe I shouldn't be trying so hard, huh?"

"Bella, it's been a long day. I'm sorry." Rico sounded sincere.

Was he?

Charlene glanced out the window and grinned at the familiar bobbing mohawks of Spence and Darla. Juleen and Marty followed them. All four were laughing. Charlene wouldn't be surprised if they would remain lasting friends.

Pointing out the window, Charlene said, "There's the rest of our crew. Let's go!"

She hurried toward the door and pushed it open to the brisk midnight air. Leo and Patrick trailed the group, chatting animatedly about ghosts. Clouds obscured the moon and stars.

Isabella, Rico, Timothy, and Dotty followed Charlene as she crossed the street to the parking garage. Hundreds of people were out and about on this eerie Saturday night.

All her guests were accounted for, which made Charlene a happy hostess. "Hi, guys!"

The mohawked couple turned, with Juleen and Marty. Leo and Patrick stayed on their heels. The rental van seated fifteen, with plenty of room in the back for the packages they carried, filled with Halloween treasures.

"Hey, Charlene," Leo said. "Salem is the coolest city ever. We'll be back to the B-and-B later." His expression glowed. "Don't wake us up for breakfast. What's the plan for tomorrow night, again? The main event?"

"We are going with Kevin from Brews and Broomsticks on a ghost tour," Charlene reminded them. "To the cemeteries too."

"Cool!" Patrick said. "Def sign us up for that. Bye, guys!" He grabbed Leo by the shoulder. "Those girls might be waiting for us if we hurry."

The pair rushed off.

"I can't imagine being twenty-one again," Charlene said, exhausted by their energy.

"Babes in the woods," Timothy concurred.

Spence shook his head. "They make me feel old and I'm not even thirty."

"Just wait until you hit forty," Marty said, clapping his hand on Spence's shoulder.

Charlene silently concurred.

They all piled into the van, and Charlene carefully drove them back to the B&B. Avery's sedan was parked next to Isabella and Rico's car. Charlene's Pilot was in the freestanding garage.

They went into the mansion. Jack waited in the living room, Silva resting on the armchair. Her guests were all still having a good time and it wasn't even twelve thirty.

"Shall we keep the party going?" Dotty gave her hips a shimmy.

"I don't know how you do it," Juleen said. "I'm ready for bed and another awesome day tomorrow."

Darla and Spence raised their entwined hands. "Mr. Sandman calls to us as well," Spence said. "Totally dig the mattresses here, Charlene. We might need to upgrade at home."

Timothy smiled at Charlene. "It seems you will be drinking your nightcap alone."

"I don't mind unwinding in silence," Charlene said. Besides, she was never alone. She had Jack. "Night!"

Her guests ambled up the stairs with quieter murmurs. Leo and Patrick, college singles, were not on the same page as her couples. Even Avery must be in bed asleep.

Charlene went to the bar in the living room and poured herself a glass of red to take to her suite, where she and Jack could catch up. She picked up Silva in her free hand—the cat seemed extra fluffy after all of the Halloween treats—and listened for everyone to be in bed as she paused in the foyer. When she didn't hear a peep, she allowed herself to relax.

She had to put Silva down to enter her suite, and the cat rubbed against her ankles in protest. "Hang on, kitty cat."

Once in her suite, Charlene locked the door behind her and Silva as Jack materialized by his chair.

"You look tired, Charlene," Jack said.

"Not something you should say to a lady." Charlene sank down into the cushions of her love seat.

"Sorry." Jack peered at her with an appraising gaze. "Still, a good night's sleep is in order."

"I didn't have any garlic today," Charlene promised, petting Silva's soft fur. "Can you imagine if she was as big as the house? I mean, we joke about it, but that was terrifying. Big gold eyes—bigger than the moon even."

"It would be scary," Jack agreed.

Charlene sipped her wine and let the flavors of red grape coat her tongue. It was an immediate de-stresser. "I wonder if the Flints cast spells over their harvest to make their wine taste so good?"

Jack snorted. "Well, you could ask Brandy. She

would tell you. Would it ruin the pleasure of the wine for you?"

Taking a bigger drink, Charlene shook her head. "No. They still have to do all of the hard work, like fertilizing and pruning and harvesting. If a spell makes it that little bit better, I'm okay with it."

Jack sat on his chair and propped his socked feet on the coffee table. "How was the festival?"

"So many people were downtown, Jack, that I can't even imagine what tomorrow, Halloween, will be like. Costumes and parties. It's fun." Charlene relaxed her back against the cushions and sighed with happiness. "Our guests all got a tea leaf reading with Kass—even the guys."

"Any secrets uncovered?" Jack watched her with contentment.

"Yep." Charlene chuckled. "It seems Juleen has a secret dream to be a romance author! She hadn't even hinted at it to Marty, but he's on board and she's going to do it. Gothic romance."

"Romance is a good thing." Jack studied her and cleared his throat as if to prepare her for something.

Her stomach clenched and her happy vibes scooted toward the window. Charlene held them with her fingertips before they escaped. She wanted to be content for just another minute or two.

Did she want to know what Jack was going to say? She got the feeling, because he'd brought up the word *romance* . . . OMG. Had Avery brought Seth home?

They were both adults in a committed relationship. Should Charlene have the sex talk with Avery? No, she'd surely missed the boat on that.

Charlene had known the teen since she was sixteen and she was now nineteen, almost twenty? Just in case, Charlene would test the waters. She'd read an article that young adults were waiting to have sex. If that was the case, then Charlene could be a sounding board.

"Charlene." Jack snapped his fingers, soundlessly, before her nose. "Where did you go?"

"Avery and Seth." Charlene's cheeks burned. "You know."

"Oh . . ." Jack seemed surprised by her deduction, which meant she was way off base.

"Why?" Charlene straightened. "What were *you* thinking?"

"You, and Sam. How is your relationship going?" Jack stood and paced before the TV as if about to broach an uncomfortable subject. He was using his doctor tone. "I realize that you care for each other." He stopped abruptly.

Charlene's entire body flooded with heat. "Uh . . ."

"It occurred to me that we need to have a signal or something, you know, so that you can feel free to have Sam here." Jack's words came out intermittently, as if not on a solid frequency of energy.

"What?" Charlene tightened her grip on her wine-glass before she dropped it.

"This is your house, and you . . . you are in love with, Sam, right?"

Jack continued pacing, glancing her way every so often.

Charlene drank the rest of her wine in a gulp.

"Aren't you? It's okay, Charlene. He loves you; I see that every time he looks at you. Has he told you that?"

Charlene nodded, wishing she could disappear.

"Do you love him too?"

"I do. It's complicated. We, I . . ."

Looking at Jack, Charlene put her empty glass on the coffee table.

"It's hard to discuss, I realize," Jack said. "But we should do it, right? We are roommates in this house. I suppose this has a lot to do with my crisis of faith. I am dead. Stuck here. Good for nothing."

"Not true, Jack! You are loved here—not just by me and Silva, but now Avery too." Charlene gulped. This was not how she'd planned for her evening to go.

Jack sent a rush of cool air toward her to soothe her. "I realize this is awkward. We are both adults, but not really. I'm dead. A ghost. My feelings shouldn't matter. Should I even have them? Is my future to watch everyone die and become a remnant of energy slamming the refrigerator door, like the ghost in the Gambles' house?"

Tears poured down Charlene's face at his misery. "You're my best friend, Jack. But my boyfriend doesn't believe that you can possibly exist. I can't introduce you. When I first brought up to Sam that my house was haunted, he didn't believe me and thought I was crazy, remember?"

"I do. You helped me get closure with my murder." Jack manifested in his chair, exuding angst. "It was shocking. The reality of my death was devastating. I didn't know I had a son. I was not a nice person, at the end."

"You had a chance to go to Heaven and you stayed for me." Charlene held his turbulent turquoise gaze. "I was so sad, and lonely, and grieving. I was very selfish to want you to stay."

"I don't regret it," Jack said firmly.

She kept her head down. Nor her either. Again, selfish.

Jack tipped up her chin with a gust of chilly air. She could see the love he had for her written plainly in his eyes. "Listen," he said.

She sniffed.

"I am forever going to be forty-seven years old. You are going to change and grow and maybe get married to Sam, and what then?" He spread his arms to the side.

Charlene began to cry again.

She'd been asking herself that same question. What then?

"I don't know. Are you miserable, Jack?"

"My love for you is all-encompassing. It's not romantic love," Jack said with confusion. "I don't know how to explain it. I would rather be here and watch over you, and Avery, and Silva, and Minnie, than not exist without you."

Sniffing, she reached for Jack, her hand cold over the form of his knee. "I want to hug you," she said.

"Not a good idea." He disappeared and reappeared by the TV. "You'll freeze."

"I love you too, Jack." She held his gaze. "I would never, ever, want to hurt you."

"I know." Jack put his palm over his heart.

"So, what should we do?" Silva meowed and snuggled next to Charlene on the love seat. She stroked the cat's soft fur, warming her fingers.

"I've been thinking about that."

"You have a plan?" Charlene sat forward. Jack was so smart.

"No."

Charlene sighed and moved Silva to her lap. "We should come up with something, together."

Jack gave a grave nod. "I've been mulling over what will happen to me as you grow older."

Her stomach tightened as she imagined the sad scenario. It would be devastating if their roles were reversed and she had to watch him grow old and die.

"And Avery. She sees me, but she will eventually grow older too."

Tears streamed down her cheeks. "And you will be trapped here in this house, alone and unseen."

Jack's form flickered and shimmered. "Exactly. What then?"

Charlene couldn't allow that to happen. "We need to make a guidebook or something so that whoever inherits you knows how to communicate with you."

"Inherits me?" Jack laughed, the rumble deep in his chest—that sound he made just for her. He was trying to comfort her, when he was under his own emotional quandary. They did love each other—they were family.

"What's so funny?" Charlene asked, her lips twitching.

"A handbook for the dead is very *Beetlejuice*, and not a likely solution," Jack admonished playfully.

"We can try," Charlene said. "It's been something Avery and I have joked about, creating a manual for the paranormal world." But it might work to let whoever came next in her family, whoever inherited the house, know that it came with Jack.

"Really?" Jack's furrowed brow didn't seem as if he was impressed.

"Yes," Charlene said. "I think we need to figure that out, because I hate the idea of you being alone, and lonely, as much as I hated it when we first met." They'd saved each other.

"I was in the nothing, I returned to nothing. I don't remember it." Jack brought the afghan and put it over her shoulders. The soft blanket warmed her. Silva purred.

Jack was thoughtful and kind. So caring.

"So, about Sam," Jack said, returning to his position before the television.

"I don't want to talk about it right now." Charlene would prefer never.

"We need to figure something out. Like, if you have *date night*, I can be on the roof or in the tree."

"Jack!"

He teased her, "In the old college days, a sock on the door handle let your roomie know you were in having fun."

"I am not putting a sock on the door, Jack." Charlene burst out laughing at the absurdity of the scenario she found herself in.

"What?" His gaze sparkled mischievously.

"That's just such a guy thing to say."

He rubbed his knuckles against his turquoise sweater. "I am a guy."

There had never been any doubt of the doctor's masculinity, alive or dead. "I know that, Jack."

He tilted his head in question when Charlene shrugged off the blanket and moved Silva to the other cushion. She stood and strode toward her best friend.

"What?" Jack asked suspiciously.

Charlene braced herself and gave Jack a very, very quick hug. She pulled back even as her skin dotted with goose bumps and held his gaze.

The love there smote the chill within her.

"Actually, Jack, you are a true gentleman."

CHAPTER 10

Charlene was on her second cup of coffee and midway through her delicious spinach frittata when Minnie brought Sam into the dining room at nine. He was dressed casually in jeans and a flannel shirt. Her guests, except Leo and Patrick, were all around the table. Nobody had overdone it last night, so clear heads reigned this Sunday Halloween morning.

Her dreams had been tinged with sadness over Jack's emotional upheaval and her helplessness to make him feel better, but Silva's giant cat face hadn't made an appearance, menacing or otherwise.

There'd been no sign of her ghost today. A sock on the door handle! *Please.*

Charlene smiled at Sam, happy to see him.

She and her guests had been discussing the plan with Kevin for the day before the tour at ten tonight. The Hawthorne Hotel hosted an epic Halloween party, but the tickets had been sold out for months.

Charlene had kept a chair open next to her just in

case Sam was able to make it. He beelined across the room and sat while Minnie set a cup of hot black coffee before him.

"Juleen and I have our tarot readings today," Darla said.

"Noon and one, and I need a bank," Juleen said. "Dotty swears it's worth every penny. Maybe I'll find out I'll hit the *New York Times* bestseller list with my Gothic romances." She grinned. She hadn't yet put on her costume or makeup for the day, so had fresh skin and bright eyes.

Sam sat down and smiled at them all, thanking Minnie for the coffee with a nod of his head. "Morning, everyone. I'm Sam Holden."

Sam was not in police mode, which meant his demeanor was much more relaxed. Thanks to Jack's awkward conversation last night, Charlene kept thinking about socks on doorknobs and shook her head.

Lacy lingerie?

No!

Jack manifested into the dining room, nodding at Sam and Charlene, accepting Sam and Charlene.

Her eyes welled up.

Avery noticed that something had changed, and Charlene pinned a mental note to have a conversation later, without the guys around. Awkward sucked, as Jack had proved, but secrets were worse.

"Is anybody interested in one of the Salem witch tours?" Dotty suggested. "I'd love to hang around downtown for the festival in the daytime. We only have a few days left and I don't want to miss a thing."

"Cod and Capers does a great lunch, with a view of

the water. You can see the lighthouse too." Charlene didn't jump when Sam's leg brushed hers, which was pretty amazing considering her skin was on fire.

Their dates had taken place at his house, where Rover didn't care what they did. Charlene was fine with the status quo of that arrangement for now.

"We might sneak into the Hawthorne and look for ghosts," Spence said. "And Darla and I want to check out the Peabody Essex Museum. Is it worth it?"

"Yes. You can spend days at the PEM, depending on your interest," Avery said. "They change things out, too, so if you see something this go around it might not be there next time you come to Salem." She laughed. "I grew up here, so it was a popular field trip during the school year."

"Cool!" Darla said. "Spence and I love history, right, babe?"

Spence nodded and helped himself to more eggs.

Minnie entered the dining room with a carafe of fresh coffee, rounding the room to top off cups. In her other hand was a plate full of Sam's favorites, including a ham and cheese croissant.

"Too bad we can't go to the ball," Juleen said. "Any chance we can get tickets at the door?"

"I'm sorry, but no," Charlene said. "The Halloween Ball has already sold out. The party is something else. I was a judge last year."

"You've been!" Dotty exclaimed. She leaned across the table with a wink. "Can you sneak us in?"

Charlene laughed. "Uh, no."

"She'd get booted off Salem's business board," Sam said with a low chuckle.

"Charlene doesn't break the rules," Avery said, tossing a pastry crumb her way.

"I don't want to risk it. Last year the winners, both single," Charlene said, "ended up dating. People's creativity blows my mind. The costumes were out of this world."

"Literally," Sam said. "Didn't a gigantic alien take the king's crown?"

"Yes. Dima was taller than you, Sam, at seven foot four. And Aphrodite was Cassandra, who was an even six feet. They were both tall and gorgeous. I wonder if they are still together?" Charlene sipped her coffee, wishing them well.

"I can totally imagine finding true love on Halloween," Juleen said.

"You're stuck with me," Marty countered. "Discovered love in the cereal aisle at Publix when I walked into her cart."

"I love being stuck with you," Juleen said. "Our relationship is a rom-com."

"Huh?" Timothy asked.

"A romantic comedy," Juleen explained.

"A man who can make you laugh is a keeper," Dotty said in sage tones. "Timothy had me in stitches on our first date and I knew he was the one."

"How did you and Spence fall in love?" Juleen asked Darla.

The couple exchanged amused looks. "You want to tell them or should I?" Darla asked. "Or we can pass. I support your decision."

Charlene smiled and glanced at Sam as he finished

his breakfast. When had she fallen in love? It was hard to pinpoint the time; it had felt gradual and right.

"We shared the back of a police car," Spence said with a straight face.

Gasps and laughter rounded the table.

"We were in high school," Darla clarified. "Busted at a party. We were not arrested or even cuffed, and because I hadn't been drinking, I was allowed to drive home. I felt sorry for Spence and gave him a lift too."

"Fair Darla stole my heart," Spence said theatrically.

"These two are really cute," Jack said. "Too bad their music is so awful."

Avery sucked in her lips to keep from laughing at Jack's comments. Sam didn't notice. Some of the joy left Charlene's heart and she cleared her throat, scanning the diners.

She noticed that Isabella didn't volunteer how she and Rico had fallen in love while grieving over Marisol's disappearance.

"Who is dressing up for tonight, besides Juleen and Marty?" Charlene asked. Avery was letting her borrow the cat ears and Charlene had a thick cat's tail.

Avery and Seth had their costumes too. Would Sam dress up?

Charlene couldn't see it, but maybe. No. He wouldn't. What if he was called into the department while dressed as a . . . an alien? She bit the inside of her cheek to keep from laughing.

Sam saw her questioning look and raised a brow.

"Spence and I are going as Thing One and Thing Two from Dr. Seuss," Darla said.

"Dorothy and the Tin Man," Dotty said. "My Timothy is all heart."

They couldn't be any sweeter, Charlene decided.

"Leo and Patrick are not dressing up, I already asked," Darla said. "Too cool for that." She shook her head.

"What time should we start getting ready for the festival?" Isabella was dressed in a black one-piece jumper with a mock-turtleneck collar and long sleeves. Her face was expertly made up, with inch-long lashes.

Rico sat next to Isabella, wearing a silky charcoal-colored dress shirt that he'd rolled up at the sleeves, allowing the tattoo of Santa Muerte to be partially visible.

"We have all day, really," Charlene said. "I prepaid for parking in the garage, so any time after five p.m."

"Smart of you," Sam said.

"Thanks." Charlene smiled at her very handsome boyfriend and suppressed a jolt when his hand covered her knee beneath the table.

"Will we meet Kevin downtown for the tour or do we need to come back here first?" Marty asked.

Charlene and Kevin had been texting earlier that morning about the semantics of the tour. She'd offered to pick Kevin up in the rental van, but he wanted his own transportation. Amy was starting to feel better but still not up to going out, and he wanted to bring her chicken soup. Though they'd been dating for some time, they lived separately. Whatever worked for people so long as it didn't hurt anyone was fine with her.

"Kevin will meet us downtown," Charlene said. "After the tour is over I will drive us all home."

"Charlene, we need to be here at the B-and-B way before midnight for Marisol's *ofrenda*. We can't be late," Isabella said. She brought a long almond-shaped fingernail to her lower lip. "Maybe we shouldn't go?"

Charlene heard the panic in Isabella's voice. "It takes twenty minutes, thirty max, to walk from downtown to here. You have your own car, or you can take an Uber at any time."

"*Ofrenda*?" Sam asked.

"It's an altar to honor the dead during *Dia de los Muertos*," Isabella explained. "We worship Santa Muerte, who offers divine protection in this life."

"And abundance. We are trying to reach Isabella's sister, Marisol, when the veil is thinnest over the next three nights, but Tuesday will be more difficult, as the portals begin to close," Rico said. He hunched over his coffee cup, his knee jiggling. "Tomorrow night will be the best chance to reach across dimensions."

Sam kept a neutral expression, but Jack burst out laughing at Sam's discomfort.

"I don't think he's buying it," Jack said.

Avery coughed and bowed her head, her shoulders shaking. Marty smacked her on the back. "You okay?"

"Swallowed wrong, thanks." Avery slowly drew in a steady breath.

"Who is Marisol?" Sam asked.

"My sister," Isabella said. "She's missing. She disappeared over two years ago."

Sam nodded at Charlene, remembering that she'd had a guest who'd wanted to talk to him about a relative she couldn't locate.

Charlene waited for Sam to finish his breakfast and

enjoy a final sip of coffee before she stood. "Shall we?" Sam, Rico, and Isabella did the same. "Avery, we're going to be in the living room for a little while."

"We are all good here." Avery rose and went to the carafes on the tall sideboard. "Can I get anyone something more to drink?"

Isabella and Rico followed Charlene and Sam to the living room. Jack appeared by the mantel.

Even though he wasn't in uniform or even on duty, Sam always had his notebook and pen with him. He preferred old school notes to using his phone app.

Same as her, Charlene thought with a smile. You couldn't doodle with your phone. There was something satisfying about tearing off a sheet of paper and tossing it away that, again, you couldn't do with your cell.

Isabella and Rico sat on the sofa, and Sam and Charlene took armchairs, swiveling them so they faced the couple.

"Let's start over," Sam said in a congenial tone. "I'm Detective Sam Holden. Can I get your names?"

"Isabella Perez and Rico Flores," Isabella said.

"Your sister's name?"

"Marisol Perez." Isabella crossed her legs. She'd tucked the legs of her one-piece outfit into black boots that had a wedge heel and so added height and traction while being cute.

Sam turned to Rico. "What is your relationship to Marisol?"

"Marisol and I were dating. In love," Rico said with a slight squirm. His dark jeans were stylishly creased, and he had on black loafers that looked like leather.

Santa Muerte peeked at Charlene from the cuff of his shirtsleeve.

"I see. And now?" Sam managed to keep his tone and expression nonjudgmental. Charlene was impressed.

Jack manifested behind the sofa and crossed his arms. His black T-shirt had a white ghost on it with turquoise eyes for Halloween.

"Well, Marisol is missing. I can't be in love with someone who isn't here," Rico said, as if explaining to an idiot what went into a peanut butter and jelly sandwich.

"And your relationship to Isabella?" Sam asked.

"We are in love." Rico took Isabella's hand.

"Because she's here," Jack said, shaking his head.

"We did not mean to fall in love," Isabella said with emotion-filled eyes. "It was an accident and nothing that we meant to happen. If Marisol had been here, it wouldn't have. I can't marry Rico until I know what happened to my sister."

"All right," Sam said. "Do you know where Marisol might be?"

"Possibly. We plan to contact her over the next few nights when the veil through the dimensions is thinnest," Rico said. "This time of year is when many religions honor their dead for that reason. It's not unusual to reach out to them."

"You think Marisol Perez is deceased?" Sam asked sharply.

"She has to be dead," Isabella said.

"Explain." Sam's pen hovered over the paper, his grip so tight his knuckles were white.

"Well," Isabella said, averting her gaze. "I don't feel her in my heart."

"I need something tangible." Sam tapped the pen to the paper and regained his composure. "When was the last time you saw Marisol, Isabella?"

"I know exactly." Isabella released Rico's hand and scooted toward the edge of the sofa. "We lived in the same house and shared a business here in Salem. A bank account. For ten years! Since we moved from New Orleans after our mother died."

"The date, please?"

"July fourth weekend," Isabella said. "I can check my texts with my other phone. I had to get a new one but saved the other just for those texts. I read them when I'm sad."

"Do you have it with you?" Sam's body hummed with adrenaline as he grew invested in the case.

"No." Isabella clasped her hands together. "It's at home in New York."

"Did you file a police report?" Sam glanced up from his notes to see her answer.

"Yes. On July sixth," Isabella said.

Rico tapped his thumb to his knee. "They wouldn't take the report on the fourth because Marisol hadn't been gone for forty-eight hours."

"They didn't believe us," Isabella said.

"I didn't see a police report," Jack said. "But I will look again now that I know the exact dates."

Charlene gave Jack a slight nod.

Sam flipped his notebook to a fresh page. "I'll check out the report and see what happened."

"Thank you," Isabella said. "I trust you a lot more than I did the two officers at the station."

"Do you remember their names?" Sam asked.

"One was Officer Button. I remembered because of the funny name." Isabella looked at Rico. "Do you remember the other officer?"

"No," Rico said, sounding bored.

"How old is Marisol?" Sam asked.

"My sister would be thirty. She disappeared at twenty-eight, the same age I am now. You have to understand that she took care of me always." Isabella glanced at Rico but then focused on Sam. "She wouldn't just walk away from me or our business, no matter what was going on in her personal life."

"Which was?" Sam asked.

"Thanks a lot, Bella." Rico jumped up from the sofa. "I can feel the skid marks on my back from where you just tossed me under the bus."

Isabella's cheeks flamed as she peered up at Rico. "I didn't mean to! We are trying to find Marisol. It's in the past, Rico."

"The more information you can give me, the more leads I'll be able to follow," Sam said. "Why don't you sit back down, sir?"

Rico did, still bristling with affronted pride.

"Where is your place of business?" Sam asked, changing the direction of questioning to something more general, possibly to give Rico time to cool off.

Charlene knew Sam, and knew that he didn't forget a thing. He would come back around to the question.

"I work at a coffee shop in the City, and Rico is a

tattoo artist. He freelances from our apartment." Isabella gave the address. "My sister was a gifted psychic and tarot card reader. I am a crystal healer. As I said, we owned a thriving business in the Pedestrian Mall that she wouldn't just leave behind."

"So why is Isabella working at a coffee shop?" Jack pondered.

"Where was the shop you used to own here in Salem?" Sam asked.

"The two-story brick building across from the church." Rico rolled his pointer finger around near his temple. "That crazy Sister Elizabeth Abbott always complained that our Santa Muerte was leaking evil into her consecrated ground. As if!"

Sam drummed his pen to the paper. "I'm familiar with Sister Abbott. She has a lot of opinions that she doesn't mind sharing at the station."

"Yeah, that sounds like her." Rico sat back against the sofa's cushions.

Isabella's tone was firm as she shared, "Persephone Lowell has the tarot card reading business opposite where ours used to be. She is also accused of devil worship by the Sister."

Sam sighed but continued writing. "Let's focus on Marisol. Rico, do you want to elaborate on the nature of your relationship with Marisol Perez?"

"It was open," Rico said.

Sam looked at Isabella, who nodded. "It's not something I am okay with in our relationship, but it worked for Rico and Marisol. I guess. You got into an argument that weekend."

"Because of Brian Preston," Rico said.

"Another lover?" Sam asked.

"Yes." Isabella fidgeted on the sofa. "He's a security guard in downtown Salem. I thought he was stalking Marisol, but I may have been wrong."

"B-R-I-A-N for Brian?" Sam asked.

Isabella nodded.

Rico puffed out his chest, reminding Charlene of a little bulldog trying to protect his property from a Great Dane.

"What was the nature of your business?" Sam asked.

"Marisol was the best psychic in Salem," Isabella said. "She read tarot cards."

"I designed Marisol's personal set," Rico interjected. "All Santa Muerte, per Marisol's wishes."

"That's true. We sold other tarot cards Rico created in the shop," Isabella said. "Marisol could also divine the future with a pendulum. She was as gifted as our mother."

"Isabella is only good with crystals," Rico said with a sniff. "We couldn't afford to stay in Salem with Marisol gone."

"And what can he do besides draw?" Jack demanded. "I feel like we need to keep Isabella from making a mistake with Rico."

Sam, to his credit, didn't show any judgment as he took notes. "Rico, tell me what happened the last day that you saw Marisol. It's very important—any small detail might help."

"We argued that morning, but we'd made up by noon," Rico said. "Marisol and I had passion. A witch has different rules than the rest of us."

"I only care about whether or not a law was broken,"

Sam assured him. "Isabella, did you see your sister after the argument with Rico?"

Isabella shook her head. "I didn't."

"Bella!" Rico said.

"It's true," Isabella said, keeping her shoulder to Rico as she answered Sam's questions. "I was working in the shop. We carried a lot of Santa Muerte merchandise. Our family brought the Bony Lady to Salem from New Orleans. Santa Muerte's worship has now spread rapidly, but we were the first to introduce her here."

"Bony Lady?" Sam queried. His nostrils flared slightly, but he made no other expression to show his reaction.

"Santa Muerte has many monikers," Isabella said. "She is a saint from Mexican folklore with similar ceremonies as the Catholic Church. That really angered Sister Abbott, who felt Santa Muerte mocked her faith, but the thing about Santa Muerte is that she welcomes all. It is Sister Abbott who was so judgy."

"Santa Muerte provides miracles in exchange for gifts," Rico said. "If you are devout, she will escort you into the afterlife after a lifetime full of blessings."

"What does Santa Muerte look like?" Sam asked.

"She has a skeletal figure and has many colored robes, for different requests." Isabella found an image on her phone and showed it to Sam, who just nodded, so Isabella brought her phone back to her lap. "When we put together the *ofrenda* for Marisol, we will invoke Santa Muerte's name."

"I see," Sam said. He clicked his pen several times.

Charlene looked at Jack, who watched Rico closely,

as if he suspected the man to be up to some sort of trick.

"Marisol was young and talented," Sam said.

"And very beautiful!" Rico interjected.

Isabella's chin lifted, but she didn't look at Rico. "Yes, all of those things are true."

"The storefronts are expensive downtown," Sam continued. "Were you wealthy?"

"Our shop did very well." Isabella kept her attention on Sam. "Marisol and I had a gold statue of Santa Muerte in a place of honor where all who believed could ask a blessing from her, in exchange for a donation."

Again with the gold.

"How much of a donation?" Sam asked suspiciously.

"It would depend on the request. A cigarette, or a coin," Isabella said. "It was about the intent, not the dollar amount."

"I'd like to see this statue," Sam said.

"So would I," Jack seconded.

"Well," Isabella said. "The problem is that our gold Santa Muerte is missing."

"What do you mean?" Sam speared both Isabella and Rico with a hard gaze.

"It went missing the same day as Marisol," Isabella practically whispered.

Sam sat back. "A gold statue. Was it painted gold or gold plate?"

Isabella straightened, her hands trembling, but she held Sam's gaze. "Solid gold. It was covered with gemstones and supposed to be hundreds of years old. Our mother got it from a believer in New Orleans. It was very important to our family."

"I hate to say this to you," Sam said, his tone hinting at disbelief, "but have you considered that Marisol took off with this valuable statue to start over somewhere else?"

"She wouldn't have," Isabella insisted.

"Why not?" Sam asked. "Maybe things were getting tough for her with Rico here in Salem. Or with Brian. Or one of her clients."

"We are family!" Isabella clutched her phone tightly.

"Families do terrible things to one another all the time," Sam said. "Stealing a statue to start over is not the worst crime, believe me."

"Marisol protected me," Isabella said. "She wouldn't leave me."

"Do you have a picture of Marisol? And the statue?" Sam asked.

"On my old phone, yes." Isabella sniffed back tears.

"What about money?" Sam persisted. "You shared a bank account. Was any cash missing?"

"No." Isabella's lip wobbled.

"You're sure?" Sam's brow arched.

"I do the accounting," Isabella said. "Her bank card was not used; our bank balance wasn't touched by anyone but Rico and me."

"And now we are broke," Rico said. "We need our Santa Muerte statue back to bring us good fortune."

Isabella edged away from Rico. "Excuse me?"

"You know what I mean, Bella," Rico said. "I love you, I want to marry you, but you won't without discovering what happened to Marisol. If we find the statue, maybe it will lead us to Marisol."

Isabella nodded, while Jack spluttered with indignation.

"How far away is your home in the City?" Sam asked.

"A couple of hour's drive," Isabella answered. "Why?"

"I'd really like to see your phone and the messages," Sam said. "The pictures."

"I could draw it for you," Rico said. "The golden statue of Santa Muerte is on some of the tarot cards I made too."

"I have a picture of Marisol and me when we were teenagers."

Sam stood and put his notebook in his pocket. "Let me do some digging around. You'll be here through when?"

"Wednesday," Isabella said. "Hopefully my sister will come through the veil tonight at midnight."

"But if not," Rico said, "there is always tomorrow, when the dimension is at its thinnest. I bet we will hear from her then."

Charlene saw Sam's jaw clench and knew he didn't believe it.

CHAPTER 11

Sam thanked Isabella and Rico for the information they'd shared, saying he would be in touch regarding the missing Marisol. He looked at Charlene. "Walk me to my car?"

Jack rubbed his hands together. "I'll wait inside with the happy couple, just in case Rico turns out to be dangerous and not full of machismo."

Charlene nodded and followed Sam, who could set a record for his brisk pace across the foyer and outside to the porch.

Once there, Sam shook his head at her. "This is crazy, right? You understand that Marisol Perez probably took off with that valuable statue and is drinking margaritas in the Bahamas."

Charlene blew out a breath but nodded. "If that's the case, then Isabella and Rico can deal with it and start their lives together."

Sam tapped his phone, brow raised. "I'm intrigued, damn it. She didn't use the bank account or take cash that Isabella was aware of . . . she could have been stashing it away. I would prefer for Marisol to be alive, Charlene."

"Me too!" She took Sam's hand, very much on the same page with him.

"But if she had an argument with Rico . . . and that was the last time Isabella saw her sister, well, I don't have to remind you that victims often know their killers."

"No, you don't." She recalled Jack saying the same thing.

"Which means Rico Flores . . ." Sam drew out the man's name.

"I get it, Sam! Rico was the last to see her after an argument. We have the security cameras now, and mace stashed in the kitchen drawer, the pantry, and the laundry room. Avery has some in her car and so do I— we are not being obtuse or careless." And Jack was protecting Isabella right now in the living room.

Sam slid his hand around the back of her neck to tangle his fingers in her hair, bringing her face close to his. She leaned into his body, their mouths meeting and fusing in heat and desire.

"Sam," she whispered.

"I'm really sorry that I missed our date yesterday," Sam said. "Halloween in Salem jumps everyone up from zero to a thousand on the wacko scale."

He rubbed his thumb over her bottom lip. Her skin sang, wanting more.

"It's all right," Charlene said. "Friday night was fun, hanging out with Avery and Seth, eating pizza and watching movies."

They kissed, deeper. After she finished the kiss, she leaned against his chest and nuzzled his neck. Sam was perfect for her.

"What does your November look like?" Sam asked. His warm breath tickled her ear.

"Not as busy. Wednesdays are always pretty open."

Sam groaned. "Mom and Dad want to come back for Thanksgiving."

Charlene smiled. "They had a good time."

"And then what happens if they decide to stay through Christmas?" She could tell that Sam was only partially joking. "I've been waiting a long time for you, Charlene. I'll take what I can get." He brushed his thumb across her cheekbone in a soft caress as he held her gaze. "Are you okay with our relationship?"

"Yes. Like you, I'm happy with what we've built together. So what if it's not the norm? If your parents come to stay, we can rent a romantic getaway," Charlene suggested. "Someplace with a view of the water and a hot tub."

"I'll look into it. You have someone to watch the B-and-B?"

"Depending on the dates, I can ask Minnie and Will to stay. Midweek means less chance of having guests, so that might be best."

Sam kissed her so thoroughly that her temperature rocketed. "I'll check things out. A romantic, secluded vacation for two will be wonderful." He stared into her eyes. "You've changed. You're not scared of the future with me anymore."

Charlene kept her palm over his heart. His jacket

and shirt muffled the beating of it, but she knew it was steady. "Is your intuition telling you that?"

Sam groaned.

Charlene stood on her tiptoes to kiss him again. "You're right, anyway. I'm really sorry about Valentine's Day."

"Don't be," Sam said. "I feel very fortunate to have found you. You wouldn't be you without your past." He peered into her eyes. "I can never be Jared. I worry that I won't stack up to his memory."

"I wouldn't ask you to be any different from who you are," Charlene said. "I just feel very lucky to have several great loves in my life."

"Several?" Sam said, mustache twitching.

Charlene's phone rang, saving her. "Mom. She has insane timing."

"My parents love your parents," Sam said. "They like you very much. I think they noticed how often I brought up your name in conversation."

Her mother texted, **Coffee today at the festival?**

Crap. Had she arranged to do that?

Sam cleared his throat and she pocketed her phone.

"I'll make them love me too. I love you, Avery, Silva, and Minnie, and . . ." Jack. But Charlene kept that to herself. If Sam didn't believe, she couldn't explain.

"I love you, Charlene," Sam said. He raised his keys. "In my free time I'll be looking for a midweek getaway for us with a hot tub. And I'll read through Marisol Perez's missing person report."

"Thank you!" She waited until Sam drove away and

brought her finger to her lip. She'd never dreamed she could be so happy again.

Charlene called her mom back as she walked into the B-and-B. "Hey, Mom! Let me see what my schedule is with the guests and then I can let you know about coffee."

"All right. I'm worried I won't have enough Halloween candy for trick-or-treaters. I always bought two bags for the kids in our neighborhood. I don't know what to expect this year. I had your dad go to the store and buy an extra one. He bought the dark chocolate Snickers."

Charlene laughed. "He's probably hoping you don't have any kids. Those are his favorite."

The phone grew muffled, then her mom returned. "I told him what you said and he just laughed. How many kids do you get?"

"None." Charlene held the phone to her ear and waited in the foyer. She could see Isabella and Rico in the living room with Jack. The dining room was empty. Minnie banged dishes in the kitchen. "My house is too far back from the road. Plus, we're going to be at the festival, and then with Kevin Hughes, searching for the Lady in White at the Old Burying Point Cemetery."

"Well, you can always come here if you ever want to hand out candy," her mom said. "I just love seeing the kids in their costumes."

"I'll get to see a bunch of kiddos downtown. Are you dressing up?"

"Raggedy Ann and Raggedy Andy. Same costumes every year. But these kids haven't seen us before."

"True." Charlene would have to be completely uncaring to miss the wistful tone in her mom's voice. "Are you feeling homesick?"

"Maybe a little," Mom admitted. "Your dad and I usually help with the harvest party at the church, bobbing for apples, that kind of thing."

"I'm sorry, Mom."

"Don't be! It will pass."

Her mom was not one to wallow, which was a good thing. Charlene walked closer to the living room, peeking inside. Isabella and Rico seemed to be arguing. "You should call your friends, just to say hi."

"I will—text me about coffee."

"Bye, Mom."

Jack joined her in the foyer, alarm in his expression. "We have got to talk about Isabella and Rico. Your suite?"

Nodding, she kept the phone to her ear though her mother wasn't on the line. "I'll get Avery. She'll want to be included."

With that, Jack was gone.

Charlene decided on a cup of tea, if she was going to have coffee with her mother later. Isabella and Rico stormed by her as they left the living room and stomped up the stairs. Neither said a word to Charlene.

Well. Trouble in paradise.

Did that mean Isabella could be in danger? Maybe Jack had answers. She went to the kitchen and discovered that Avery and Minnie had already cleaned up the mess from breakfast. "Thanks—you guys are fast."

She turned on the electric kettle and got a mug and herbal tea.

"How's Sam?" Minnie asked.

"Great," Charlene said. "He's going to look into the missing person report for Marisol Perez."

Jack appeared in the kitchen. "Hurry, Charlene."

Charlene shrugged, not sure how to get Avery in her suite without Minnie being suspicious.

She dunked her tea bag, not as zealous as Kass about the steeping process.

"Isabella seems like a sweet girl," Minnie said.

"Yes, I agree. I had no idea that they owned a gold statue covered in gemstones," Charlene said. "And that it is missing, along with Marisol."

"What?" Avery asked.

"I know . . . Marisol is gone and the statue is gone. Sam thinks she might be in the Bahamas somewhere."

"That would be better than the alternative," Avery said. "The *ofrenda* altar they've made is very specific to calling for Marisol's spirit . . . what if Marisol were to come through tonight?"

Minnie's eyes widened. "No way. Could that happen?"

"We should think of some contingencies," Charlene said. "Just in case we are flooded with spirits by opening the door, or portal, or whatever you call it."

Minnie laughed. "*Ghostbusters*? Sorry. Bad joke. Seriously, who will you call if there is a wild ghost in this mansion, looking for her sister?"

Jack rolled his eyes.

"We can handle it," Charlene said, having no idea if this was true.

Minnie raised a doubtful brow. "Maybe that nice girl Kass could help? And doesn't Seth's mother have a ghost in her kitchen?"

"Good ideas," Avery said. "Dani and Kass are experts."

"Persephone too," Charlene said. "It's really inconvenient that the Flint ladies are so involved with their coven this weekend, because I trust them and their powers." She took out the tea bag and put it on a saucer. "And Kass isn't available tonight for the same reason, but she can help tomorrow if necessary."

"Good options," Jack said. "You're ignoring me, so I'll spill here that Isabella and Rico were arguing about the statue while you were outside with Sam. Rico thinks Isabella should have covered for him by lying to Sam, and saying that she'd seen Rico after the morning argument he'd had with Marisol."

Avery started to reply but remembered not to answer Jack just in time.

Charlene nodded. "Avery, honey, could you help me with my costume really quick?"

"Yes!" Avery lowered her tone to one not so eager. "Yes, I could."

"Be right back Minnie," Charlene said, tugging Avery with her. She shut the door and locked it.

"Clever thinking," Jack said with approval. He'd already turned the TV up.

Charlene arched her brow at Jack. "I wasn't ignoring you."

"Sorry," Jack said. "But was it important?"

"Yes," Charlene conceded. "We should call Sam. He doesn't believe in the paranormal but will see about the missing person report an Officer Button filed on July sixth two years ago."

"Tonight we could know if Marisol is in fact a

spirit," Avery said. "Jack, will you be able to help light the way for her?"

"I have no idea," Jack said in speculation. "I've never tried to and don't have the first clue. I'll see if there are any tips online."

"Tonight is not the most powerful night," Charlene said. "That would be tomorrow at midnight. It's possible Marisol could come through over the next three days, but November first at midnight is the key time."

"If Marisol is dead," Jack reminded them.

"If," Charlene and Avery said in unison.

Charlene's phone dinged and she read the text, thinking it would be her mother.

Sam!

No missing persons report ever filed.

A second text quickly followed.

You and Avery be careful.

Charlene showed Avery and Jack the messages.

"Rico had said it would be a waste of time to file the report because the cops thought Marisol had left of her own accord. What if they didn't bother? Here it is, two years later, and she hasn't surfaced?" Charlene's stomach clenched. "I'm beginning to think the worst."

A knock sounded on her door.

Charlene answered it. "Hey!"

"I was wondering if we could get everyone together who wanted to decorate a sugar skull for Day of the Dead." Minnie shook her head and backed up. "Never mind. We should save it for tomorrow, the actual day. It seems like this group likes to stick together. You'll be headed out at five?"

"Yes. What time did you want to take off?"

"Now okay? I have lunch fixings prepped if people are hungry for sandwiches. There's chili in the fridge that just needs to be heated." Minnie took off her apron and hung it in the pantry. "Nobody will be around tonight, so I'll be back in the morning at eight for breakfast."

"Let's make it eight thirty," Charlene said. "I can handle coffee."

"I'll help," Avery said.

Minnie tilted her head, her expression uncertain. "You're sure?"

"Positive! You should go and tell your adorable family hello and have fun," Charlene said. "Thank you!"

"You're welcome. We might see you at the festival—it's way better than trick-or-treating with the grands being tweens." Minnie retrieved her purse and got out her car keys. Charlene and Avery left her suite and followed Minnie through the kitchen.

They exchanged hugs in the foyer.

"Please, be careful tonight with the ghosty thing," Minnie said just before she left. "You don't want the wrong entity getting in."

That was something Charlene hadn't thought of but would ask Kass about.

"Ghosty?" Jack spluttered with indignation.

Minnie left, and Charlene and Avery were able to talk freely with Jack, returning to the warmth of the kitchen.

"I am the only spirit in this house," Jack promised them. "I would notice."

Silva demanded Avery's attention, so the teenager sat down to pet the cat, scratching just under her chin the way she liked it. "Darla, Juleen, Spence, and Marty walked downtown for the tarot card readings with Persephone. Dotty and Timothy plan to Uber. Everyone will be back here at four forty-five to leave at five. Seth and I will meet downtown. I don't think you really need my help with your cat ears?"

"No. Thanks for letting me borrow them. Would you like a hand with your Agatha Christie? How long do you need to get ready?"

"Half an hour maybe." Avery shrugged.

Charlene sipped her now cool tea.

A knock sounded on the front door.

Jack disappeared and reappeared as Charlene was walking to answer it.

"Sam," Jack announced.

Charlene smiled wider when she opened it. Sure enough, it was her handsome detective.

"Miss me?" Sam asked.

"Always." Charlene pulled him inside and out of the crisp autumn air. He'd donned a warmer canvas jacket over the lighter flannel.

"Are Isabella and Rico here?" Sam asked. "It sounds quiet."

Jack again disappeared and reappeared. "Yes, Rico and Isabella are in their room. Isabella is crying."

"Most of our guests are downtown, but I believe they are upstairs," Charlene said.

Sam smoothed his mustache. "I'd like to talk to them."

Avery came out of the kitchen. "Hey Sam!" She gave him a hug. "How's it going? Things nuts today or what?"

"Nuts is accurate," Sam said in a dry tone.

"Let me run upstairs and get them." Charlene said. "Want some coffee or tea? We have the Keurig, so whatever you want."

"Black coffee would hit the spot. The living room?"

"Great." Charlene walked up the stairs. Why would Isabella be crying? Maybe she was just now finding out that Rico was a slimeball who expected her to lie for him to the police. All he seemed to care about was the gold statue.

She knocked on the door of the blue suite.

Rico answered, exasperation on his features. "Yes? Oh, Charlene."

"Charlene?" Isabella queried, looking up from the silver bracelet with a variety of charms in her palm with concern. "Please come in."

Rico widened the door.

"What's wrong?" Charlene asked, forgetting about Sam downstairs for a moment in her desire to help Isabella.

"You might think this is silly, but I haven't really looked at my sister's things since we moved." Isabella sighed. "It's too painful."

"Not at all silly, Isabella." After Jared died her mother had helped her pack up his clothes for charity or she wouldn't have been able to get through it.

"The owl charm on her Santa Muerte bracelet is missing." Isabella raised her gaze to Charlene and jiggled the bracelet. The small white ceramic disks teased her memory. Where had she seen it?

"I keep telling her that it's probably *been* missing and she just noticed," Rico said. "It's not important."

"I know how much she liked this bracelet," Isabella

said defiantly. "Marisol would have told me if it was broken so I could fix it. The symbol of the owl is very important between Marisol and Santa Muerte because the owl is a sign of psychic wisdom."

"It's true," Rico said. "Marisol had a tattoo of the owl on her shoulder."

Charlene wished she had time to study the *ofrenda* more closely but took a quick look to discuss with Jack and Avery, and possibly Sam, later. The salt, water, candles, and paper. The box from Jonas at the wharf, half full. "Sam is here, downstairs. He wants to talk to you." The tarot cards, the small white plastic statue of the Bony Lady, the Mexican tequila, the cigarettes. A brass key. "He has more questions for you. I think it would be helpful for him to see this altar. Marisol's things."

Rico scowled. "The policeman? They didn't do anything for us earlier. Why should he care now?"

"Sam is a detective," Charlene corrected Rico. "A very good one."

"Charlene thinks it's important," Isabella said. "Let's show him."

"Thank you." Charlene left the room and beckoned to Sam and Avery, who both came upstairs.

"Hello again." Sam entered the suite, his gaze on the *ofrenda*.

"Hi," Isabella said, her eyes swimming with unshed tears.

Sam braced his shoulders. "Miss Perez, I regret to inform you that no missing person report was ever filed."

"What?" Isabella asked, clutching the bracelet.

Jack hovered around the altar, as interested as Charlene. Could the charm have been missing all along? Was it a clue?

It was possible that Marisol hadn't mentioned it so as not to worry her sister.

Sam took out his notebook and pen. "I would like to officially open an inquiry into Marisol Perez's location."

CHAPTER 12

Charlene could feel Sam's earnest energy as he apologized very sincerely to Isabella. "Officer Button was let go a year ago and so no longer works at the station or I would file a complaint."

"I knew it," Rico said, sounding victorious as well as arrogant. Not a winning combo.

"I appreciate your apology, Detective," Isabella said. "I had a feeling the officers didn't take her disappearance very seriously. Missing valuable statue, missing pretty witch."

Sam nodded. "I'd like for you to come to the station and fill out a report. I wish you had your old phone with pictures and texts, but we can add that later. Let's get Marisol's information into the database and start shaking trees."

"It's been over two years. I miss her so much." Isabella placed the bracelet back on the *ofrenda*. "I can come right now."

"All right. I'll add the details myself," Sam assured her, "and see what's out there. Let me take a few pictures of the altar first." He snapped several photos, but Charlene could tell he was in a hurry to get the report done.

"Thank you!" Isabella said, crying softly.

"I'm coming with you," Rico said.

They all left the bedroom.

"Sucks for Sam," Jack said. Charlene could hear him but not see him as he went from the blue suite to the foyer. "He's got to feel terrible on behalf of his fellow police officers. The department let Isabella down."

Avery shut the door to the suite and then they all descended the stairs.

"I drove from New York," Isabella said, "so we can follow you to the station. I appreciate you doing this on a holiday."

"Crime doesn't take a vacation." Sam turned to Charlene. "This will probably take around an hour."

"They have the code to come and go as they wish," Charlene said. "I promised Mom that I'd meet her for coffee downtown."

"You are lucky to have your mother around," Isabella said. "I miss mine every single day."

Charlene couldn't imagine life without Brenda and Michael Woodbridge.

Sam, knowing her complicated history with her mother, patted her shoulder. "Good luck."

Sam left, as did Isabella and Rico, to finally file a missing person report, over two years later.

Avery sank down on the midstep of the staircase.

Silva climbed into her lap and plopped into a ball of fur. "Sam will oversee the report and ensure it gets done correctly. I'm going to be a detective just like him. One that can be counted on."

"I know you will," Jack said. "But you are going to be even better because you don't close your mind off to the paranormal. Even before you could see me, you didn't discount the possibility."

"That's true," Charlene said. "But wishing for Sam to change is like wishing we could control the weather."

"In Salem?" Avery scrunched her nose.

Her phone dinged and she pulled it from her back pocket. "Mom. If you guys are fine, I'll meet her at Witch's Brew downtown. It's got great people-watching windows, and the costumes should be awesome."

"Don't forget your cat ears," Avery reminded her.

"I'll save the big reveal for this evening," Charlene joked.

"Cool—Jack and I are gonna watch a documentary on the making of jump scares. It might come in handy for tonight." Avery rubbed her hands together.

Laughing, Charlene left and drove her Pilot to the popular coffee shop. Her mom was already there and had gotten a prime seat.

"Should I order, or should you?" Her mom grinned and patted the wooden top. "One of us needs to stay with the table."

"I'll order—what do you want?"

"Pumpkin spice latte with whipped cream," her mom said. "And a pumpkin scone."

"On it!" Charlene joined the line and decided her mom's order sounded so good she'd have the same. Ten minutes later she brought their drinks and plates to the table.

"Thank you," her mom said, passing her a twenty.

"It's my treat," Charlene said. "You can buy next time. This is a primo location." There was a stream of people in various stages of costume for Halloween. Laughter abounded, which always lifted one's spirits.

Charlene took off her jacket and put it on the chair, snagging a long brunette lock on a button. She yanked it free.

"Careful, honey. You have such pretty hair." Smiling, her mom tucked the twenty back into her purse. "That sounds nice."

"I like yours too."

In fact, Charlene envied her mother's snow-white hair and hoped that hers would someday be as lovely. Her glasses were orange for the season, and she wore a T-shirt with a giant pumpkin on the front, which went with her festive pumpkin earrings.

"Dad and I come here at least twice a week," her mom said. "He reads and I crochet, but mostly I just love to watch everyone go by. It's better than reality TV. Our favorite, though, is to watch the boats in the bay. We've even seen dolphins."

"That's supposed to be lucky, right?" Charlene breathed in the scent of pumpkin and cinnamon. "It's been a while since I've had a latte, and good call on the whipped cream." She studied her mother for signs of distress, but she seemed back to her normal self.

"So, how are your guests?"

Oh, now they were getting to the bottom of the insistence for coffee. Brenda wanted gossip.

Charlene broke off a corner of the pumpkin scone and placed it on a napkin. She could oblige. "We learned a little more about Isabella's missing sister, Marisol."

Her mom propped her forearm on the table and leaned closer. "You did?"

"Well, Sam discovered a missing person report was never filed." Charlene loved the look of surprise on her mom's face.

"No!"

"Yeah—he's at the station right now with Isabella and Rico." She sipped her latte. "It seems the officer who was supposed to take the report no longer works there. He was let go, and I think we can guess why."

Her mom swiped her finger through the whipped cream and put it in her mouth. "Sam will get to the bottom of this situation."

"I know it. He's a great detective. Avery wants to be just like him."

"Rico used to be in a relationship with Marisol, correct?" Her mom wiped her lips and bit into the scone.

"Yes." Would her mom judge?

"He'd better have a solid alibi or Sam has his first suspect." Charlene should have known that Brenda Woodbridge would be about solving the crime.

"You're right. Did I tell you about the golden statue of Santa Muerte? It's missing too."

"Interesting. What about her bank account?"

"Never touched. Isabella and Marisol shared everything. House, business, and finances."

"And now a man." Her mom shook her head and sipped her latte. "That doesn't sound good for poor Marisol. What's the plan?"

"Sam is going to *shake trees*, he said. Look for Jane Does in the last two years. She had long dark hair, like Isabella, and from all accounts was a lovely woman and talented witch."

This didn't bother her mother at all, as it might have done in the past. "Kass is a skilled witch with long dark hair. The Flints have red, though. What about Persephone? Is she dark-haired?"

"Pink, so probably not natural," Charlene teased. "Are you interested in getting a psychic reading done?"

"Nah. My life is great. I don't need to know the future. What about you?"

"We have the same feelings about it, Mom. I'm not against it, but I don't want to know either."

Her mom lifted her mug and clicked it to Charlene's.

Just then Kass walked by outside, with Persephone. Kass waved at her through the window. Juleen and Darla must have finished with their psychic readings. Charlene checked the time on her phone. Yep, three.

The pair suddenly turned around and entered the coffee shop, heading for their table.

"Brenda and Charlene!" Kass said, her eyes twinkling with happiness. She was wearing fringe for her costume, rocking the Cher vibe. "We can't stay, but Persephone has a message for you, Charlene."

"A psychic message?" Charlene asked. What other kind could it be?

"No," Persephone replied with a smile. Her bright

pink hair was tied back with a purple bow. She pulled a business card from her leather cross-body purse. "A note from one of my clients who saw you yesterday and is besotted. He sells luxury boats and is very, very rich."

Her mom chuckled. "My Charlene is very beautiful. We'll have to let Sam know he has competition."

"No, we don't, and no, Sam doesn't." Charlene didn't take the card. "Tell . . ."

"Benjamin Fiske," Persephone supplied. "Millionaire."

"Mr. Fiske, that I am engaged."

Her mom sucked in a surprised breath. "You're engaged?"

"No, Mom, but that's a nice way to let someone know you're not interested. No matter how much money they have," Charlene said. "Isn't that the guy with all the benches? There's one by your condo. It's a brilliant strategy and not cheap. I'm considering it myself for the slow months."

"Oh, he is handsome," her mom agreed.

Kass shimmied her hips. "Let them down gently," she said. "Benjamin is the whole package, but I understand. Franco has my heart, so there is nobody else."

"I wish Benjamin would fall head over heels for me," Persephone said. "But I just guide his life, that's all. Nothing important." She rolled her eyes, poking fun at herself. "Do you still need me on call tonight?"

"I don't know," Charlene said. "Isabella is at the police station with Sam to file an official missing person report. I guess it wasn't done two years ago."

"I feel terrible for Isabella," Persephone said. "She's so innocent still compared to Marisol. Or even myself.

Maybe because she doesn't have the connection with the other side. It's a blessing and a curse."

Charlene supposed it would be a heavy burden to be a messenger between dimensions.

A tap sounded at the window. Persephone groaned. "This guy won't leave me alone."

Shifting toward the glass, Charlene recognized the security officer, Brian Preston. He wore his uniform but took off his hat to ruffle his brown hair.

Charlene recalled that she'd seen him last night coming out of what she thought was Persephone's business. He'd followed Isabella into Kass's shop last month. The memory landed at last of the key chain, with the disk that she'd thought was an owl. Or a cat. Could it be the missing charm? He'd been close to Marisol. Maybe she'd given it to him as a lover's token.

"I was happy to take on Marisol's clients when she left . . . and I pray every day that she left of her own volition . . . but this dude is too much," Persephone said.

Persephone had Marisol's clients. That was quite an influx of money, according to Isabella. "I thought I saw Brian at your business last night," Charlene said. "You should file a complaint against him if he's bothering you."

Persephone tilted her head. "That's right—Dotty was getting her psychic reading last night. She's an old soul and simply adorable. The space you must be thinking of is a mail center. Anyone with a key has access to it."

"Huh," Charlene said. Her confusion must have been clear because Persephone grinned and leaned toward the table.

"The mail center is an address holder for people who need a place to mail documents or packages," Persephone explained. "Ship captains in the old days especially used them. Now there are folks who live on boats or travel in vans, or RVs, who require an address that isn't a post office box."

"Like Jonas McCarthy," Charlene said. "He's got his own boat."

Persephone studied Charlene. "How do you know Jonas? I haven't seen him . . . well, not since Marisol disappeared." She pressed her fingers to her lower lip. "Does Isabella know?"

"I met him last night—he was at the Captain's Wheel with Rico and Isabella. He'd brought some of Marisol's favorite things for her *ofrenda*. Items from New Orleans."

"*Ofrenda*?" her mom asked, ever curious. Something else she and Charlene had in common.

"It's an altar meant to tempt a loved one's spirit from the other side. It's what I do using my tarot cards and mediumship," Persephone explained. "The veil between dimensions is the thinnest at this time of year and over the next three days in particular."

"Have you tried to reach Marisol?" Charlene blurted out. It would cut to the chase if Persephone could reach out on her own.

Persephone shrugged. "I did, but I'm not surprised Marisol wouldn't answer me. We weren't friends, really. Unfortunately, we saw each other as competition."

"And she might not be dead," Kass said gently.

"True." Persephone sighed. Brian made the call-me signal and walked off with a cheerful deluded whistle.

"I don't like him," her mother said.

"Join the team, Brenda," Kass said. "We have to scoot. Good luck—and say hi to Kevin for me. You're doing the cemetery tour, right? I wish I could help, but I've got coven plans. I'm on the list for tomorrow if Marisol doesn't come through tonight."

The ladies left and her mom tapped her finger to her mug. "Interesting young women. They seem sincere in their wish to help. Where is the gold statue? Maybe that would be easier to find than Marisol. Or an additional avenue to go down."

"I have no idea. I haven't even seen what it looks like yet." Charlene crossed her ankles. "I foolishly imagined it to be plastic, like the white figurine already on the *ofrenda*. I had no clue it was solid gold. Isabella's old phone has text messages and photos between her and Marisol, but it's at their apartment in New York."

Where Isabella didn't use her own gifts as a crystal healer but worked in a coffee shop. She didn't like how Rico talked down to Isabella, as if she wasn't as good as Marisol, when he didn't have any psychic talent at all.

"What do you think about this rich cutie?" Mom picked up the business card with Benjamin's handsome face and flipped it over. "He wrote his private cell phone number with a message to call him, day or night."

Charlene remembered the man in the nice suit who had winked at her. No wonder he'd looked familiar. Benjamin's face was plastered everywhere. "He is cute— but clean-shaven. I prefer my men to have a mustache."

"I don't blame you." Her mom lowered the card. "Will you be attending the Day of the Dead parade?"

"Depends. I promised Isabella that I would help her with her sister. Hopefully we get answers tonight and then yes, it would be a lot of fun."

"Should you try to reach out to Jared?" her mom asked gently.

"I am at peace with Jared and his death," Charlene said. "It gutted me, as you know, but having answers as to how he died, and that the person responsible is in jail, allows me to let his memory live in my heart without anger."

Mom patted her hand. "That's wise."

"If I didn't have those answers, I'd be a basket case for sure." Charlene finished her scone. "I understand why Isabella wants to know, one way or the other, about Marisol. I'm worried because if Persephone has no contact, and the leaves are murky for Kass, well, does that mean Marisol is alive and just wanted to disappear?"

"It's very strange." Her mom pointed to the steeple visible from the window. "We went to church this morning, and Sister Abbott handed out pamphlets against the parade tomorrow night, saying it was the Devil's work."

"I haven't met Sister Abbott," Charlene said. "I hear she's quite the activist. She has Kass shaking in her braids. I guess Santa Muerte is worshipped in a similar way to Catholicism, which is why the church is up in arms."

"In Sister Abbott's world, there is no room for other faiths."

Charlene sipped her latte. "That's kind of narrow-minded."

"I used to be like that, but I've seen a lot of good *and* bad done in the name of religion," her mom said. "I'm comfortable with my priest and Catholic faith, but I don't think it's the only way to pray or worship."

Charlene's mouth gaped in surprise and she snapped it closed. "That is very evolved of you, Mom."

"The Beatles said it best. All we need is love, right?"

"Right." Charlene nodded at the business card. "We should probably toss that so that Benjamin doesn't get crazy prank phone calls."

"I'll do it," her mom offered. "Don't want Sam to get jealous."

"Sam has nothing to worry about," Charlene said with assurance.

"It makes me happy to know that you care for him," her mom said. She put the card next to the twenty in her purse.

"Thanks, Mom. It means a lot to know I have your support." Charlene checked the time on her phone, ready to get going.

"Always!" Her mom piled the empty dishes on the tray. "I'm very curious about what happens tonight with the *ofrenda*, so you have to call me tomorrow to let me know if you've made contact."

Charlene laughed and reached for her jacket. "Got it. First, though, I am going to show my guests a rousing time downtown with costumes and food, and then go ghost hunting for the Lady in White with Kevin."

"That sounds like fun, but I'd prefer handing out candy and visiting with the kids." Her mom wrapped an orange shawl around her shoulders. "I hope we have a bunch of trick-or-treaters. You know the town of Salem will be live streaming the festivities?"

"I didn't." But it was a very modern idea for the historic city. "I don't have to warn you to monitor Dad's Snickers intake?"

"I don't relish that." Charlene's mom gave an exasperated shrug. "That man loves his sweets."

CHAPTER 13

That evening, dressed in cat ears and a cat's tail that had Jack laughing hysterically because Silva's was much fluffier, Charlene captured a photo of her and her guests all in costumes for the party downtown. Leo and Patrick had joined the crew, deciding to dress as pirates, though they hadn't originally thought to participate.

Isabella and Rico had gone all out to be skeletons in honor of Santa Muerte and had the most gorgeous makeup, which had taken them from the time they'd returned from the police station at two thirty until they'd come downstairs in solid black clothes and white faces with white gloves for hands. Isabella wore a wig of white curls with bloodred silk roses. Rico wore a top hat in black.

"Everyone looks amazing!" Charlene said.

"Maybe you could have put in a little more effort," Jack teased.

She'd added a pink nose and whiskers, so she'd upped her game a little from the original idea.

"I think you're cute too," Avery said, the only one other than Charlene and Silva to hear Jack. Her Agatha Christie costume was warm, as it consisted of a trench coat and hat. She looked at Silva and Jack. "We'll be back before midnight, so stay out of trouble, will you?"

It seemed that her ghost was interested in whether or not he could access the other side when the veil was thin and was doing a deep dive on the internet for research purposes. Seth had to work, but Avery planned on meeting him later with their friends at the beach.

Sam had sent her another cautionary text without any details. Charlene knew he would share what he could as soon as he was able.

Charlene drove the rental van downtown, going slow because of the crazy traffic. Luckily, the city had prepared for the insanity and had traffic patrol and orange cones marked for pedestrian safety. She arrived at the parking garage without mishap.

Brian Preston wasn't around that she could see. Isabella seemed relieved, and they all piled out.

"Food!" Patrick shouted.

"Beer!" Leo yelled.

"Both, my lads, both," Spence intoned, putting his arms around their shoulders.

The Pedestrian Mall had everything to offer, from caramel apples, candy corn, corn on the cob, and chicken on a stick, all within a five-block radius.

Whoever had invented that tasty chicken treat deserved their millions. Charlene and Avery ate until they couldn't eat another bite. The kids, dressed to the nines, were so adorable that it was impossible to choose a favorite, and the adult costumes blew her mind. Maybe next year Avery, Charlene, and Minnie could be the Sanderson sisters from *Hocus Pocus*. What would Jack think of that?

An hour or so later a forlorn Isabella joined Avery and Charlene. "I seem to have lost Rico somewhere. Probably a bar." She tipped her chin. "I told him I'd go with him, but we had a bit of a tiff."

The last person to have a tiff with Rico had disappeared, so Charlene hoped that Isabella would stick with Avery and her.

"You're welcome to join us. We've been people watching. Would you like something to drink?" Charlene asked. "They have carts offering everything from mixed drinks to wine spritzers."

"What are you guys drinking?" Isabella asked.

"Tea," Charlene said.

"Hot chocolate," Avery said.

"Oh—do they have any hot cider?" Isabella's tone lifted. "Avery gave me a taste the other day and it was so good. I'd never had it before."

"Let's stand in line and see," Charlene suggested.

The line moved quickly, and they were in luck. Isabella ordered a hot cider with whipped cream and cinnamon candy sprinkles.

"This is more sugar than I normally consume, but it tastes so good," Isabella said. Her perfect white make-up still hadn't smudged.

"It's that time of year," Avery said with an unrepentant shrug.

"How was your trip to the station with Sam today?" Charlene asked.

"Sad, actually. The detective needed to know things that made it real, like Marisol's social security number, banking information, our past addresses. Her driver's license information." Isabella sighed. "I just know that one way or another we will get answers at last. I felt compelled to be here in Salem."

Avery hugged Isabella from the side. "I'm sorry."

"Thanks. You're very empathetic. Are you psychic at all?" Isabella asked.

"I don't get messages or anything," Avery said. "But I am open to the possibility of more out there."

Charlene appreciated the teen's vague answer rather than her giving a detailed explanation about how her ability to see Jack, their resident ghost, had come to her after her head injury.

"I want you to be with us tonight, all right?" Isabella didn't let go of Avery's hand until the teen agreed.

"Sure." Avery sipped her cocoa. "I'm happy to help."

Juleen and Darla joined them, and pulled Isabella toward the others because Dotty was blindfolded and trying to smack a piñata shaped like a giant skull.

Jonas and Rico exited the Captain's Wheel, singing a song in Spanish. "I didn't realize that Jonas spoke Spanish. Last night he had a Louisiana drawl," Charlene murmured to Avery with a laugh.

"People are multifaceted," Avery remarked.

At nine thirty the music and party atmosphere were still going strong. Kevin had texted her to remind her they were meeting at the corner of Central and Charter.

"How many times have you been on the cemetery tour?" Avery murmured, for Charlene's ears alone.

"Several, but I learn something new every time," Charlene said. She'd had no idea when she'd chosen Salem how quickly it would become home.

"Have you ever gotten an orb in a photo, or seen a ghost there?" Avery asked.

"No. I'm curious if you'll be able to see any ghosts. Whatever happened when you hit your head changed your perception. For me, it was an emotional connection to Jack, to help find out how he'd died."

"I can see more than just Jack." Avery shivered. "But I've figured out how to block it or else it would make me certifiable. Some ghosts, similar to Jack, are very real, while others are just wisps from the corner of my eye."

"It must be different for everyone and every spirit. Jack has never shown up on film," Charlene said. "And too bad about our guidebook. Jack reminded me that it was already done in *Beetlejuice*."

Avery laughed. "Figures. There goes our million-dollar idea."

Isabella pulled away from where she'd been hanging out with Darla with a concerned look on her face. She shaded her eyes and peered into the throng of festival-goers. "I swear, I feel like I'm being followed. Is it Brian, the creeper who stalked my sister?"

The three women looked for the security guard. Five foot ten and average height. Brown hair and eyes. The problem was, this was the night when people were in costume and weren't who they appeared to be.

"Stay with us." Avery pulled her mace from her coat pocket.

"I have mine too," Charlene said, patting the side of her purse.

"What if I'm feeling Marisol?" Isabella gave a hopeful smile. "I've felt the pull to come here during my crystal meditations. There has to be a reason."

Darla had befriended a woman in a Puritan costume with long brown hair. Darla was very friendly and so far had defied all the rock star stereotypes. Nice manners, inclusive, the drummer and not the singer, and drug-free.

Charlene didn't want to go down a tangent of times changing, but this was a good example of how men and women could be their most authentic selves.

Even her mother knew that. Shocking.

By the time they reached the cemetery, it was eleven at night. Chilly and foggy. Perfectly eerie for Halloween.

The moon played peekaboo with clouds and barren trees.

It was the perfect place for a ghost sighting, and the best night of the year—All Hallow's Eve.

"Well?" Charlene asked Avery. "What do you see?"

"I see mist," Avery said. "It could be something . . . but I don't know. I would need to concentrate and have it be very quiet, but this is sheer chaos."

"We need to go, Charlene." Isabella sounded tense. "It's eleven fifteen, and we must be at the house at midnight. I don't care about these ghosts here, I want my ghost. If Marisol is a ghost. Sam seemed to think that either she stole the statue and started over or something happened to her. Not that he said that in so many words."

Sam was very good at responding with nonanswers.

Kevin had known that the four of them would be ducking out. She'd given him the keys to drive her guests home after the tour. They would possibly stop at Brews and Broomsticks. Charlene wasn't worried; trusting Kevin would keep her crew safe from harm.

Charlene, Avery, Isabella, and Rico Ubered to the bed-and-breakfast. The couple held hands as if all was forgiven. The mansion looked a tiny bit spooky against the shadowed sky.

Charlene shivered on the porch and quickly unlocked the front door.

"Does anybody else feel chills besides me?" Isabella asked.

"The doctor that was murdered here," Rico said. "I know Isabella doesn't want to talk about it, but he's probably haunting the place."

Rico happened to be correct on his long-shot theory, but she wouldn't tell him so.

"Been watching the news." Jack was in the foyer. "Crazy night tonight. I think people are losing their minds over Halloween fun. The only thing to top this off would be a full moon, which is next week. Small favors."

"I'm going to drop my purse off in my room. Avery and I will meet you in a few minutes in your suite, all right?"

"Thank you," Isabella said. Rico hurried up the stairs, intention in each step. No matter the motivation behind it, he wanted to contact Marisol.

Jack met them in her suite. Avery took off her jacket as did Charlene, and they draped them on the love seat.

"I've been watching the live streaming of the park," Jack said. "They're showing *Hocus Pocus* at the bandstand. The cameras switch from the Hawthorne to the festival at the Pedestrian Mall. This has got to bring in a lot of money for Salem."

"Brandy will be happy." Charlene studied Jack. "I don't understand how the opening of the veil works, and I don't want you caught up in it. I don't want to lose you to a random crack that sucks you out into the abyss."

Jack glowered. "What do you suggest?"

"How about just be aware, like you do, but out of sight. If we call for you, then come, but stay away from the suite and the *ofrenda* altar."

"I think that's smart too," Avery said. "We have no idea how this stuff works. It's different for everyone."

"We should get up there," Charlene said. It was now eleven forty.

"And I'm supposed to be *aware* if you need me?" Jack conveyed disapproval, shooting his arms to his sides, palms up.

"Just in case!" Charlene glanced toward the ceiling. "We can compare notes afterward for tomorrow if Marisol's spirit doesn't come through tonight."

"All right," Jack agreed reluctantly.

"Thank you," Charlene said.

Avery made heart fingers for Jack as they left Charlene's suite and climbed the stairs to the second floor.

Isabella and Rico had cleared off the desk in the room and covered it with a black silk fabric that had owls imprinted on it. Everything Jonas had brought had been unpacked. There was a framed picture of

Isabella and Marisol when they were young teens, with grinning faces. A large white candle was in the center that flickered merrily.

"What would you like us to do?" Charlene asked.

"Come in. Close the door," Rico said. "We will each light candles and call to Marisol, lighting the way from the spirit world. We must have open minds. I don't think you should be here, but Isabella disagrees. She feels psychic energy in this house. Perhaps you have powers that are untapped."

Charlene and Avery exchanged a look. Isabella had to sense Jack's presence, unless she was picking up on Charlene and Avery being able to see him . . . the paranormal rules were not straightforward.

"We are both open to the possibilities of there being more than what we see, touch, taste, hear, or feel," Charlene said.

"Perfect." Isabella straightened the charm bracelet on the cloth before facing Charlene and Avery. "Let me explain our offerings to tempt the soul of my beloved sister, if she is among the dead, to contact us and let us know what happened to her, and that she's all right."

"Okay," Avery said. "I'm nervous that I might make a mistake."

"You can't." Isabella handed Charlene and Avery each a white candle in a silver holder. "We will light these at midnight, as we sing Marisol's name."

Rico dropped to his knees before the picture of Marisol he must have drawn. Isabella and her sister looked a lot alike, though Marisol's features were slightly harder, which, Charlene admitted, could be Rico's rendition.

"Did you make that, Rico?" Avery pointed to the eight-by-ten-colored drawing. Marisol had shoulder-length dark brown hair, like Isabella's, and oval-shaped brown eyes. Her rosebud mouth and upturned nose hinted at her beauty.

"Yes," Rico said with disappointment. "It doesn't do her justice."

Isabella crossed her arms and studied it. "It's pretty, Rico. Where is the picture of the statue?"

"It's not as good—it is for Santa Muerte and should be perfect." Rico's voice bordered on whining.

"Rico, please," Isabella said. "It's important. I have the tarot card with the statue on it that you made, and the lover's card. What if it isn't enough?"

"Fine." Rico got up and went to his side of the bed, pulling his suitcase from under it. He placed it on the mattress, where Charlene and Avery sat on the end, and removed a dozen drawings in full color. "None do our Santa Muerte honor. She is solid gold and decorated in diamonds, sapphires, and rubies. Emeralds. We cannot afford to lose the Death Goddess's favor. We need her back."

"This is about Marisol, first and foremost," Isabella said, tilting her head at Rico with narrowed eyes.

"Yes, but they are entwined." Rico twisted his fore-fingers together.

"Let me see them," Isabella said. "We must hurry. It's almost midnight."

He handed her the drawings with a bowed head.

"These will do the job," Isabella said. She handed them to Charlene and Avery. "Which is the best?"

Charlene had no clue. They looked the same to her untrained eye. She was a doodler, not an artist.

"This one," Avery said. "It's got the most detail."

Rico, definitely an artist, sighed. "I suppose it does. Do you see the shading of the gold behind the diamonds?"

"Rico." Isabella was not catering to his moods right now. "Did you get the Santa Muerte pendant from Jonas? I was surprised he still had any."

Rico pulled the pendant from his pocket and placed it on the *ofrenda* rather than Isabella's outstretched palm.

"It's eleven fifty-five." Isabella blew out a breath. "My sister's charm bracelet had the five symbols of Santa Muerte on it. The scythe, the globe, the hourglass, the scales of justice, and the owl. The owl is missing. This brass key was in her jewelry box. What does it unlock?"

Charlene knew from Jared's death that sometimes there were questions when a loved one died, like receipts to a bowling alley when she hadn't realized he'd like to bowl to unwind. He'd gone with a friend when she and her dad had visited the occasional museum; not his thing.

No matter how well you thought you knew someone, it was impossible to be inside their head, to understand everything.

She had the feeling that bringing up Brian Preston and the charm wouldn't be a good idea until she knew it was a match. She'd tell Sam about it.

Isabella wiped a tear from her cheek. "Marisol, please, please join us."

"The lover's tarot card," Rico implored the ceiling, "that I drew for you, my passionate one. A pendant to remind you of the success of our shop's Santa Muerte merchandise. Your favorite Mexican tequila, your brand of cigarettes."

Isabella touched the grits from Louisiana, and the single pink hibiscus blossom. "Marisol, my sister, my love, my companion. I miss you so much. Please come through if you are able."

"It's midnight!" Rico lit a white candle, then passed the lighter to Charlene, who lit hers, and passed the lighter to Avery, who lit hers, and handed the lighter to Isabella. Once all were lit, they placed the silver holders on the desk.

"This will light the way," Isabella said. "Let's hold hands and pray, thinking of Marisol's name, over and over."

Charlene clasped Avery's hand and Rico's. Isabella took Avery's and Rico's to make a circle. Rico started to hum.

"This sound alerts the spirits that we are here," Isabella whispered.

"Should we do it too?" Avery asked.

"If you want, or you can sing Marisol's name."

Charlene and Avery hummed along with Rico and Isabella.

At ten minutes after midnight, Rico looked around and entreated the spirit of Marisol to come forward.

"*Only* the spirit of Marisol Perez," Isabella clarified.

"Only the spirit of Marisol Perez. Please come forward and speak to us, explain to us what happened. We love you and miss you." Rico bowed his head.

"Marisol, my sister, so talented. If you are at peace, I want to know. Is it selfish? Yes, but it comes from love," Isabella entreated the room.

"Love, we love you," Rico intoned. He stopped and looked around. "I feel her here."

"You do?" Isabella rocked backward and released Avery's hand, breaking the circle to press her hand to her heart. "Mari? Are you here?"

"She is," Rico assured Isabella.

Charlene glanced at Avery, who gave a tiny head-shake.

She didn't either.

Problem was, they couldn't call for Jack in the event some weird fissure in the world was open and he was caught in it.

She didn't want Jack in danger.

Unless the veil wasn't at all open. There was no way to prove it, and that meant acting on faith; in this case, Isabella's faith in the Death Goddess, Santa Muerte.

They prayed for an hour, earnestly entreating Marisol to communicate.

"Knock once if you can hear me," Isabella said.

"Or move the blinds," Rico said, standing up.

Probably to try to move them himself, Charlene thought, narrowing her eyes in the dim room to watch Rico.

"Marisol?" Isabella closed her eyes and squeezed her hands together. "I'm here. I'm here. I've felt you call-ing me to Salem. Now I am here. How can I serve you?"

Jack appeared next to Rico who was standing very close to the blinds.

Charlene bit her tongue to keep from calling Jack's name.

They'd agreed this wasn't a safe space for him to be just in case there was an open portal in time somewhere.

"I'm sorry to interrupt," Jack said. "Some of our guests are on the news being interviewed—a woman was shot and killed at the Old Burying Point Cemetery."

CHAPTER 14

Avery stood in alarm, bringing Charlene with her. "Do you feel Marisol too?" Rico asked Avery. He rubbed his arms. "She's here, like I told you. It's cold here!"

"You're by the window," Avery said.

"I don't see or feel Marisol. I'm sorry," Charlene said. "Perhaps tomorrow would be the best day for her to come through? This room is small—so what if we . . . yes, what if we moved the altar to the living room and invite all of the powerful witches who can come to support your efforts?"

Woman shot. Who? Charlene should go get her guests, but she'd Ubered to the B & B. Kevin would drive them all home safely. She needed to get out of here and help her other guests. She had to find out what had happened and who was dead.

Avery put her hand to her temple and closed her eyes. "I . . . sense that tomorrow night will be a better time. I know you're right, Rico, about this house having energy. Isabella, I sometimes feel things downstairs in the living room."

"I bet that was where that doctor was killed," Rico said. "Isabella, my love, what do you want to do?"

"I will pray all night for her to hear me," Isabella said. "But I know you're all right—tomorrow, when we have a powerful coven together, Marisol will hear me clearly. I know she is not alive. She would never leave me without a goodbye."

Jack shimmered with concern.

"I will pray with you. Go, go," Rico said, shooing them out of the room. "I swear I felt Marisol, but maybe she needs help from real brujas, not normal humans."

"I'm sure that's it," Charlene said.

She hurried down the stairs, and she and Avery raced for her suite. The television was on and both of their cell phones were ringing, as was the house phone.

On the television, Kevin Hughes was commiserating with Darla, easily recognizable in her pink mohawk and leather jacket. Where was Spence? Dotty or Juleen?

"What happened?" A reporter stuck a mic in Darla's face. Kevin edged the guy back to give her some room.

"Cindy was shot; she was a friend we just met today," Darla said with a trembling lower lip. "She's a local. We were talking and then she crumpled over. Dead. I've never, this is awful. I—"

Spence took a step toward the reporter. "Back off, man. My wife is upset and doesn't need you in her face."

Timothy, Marty, Dotty, and Juleen were visible in

the next camera angle. Everyone was okay. They could have been killed by a crazy shooter.

"Kevin has the keys to the van." Charlene dragged her phone from her purse. Kass had texted, Sam had texted, her mom had texted.

She answered everyone that she and Avery were okay at the B&B with Isabella and Rico.

Next on the news was a woman with lovely long brown hair and big brown eyes. Cindy Sherman. Local schoolteacher.

Avery sank down to the love seat with a gasp.

"Did you know her?" Charlene asked.

"No. No, but you know who she looks like?"

Charlene considered this and snapped her fingers. "Isabella."

"She's right," Jack said. "I didn't see it because of her costume, but the teacher photo shows it perfectly."

Sam called, and Charlene answered right away. "Hello? Yes, Avery and I are in my room watching the news. It's so sad."

"Detective Jimenez picked up the case."

"Oh . . . okay." Charlene and the detective didn't get along, and she knew it was because Jimenez was in love with Sam, though she'd never said so. Charlene had kept the detective's secret.

"Are you staying home for the night, please?" Sam stressed the last word.

"We have to make sure the guests are taken care of," Charlene protested. "I'll call Kevin next to check on everyone. He's got the keys to the rental van and was going to drive everyone home."

"They have that area completely shut down to find the shooter," Sam said. "Where's it parked?"

"The garage across from the Captain's Wheel pub." Charlene hugged her arm to her middle.

The sound of the front door opening had Charlene and Avery hustling out of the suite down the hall to the foyer. She held the phone to her ear, glad to have Sam on standby.

"Charlene!" Leo called. Patrick was next to him, the young men sobered after the tragedy.

"Hey—are you okay? We just saw the news," Charlene said. "Sam, I'll text you later to keep you in the loop."

"Same."

Phone call over, Charlene read the stream of texts from Kass and her mom, and now Kevin.

"Hang on," Charlene said, reading the messages. "This is from Kevin. Did you two walk?"

"Yeah. Traffic was blocked and we didn't know if you were okay, so Kevin had us check on you and Avery," Patrick said. "Where are Rico and Isabella?"

"In their suite," Avery said.

"Okay. Holy crap." Leo patted his chest and his rapidly beating heart. "We ran the whole way."

"What did you see?" Avery asked. The perfect question from a police officer in training, Charlene thought.

"Nothing, really. We were taking pictures of orbs, trying to get the Lady in White. Not sure what we have." Patrick shrugged as he gripped his phone.

"Not important," Leo interrupted. "We heard Darla scream, worst sound in the world, and it will haunt me forever. We were on the other side of a tree, with Timothy and Dotty, reading headstones. Spence was helping Darla, pulling Darla off that friend she made, Cindy. Cool woman. She lives—lived—in Salem all her life."

"That's tragic." Avery's brow knit. "Did you have your phone anywhere near Darla and Cindy? For background images?"

"Oh, to see if the shooter would be visible," Jack said. "Thinking like a cop. Proud of you, Avery."

"It would be a long shot. You might want to let the detective on the case, Detective Jimenez, know if you do," Avery said.

"All our video was of the headstones." Patrick opened his photo app. "But I'll check to be sure."

Avery nodded. "Thanks. The timing of the gunshot makes it a simple section to study on your phones."

"We will," Leo said. "I'm so amped up!"

"Adrenaline will do that," Jack said.

Charlene's phone rang. "It's Kevin!" she answered. "Hey! Are you all right?"

"Sam pulled some strings and got us to the parking garage," Kevin said. "We are on our way home now. Did Leo and Patrick reach you?"

"Yes, they're here." Charlene expelled a breath. "Come in with the others and I'll pour you a giant whiskey, Kevin."

"Deal," he said without argument. "We could all use a nightcap."

"I've got you covered." Charlene said a heartfelt prayer of thanks that they were safe. And for Sam's assistance in getting her guests home.

She sent Sam a thank-you text and invited him for a nightcap, but he declined. Jimenez had asked for his assistance with the shooting.

That was good, then. Charlene messaged him that Isabella and Cindy Sherman looked very much alike. Closer than sisters. Like Marisol too.

Sam sent a thumbs-up.

Charlene pocketed her phone and hurried to the kitchen with Leo and Patrick, and Avery, following her. Of course Jack was already there.

"Let's get snacks set out—crackers and cheese, water, tea, and ice in a bucket. I promised Kevin some liquid fortification," Charlene said. Caring for others helped with her own nerves.

"Where should we set up?" Avery retrieved a metal ice bucket from the cupboard by the fridge. "Dining room or living room?"

"Dining room," Charlene said. "It will be easier to have a conversation over food and drinks with an actual table."

"Done." Avery handed Patrick the ice bucket. He went to the freezer and filled it.

"Leo, grab the cheese, please," Charlene said. "Minnie has some sliced on the second shelf of the fridge."

Avery ducked into the pantry and came back with boxes of crackers. Together, they put together a platter of cheese and crackers that looked inviting, not that Charlene was hungry. Her stomach was tense with angst and would be until the guests got back in one piece.

"Veggies?" Charlene rifled through the crisper drawer

and blessed Minnie again. "They are already trimmed and washed."

Avery got out a dish for those, too, as well as spreadable cheese.

"I'm getting hungry," Leo said.

"Adrenaline wore off," Jack observed. "To be twenty-one again."

"To be alive again," Avery teased.

"Huh?" Leo asked.

Avery shook a celery stick at Leo. "To be hungry is to be alive—a good thing."

Charlene knew Jack was sure to get the lecture he had coming—not that he could hear it now through his laughter.

"Kevin's here," Jack said a moment later. "Darla is really upset. I wouldn't be surprised if she was experiencing shock. She'll need water before drinking alcohol."

Nodding, Charlene went to the foyer as the guests streamed in from the chill outside.

"Hey!" Charlene was tempted to hug them all as they entered just to make sure nobody else was hurt. "We are set up in the dining room, with snacks and drinks."

"Our Darla could use a double," Dotty said. Her arm was wrapped around the younger woman in commiseration.

"Let's have some water first, and then I'll pour," Charlene said.

Timothy held Dotty's shopping bags. Spence was on Darla's other side. Juleen and Marty disappeared into the dining room with Leo and Patrick.

Kevin hugged Charlene and then Avery, handing Charlene the keys to the van. "What a nightmare."

"I'm so sorry." Charlene studied Kevin's beloved face. "Thank you for taking care of my guests and making sure they got home."

"It was brutal." The light of joy usually in Kevin's gaze was absent. "We would have been even later, but Sam got us through with a police escort."

"What's going on?" Rico asked from upstairs. "It's a lot of commotion. We're praying up here."

Avery ran up the stairs and murmured to Rico, letting him know about the dead schoolteacher who'd been shot at the cemetery. He put his hand to his head and pulled his hair, then returned to the suite he shared with Isabella without another complaint.

Avery quickly rejoined them, not the least out of breath. "I didn't mention that Cindy looks like Isabella."

"What?" Kevin asked.

"Did you know Cindy before she was with you tonight?" Charlene placed her hand on Kevin's forearm, offering comfort.

"No," Kevin said.

"She's a teacher and they put her school photo on the news," Avery murmured. "Exact image of Marisol and Isabella."

"Coincidence?" Kevin scowled.

"It happens." Avery gave a doubtful shrug.

"Or not," Jack said.

"We need to get more information." Charlene released her grip. "Come on. I'm buying. You are welcome to crash here in the library. We have a futon."

"I might take you up on that," Kevin said. "I've never been next to someone who was killed."

"Have you checked in with Amy?" Charlene scanned his expression with concern.

"She's knocked out at her apartment from cold medicine. I thought I'd bring her chicken soup, but she didn't want me to get sick. Can you imagine if she'd been with us? What if she'd been hurt?" Kevin raked his hands through his hair.

"It's going to be fine." Charlene urged him into the dining room.

Patrick was pouring drinks for everyone from water to whiskey. Darla sipped her water, her whiskey next to her. Charlene was ready for a well-deserved glass of wine.

"Hot cocoa for me," Avery said. "With extra chocolate sprinkles."

Once everyone was seated, Charlene asked Kevin what had happened. Nobody really knew anything, but it was good to commiserate together. By one thirty in the morning, everyone had calmed down enough to be ready for bed.

Kevin crashed in the library, and Avery took the love seat in Charlene's room to watch the news and make Charlene feel better.

"I will be on guard tonight, my darlings," Jack said.

"Thank you, Jack," Charlene and Avery said in unison.

The next morning Charlene woke up with a start. She smelled bacon. Minnie was here. It was Monday, but they were having a weekend breakfast because it was the Day of the Dead.

No Marisol coming through the other side last night, but a teacher, Cindy Sherman, had been killed—adding to the ranks of the deceased.

Kevin had stayed over after he'd brought her guests home, with a little help from Sam.

Her phone dinged and she reached for it, missing Silva's warmth, but she was probably with Avery, or the bacon.

Sam. **On my way!**

It was eight, so Charlene raced into the shower and dressed in no time flat. Minimal makeup, but clean at least. How sweet of Sam to want to check in on everyone.

Charlene braided her hair so it was long and to the side. She left her suite—no Jack, no Avery, and no Silva.

Minnie's smile held a quaver. "Morning. How are you? I can't believe what happened! What happened?"

"We don't know a lot, but Sam is on his way." Charlene hugged Minnie.

"Good. I'll warm the ham and cheese croissants he likes so much. I made the big pot of coffee so that's ready too."

"Did you have some? You've got three cups of coffee manic energy," Charlene teased.

"I've been up since five thirty this morning—Will and I saw the news about Cindy and Kevin there with our guests. I tossed and turned without sleeping a wink. What if you'd been hurt? Or Avery?"

"We don't know the motivation for the shooting,"

Charlene said. "It could be just a random crazy person, unless the schoolteacher has dark secrets."

"The news is saying that Cindy Sherman was practically a saint and there is *no* reason for anyone to want her dead," Minnie said.

"I hate random crimes, but there was a lot of drinking and excitement going on." Charlene couldn't get the connection of Isabella and Cindy's similar appearances from her thoughts.

"It's awful is what it is," Minnie declared. Her apron was white-and-black fabric with skulls on it.

"Agreed," Charlene said. "We can ask Sam, not that he will tell us much. He should be here any minute."

"Kevin left this morning already," Minnie said. "The van keys are on the hook. He wanted to see Amy and check in. She saw the news and was worried about him. I gave him some muffins to take to her."

"That was very thoughtful, Minnie—thank you." Charlene poured herself a cup of coffee and walked down the hall to peek into the dining room. Ah, Seth was there, sitting next to Avery. The young man had his arm around Avery as if he didn't want to let her go.

"So sweet," Charlene said to Jack, taking her mug to the living room. "Any news since last night?"

"No," Jack said. "Minnie was right; the young woman didn't even have a parking ticket."

"It's tragic." Her heart ached for the loss of the community.

"I agree. Poor Darla didn't sleep well either. Spence is wondering if they should go home but she doesn't want to leave. She wants to talk with the detectives to help if she can."

"I really like that couple," Charlene murmured. "Are Isabella and Rico down? We're going to set up in here for the midnight beckoning of Marisol Perez. You took a big chance last night, Jack. What if something had happened?"

"I didn't sense any cracks in the force yesterday like you were afraid of," Jack said with twitching lips.

"Still."

"I'll be careful. I want to help Isabella. I have a vague memory of her and her sister from ten years ago. They were new in town, and Marisol had cut herself while they were moving from New Orleans."

"Jack." Charlene raised her brow. She understood how much he cared about his patients. He'd been an awesome doctor.

"They didn't have insurance, so I gave them my cell number to call directly if they needed supplies, but they never did."

"You're a softy," Charlene said, daring a sip of hot, creamy coffee.

"Me?" Jack put his hand to his chest in question.

Sam knocked on the door and Charlene hurried to answer it.

The sight of Sam always made her happy inside. "Come in. We've got coffee. Minnie is making you a ham and cheese croissant."

"What a welcome!" Sam kissed her on the forehead, then checked to make sure nobody was around and kissed her firmly on the mouth.

"Sly." Jack laughed.

"How are things going?" Charlene asked. The only

thing keeping her from hugging him tight was the hot mug between them.

Sam shook his head, his joy at seeing her fading. "Cindy was a good person killed for no reason. In my business that is very rarely the case. It's up to us to find out what happened to her, and why. We won't rest until we do."

"I believe you." Charlene briefly rested her forehead to his chest. Sam was very good at catching the bad guys, or girls. He and Jimenez would be an unbeatable team.

"Where is everyone?" Sam asked.

"The dining room. Darla was standing next to Cindy when she was shot." She realized why he'd been efficient with his kiss and blew out a breath. "Are you here for the coffee, or is this official business?"

CHAPTER 15

After Sam explained that it was a bit of both, Charlene urged him toward the dining room and breakfast. "I can offer food and conversation."

"Your specialty." Jack disappeared but reappeared in the dining room by the sideboard.

"Good morning," Sam said to the guests around the table. Leo and Patrick weren't down yet, but the four couples were in various stages of coherence.

"Morning," most folks repeated.

Charlene passed Avery and Seth to sit at the end of the table, saving a seat for Sam next to her.

Darla had huge shadows beneath her eyes and her slender shoulders were slumped forward. She had some eggs and fruit on a plate before her but hadn't eaten. Even her coffee was untouched.

"And why didn't that psychic lady warn you about what was going to happen?" Spence spoke in an angry tone. "Persephone was happy to take your money with no heads-up that something bad was going down. It's a raw deal. You should ask for your money back."

"I don't know how it works." Darla shrugged and chased eggs around on her plate with her fork. "It was all good news."

Minnie had made scrambled eggs with ham chunks and fresh baked croissants. Shredded cheese was in a center dish, as were sliced green onions. Butter and jams were available.

Marty offered Juleen the bowl of eggs and she took a scoop and passed it to Avery, who had started the round.

"Did anybody get a warning about last night?" Spence continued, still peeved.

Charlene gave Sam a dish and took one for herself. There were plenty of eggs, but Minnie brought in a croissant for Sam with the ham and cheese melted inside.

Sam winked at Minnie, who blushed, scanned to see if anything needed refilled—it didn't—and left for the kitchen. Her leggings matched her apron today in honor of *Dia de los Muertos*.

"I was given a positive reading as well," Juleen said. "My books will be popular and find an audience. I would have preferred to know that someone would be shot who was near our group."

Marty sipped his orange juice, his face sad. "We can ask Kass, but I bet she'll tell us it's not a clear vision or some other crap to protect their butts."

"And keep their money," Spence said.

"These guys are just upset that their ladies could

have been hurt," Jack deduced. "It's not really about the money but wanting justice."

Charlene silently agreed with Jack.

"We could have warned Cindy," Darla said in a ragged voice. "It seems frivolous to have eggs when she won't ever have breakfast again. I held her hand."

Dotty got up from her chair and hugged Darla. "Sweetheart. This is just a terrible thing that happened. You couldn't have prevented it. She was lucky that you were able to hold her hand, because you'd befriended her. Without that, she would have been alone. It's awful to think about, but I hope, after time has passed, you can feel peace in that."

Darla sniffed. Dotty didn't let go for several minutes until Darla was ready.

"How do you know what to say?" Charlene asked softly.

"I was a counselor at our school after a shooting on campus," Dotty said. She didn't go into further details, but Charlene could imagine the tragedy that must have happened to require such empathy.

Her calm words served to lighten the mood of the group. They couldn't have prevented what happened.

"Detective Holden, I'm willing to help in any way to find out what happened with Cindy," Darla said.

"I will let Detective Jimenez know. She is running the lead on this case, and we do appreciate that." Sam nodded at the young woman in acknowledgment. "You never know where answers will come from during an investigation."

Avery sighed. "Five years before I can be on the police force feels like forever. I want to help now."

"You're going to be an officer?" Marty asked.

"Yes. It's my dream."

"A detective," Seth said with pride, smiling at his girlfriend.

"Do you have to go to the police academy?" Timothy seemed very tired after little sleep last night. Maybe Charlene could suggest naps for everyone? "Not like I know, but from the movies."

"Because I want to be a detective, I'm going to college first," Avery said.

"And then police academy training, which is no picnic," Sam said. "Not sure why you want to do this job. It's a lot of untangling of threads."

"I love puzzles." Avery exuded assurance.

"Is Sam trying to talk her out of it?" Jack asked.

Avery started to answer but caught herself.

Charlene could relate to that.

"You have to follow the rules all the time." Spence handed Darla a piece of scone. "Not sure I'd be good at that."

"I don't mind the rules, so far," Avery said. "Calculus is harder than being good."

Everyone around the table burst out laughing.

"Good for you, to follow your passion." Isabella's face was devoid of the white makeup from yesterday and she looked about twenty rather than twenty-eight.

"How did things go for you last night?" Juleen asked. "Did you reach your sister?"

"No," Isabella said softly. "We didn't."

"I felt something," Rico said.

Isabella glared at him. "You know that makes me feel bad, right?"

Rico raised his palms and sat back in his chair.

"Especially because it isn't true," Jack said.

"Will you try again tonight?" Dotty asked.

"Yes." Isabella nodded. "If any of you have a hint of psychic powers, I'd be grateful if you'd stay and help us call for Marisol. Tonight is the best night of the three possibilities."

All of her guests shook their heads.

"It was worth a try." Isabella smiled at Charlene. "In addition to you and Avery, we will have Kass, and possibly Serenity. Persephone."

"I could ask my mom, but she's got a date tonight." Seth shrugged.

Sam bristled, as if he was trying very hard to keep himself together.

"Are you okay?" Charlene asked.

"Psychic energy," Sam murmured. He finished his ham and cheese croissant, sipped his coffee, then stood. "I was wondering if I might talk to Rico and Isabella?"

Charlene hadn't been included, but she wasn't going to let her guests be badgered, so she followed Sam to the foyer.

"I'd like a picture of Marisol," Sam said.

"Besides the one of us as teenagers in New Orleans? You took pictures of the *ofrenda* already yesterday."

"Just Marisol would be best."

Isabella sighed. "Rico drew one for her *ofrenda* yesterday that is quite beautiful. My sister was as lovely as she was talented. And protective. Some of her tarot clients were very dark. I'd cleanse her aura and psychic fields with my crystals afterward."

"May I see that picture?" Sam kept his tone ultra polite. Even though the subject matter wasn't something he subscribed to, he remained professional.

"I'll bring it down," Rico said. "You can take a photo of it, but we need it for tonight's ceremony."

"All right." Sam turned to Isabella as Rico ascended the stairs to retrieve the pictures.

"What is it, Detective?" Isabella asked.

Sam clenched his jaw tight, but in the end, he just shook his head.

Charlene wondered if he'd been on the verge of giving her a lecture on believing in black and white. Facts. Proof.

Where did that leave room for faith?

Rico returned with the drawing of Marisol, the sketch of the statue, and the tarot card that had the gold statue on it. He hadn't brought the picture of Isabella and Marisol. He arranged them on the oval table by the front door.

Sam used his cell phone to take individual photos of each item. "Thank you."

"How is the search for Marisol going?" Rico asked.

"I haven't heard anything yet, but investigations take time," Sam said. Answering the question with no actual news.

Rico picked up the sketch and the tarot card. "I'm done with breakfast," he said to Isabella. "We should go upstairs and continue to plan."

Isabella blinked rapidly. "We'll have more magical people tonight, which is sure to help. This is the most powerful night of the year because the veil is the thinnest." She noticed Sam's controlled expression. "It's fine that you don't believe in the paranormal, Detective Holden. We've been faced with doubt our whole lives. Between us, we will find my sister one way or the other."

Isabella took the picture of Marisol and held it to her chest. Rico gently put his hand on her hip and the couple went upstairs.

Sam hooked his thumb over his shoulder. "Charlene, can I talk to you on the porch?"

"Of course."

Once outside, Sam faced her with a serious expression. "Tell me you don't believe in this spirit crap."

Charlene's stomach tightened. "I can't do that."

"What?" Sam rocked back as if she'd sucker punched him.

"I can't say that I don't believe in the paranormal," Charlene said softly. His expression was killing her.

"You are a logical, educated woman—from the *Midwest*," Sam said.

Tears stung her eyes.

"That I am. I also know for a fact there is more to this world than what we experience with our five senses." Charlene lowered her arms to her sides.

"Ghosts?" Sam exploded.

"Yes, Sam," Charlene said.

He shook his head so vigorously that she feared he'd lose his balance. She reached for his arm, but he shrugged her touch away. "How can you believe in ghosts? It makes no sense to me at all."

Charlene grew defensive at his attack on her beliefs

when he was actually very wrong. "Do you remember when I first moved here?"

"Yes." His golden-brown eyes remained cool. "I thought you were the most beautiful woman I'd ever seen."

"I informed you that there was something wrong at my house." Charlene pointed to the front door.

"Right," Sam said. "We discovered that the owner, a doctor, had been killed here. We arrested the *human* responsible."

She started to get angry at his tone. "I told you, and you didn't believe, that my home was haunted. It still is."

"By this dead doctor?"

"Yes." Charlene tipped her chin. "Dr. Jack Strathmore."

"Is he dangerous?"

"No! He's just . . . Jack. He looks out for me and Avery and the guests. Silva."

"Show me," Sam demanded.

"You want to meet Jack *now*?" Asking Jack to manifest was not a perfect science. He'd had anger issues, and when he was upset, he couldn't control his energy. It wasn't like she could say, *Hey Jack, tell Sam hello and be friends*. It had taken time for him to figure out how to communicate with Charlene. Not everybody could see him, let alone converse.

"Can't do it?" Sam's mustache quivered.

"I'll try. Jack!"

Jack appeared on the porch next to Sam in a blast of cold. He was so upset by what was happening that he vanished.

"Did you feel that?"

"What?" The wind picked up, and of course it was a chilly fall day. Jack's essence blended with the temperature.

Sam bowed his head as if completely undone. When he raised his gaze he appeared lost, as if he had no idea what to do. "This is a waste of time."

"Sam," Charlene said in an imploring tone. "Please believe me."

"How can I believe you if you can't prove it?"

"It's called faith."

"Faith." Sam shook his head. "Are you the only one who can see this ghost?"

"No." Charlene almost didn't want to say anymore, but secrets ruined relationships, and if she and Sam were to move forward together, they had to find common ground.

"Who?"

"Silva," Charlene said. "She's seen Jack since the beginning."

"The cat can't vouch for your story, Charlene. Anybody else?"

Charlene bowed her head, hoping she was doing the right thing. Could Sam block Avery from pursuing her dream as a detective? No! He would never do that; even if he didn't believe Charlene, he was a man with integrity. "Avery."

The betrayal on Sam's face was like a stab to her heart.

He opened the door and called, "Avery?"

Avery popped out of the dining room. "Yeah, Sam?"

"Come here, would you?" Sam radiated hurt with each breath.

Jack must've really reached deep for strength because he manifested fully to join Avery as she reached the porch. Seth stayed in the dining room at the threshold.

"What's up?" Avery asked.

"Charlene tells me that this house is haunted by a dead doctor," Sam said in a wintry tone.

Avery gulped, her smile fleeing as she saw Sam's expression of hurt and disbelief. "It's true, Sam. I couldn't see him until after my head injury, but the spirit of Jack Strathmore is here."

"Now?" Sam asked.

"Yes," Avery said quietly.

Jack's image flickered back and forth. "Sam? Sam!"

Sam looked destroyed. He bent over at the waist and walked to the railing on the porch where he sat down, his knees bent. He rammed his fingers into his hair and glared at Charlene with hurt. "Where is he?"

"By the front door," Charlene said.

Jack twisted his hands, making leaves dance in the wind. Sam didn't notice. Could be the wind.

"You should have tried harder to tell me," Sam said.

Tears spilled down her cheeks. "Over the years I've brought it up, but you bring out your show-me-the-proof argument and I can't fight that. Either you can see him or not. It was never an argument I wanted to have with you, Sam. I love you."

"You are not who I thought you were." Sam stepped down the stairs, reaching the gravel. "I'll be in touch about Marisol. I bet I'll find proof of her death before you get some ghost to cross some ridiculous veil."

Charlene felt as if her heart had been torn from her chest and stomped on.

Jack tried to stop him from going to his SUV, but Sam was so hurt he didn't notice the arctic cold. He hopped in, reversed, and left without ever acknowledging Charlene again.

"He doesn't mean that," Avery said, hugging Charlene.

Charlene didn't dare give into her grief. She'd thought she would marry Sam and they'd figure out a compromise, but this . . . this was too much.

She couldn't survive another heartache like this.

"Charlene," Jack said, his entire being filled with pain on her behalf.

"I can't go through what I did when Jared died again." Charlene froze every agonizing emotion and tipped her chin. Numb was best.

"Charlene?" Avery gripped her hand.

"I'm fine, hon. I have guests to take care of. I will be all right," Charlene released Avery's chilled fingers. "We will be okay."

"Charlene!" Avery cried, not believing her.

"I can't fall apart right now, okay?" Charlene patted Avery's arm. "Please, let me deal with this in my own way."

Avery, torn, stared down the long drive, where not even Sam's taillights were visible. He was gone and might not ever come back.

That had been a close call with her heart. Who was she kidding? It was too late. When you loved someone, you gave them the power to hurt you. Sam had looked like she'd stuck a knife in his ribs and twisted. He'd left her—by choice.

She pinched the inside of her wrist until it stung.

Charlene led the way inside, Avery at her heels. The teen slammed the door closed. Jack's frenetic energy caused him to flicker visible and not visible. Most disconcerting.

"Charlene, don't forget about decorating the sugar cookies today," Minnie said, peeking from the kitchen hall. "We can be ready in fifteen minutes with frosting and all the trimmings."

"Great idea!" Great distraction. Charlene went into the dining room and pasted on a big smile. "Hey, all, we're going to decorate our sugar skulls to celebrate the Day of the Dead. Winner gets a small prize."

"That sounds fun." Juleen peered around the table. "If Rico and Isabella were here, I'd bet on them to win."

"They're upstairs," Charlene said. "Who all wants to go to the parade downtown tonight?"

"Do you think Cindy's spirit will be there?" Darla asked.

"I don't know," Charlene said. She didn't know a lot of things. She'd been okay with that, being open. It was something she'd learned after Jack had widened her eyes.

"We could ask Persephone," Juleen suggested. "I want to go by her shop and ask why she didn't tell us about Cindy."

"Good idea," Marty said. "When are we doing the cookies?"

"Now good? Let me clear the table and bring out the cookies and frosting. There will be *Dia de los Muertos* entertainment all day downtown. Parade tonight. And you guys are checking out on Wednesday." Charlene could focus on taking the next step. It was how she'd gotten through her days after Jared died. One breath at a time.

"I'm not leaving until we know about Cindy," Darla said. "Spence and I will find another hotel if you're booked. We've already talked about it."

"The Salem Police are very skilled at finding the bad guys." Charlene, still smiling, went into the kitchen.

"How's it going?" Minnie asked after catching a glimpse of Charlene's too-bright expression.

"Fine. We're ready to decorate cookies and then I think our guests will spend the day downtown again."

"Your mom called and left another message," Minnie said.

"I'll take her and Dad some of the cookies and find out how their Halloween went too," Charlene decided. Fill each second with tasks so she didn't have time to think.

"Terrific." Minnie stopped and examined Charlene closely. "Are you sure you're okay?"

"Yep." Charlene scooted away from Minnie's laser gaze. "Why wouldn't I be?"

"Sam usually tells me goodbye before he goes." Minnie stayed next to Charlene like a second skin.

Charlene shrugged. "He was in a hurry." Now wasn't the time to break it to her housekeeper that she and Sam had split.

Jack hovered, upset, between the kitchen and dining room. "Charlene. Please talk to me in your suite."

She put up a hand. She couldn't think about what had happened or she would crumple into a million pieces.

Charlene brought the tray of undecorated cookies to the dining room. Avery quickly changed the breakfast tablecloth to a clean one. Seth helped and brought the old tablecloth to the laundry room.

Minnie carried in a tray loaded with frosting in a variety of colors and sprinkles. All things to decorate their sugar skulls.

"The winner will receive a Starbucks gift card," Minnie said.

"I love a competition," Juleen said.

Her guests worked diligently. Charlene focused on hers as well, making two for her parents specifically.

People all had plans for the day but would be back for happy hour before the Day of the Dead parade.

Charlene ignored Avery's entreating looks, and Jack's, and only paid attention to the frosting. Her dad loved chocolate, so she added chocolate nibs.

At noon she was done. Seth had to go to work, and Avery wanted to come with Charlene to visit her parents and say hello. Charlene allowed it because it would force her to be strong.

Lunch would be on their own. Maybe her parents would want to grab something to eat together? She could visit with Sharon from Cod and Capers. The Flints had coven things all day.

She'd built a life of friendships since she'd moved

from Chicago, not letting herself make the same mistake twice. And now she was grateful for her choices.

Her life had been Jared. Now it was the B&B. Jack. Avery. Silva.

Sam's rejection of her hurt like hell, but it wasn't fatal.

CHAPTER 16

Charlene, with Avery riding shotgun, drove on autopilot toward her parents' condo and the wharf.

"Are we not going to talk about what happened with Sam?" Avery demanded. "It's just you and me in the car. He's wrong, which breaks my heart, but not as much as it must be breaking yours."

Blinking back tears so they wouldn't fall, Charlene focused on the stoplight as it turned red. "I can't talk about it. If I do, I'll be a mess." She glanced at the concerned teen. "I can't afford that. We have a house full of guests, thank God, to keep me distracted."

"That's not healthy!" Avery said.

How to explain that she'd be all right? "Jared and I were so in tune with each other, so in love, that we didn't need anybody else." Charlene's heart throbbed. "When he died, I had nobody. I had my entire world one minute, and in the next Jared was gone. Poof! Can you imagine?"

Avery shook her head.

"When I moved here I vowed to create a wider existence for myself. I'm a member of Salem's new business board. I have a circle of wonderful friends that include witches. Jack, a ghost, is my best friend. And I have you, Avery. You are a daughter to me. So. While Sam's actions have really wounded me, they haven't killed me. I have to hang on to that."

The light turned green, and Charlene stepped on the gas with a little too much oomph and the Pilot jumped. She patted the dashboard.

Her chest ached and she swallowed a lump of nerves. She would survive.

"You are a very strong woman," Avery said. "I love you too. And so does Sam. I think Sam will realize that he's wrong and come around."

"How?" Charlene was glad to see Benjamin's friendly face on the bench. It meant they were nearing the condo, and she could get away from Miss That Doesn't Seem Healthy before she broke down. "Did you discover a way to make Jack visible to Sam? As much as I'm tempted to pop him on the head, it's not a viable plan."

"Are we sure?" Avery scowled, making her look much wiser than her actual age. "You're right. Violence isn't the answer. Patience, I guess. Maybe just give it some time."

"That sounds fine with me." Time would let her build a shield around her heart to protect herself from getting hurt. Charlene parked and turned off the engine. "Let's not mention it to Mom and Dad."

"I wouldn't share your stories." Avery hopped out of

the SUV and retrieved the goodies from Minnie. "You can trust me."

"I know that, sweetheart. I do." Charlene took the cookies from Avery and followed the young woman into the lobby of the condo.

"What floor?" Avery asked.

"Ten."

"I'm looking forward to seeing their place. Curious as to what style dominates in the Woodbridge household," Avery said. "Books and art, or a casual vibe?"

"I love the view of the bay," Charlene said. "And I forget about the style once I'm in, drawn to the picture window. It's peaceful."

They exited on the tenth floor.

Charlene knocked firmly.

"Come in," her mother sang. She studied first Charlene and then Avery from head to toe before stepping back and tugging them inside. Did their casual attire, jeans and jackets, pass muster? "Michael! The girls are here."

Mom wore a coordinated pantsuit in shades of blue with a blue pair of glasses to match.

Charlene gave her mom the covered dish of cookies. "You know the way to his heart," she said. "With treats!"

Her dad ambled out of the second bedroom they used as an office. "Hello! How nice to see you both. Do you have time to stay? I'll put the kettle on."

"Yes." Charlene had all the time in the world.

Her mom lifted a brow at Charlene's forced cheeriness. "If you have other things to do . . ."

"I don't," Charlene said.

Avery exhaled and looked out the window. "You're right Charlene. This is a great view of the wharf, and the lighthouse."

"Thanks. We like it," her dad said.

"We are so glad you came by," Mom said. "My heart stopped for a full sixty seconds, seeing the news of Cindy's death and Kevin being interviewed. The poor young lady from your group—she had the mohawk costume—was just so upset. How is she?"

"Darla was devastated by what had happened," Charlene said. "Luckily, one of our other guests, Dotty, has some experience with counseling, so that helped everyone this morning at breakfast. Reminded us all that there was nothing we could have done."

"Darla had befriended Cindy and included her in our group, so she felt guilty," Avery explained.

"Oh no!" Her mother put her hand to her chest.

Her dad patted her mom's shoulder. "It's good to see you both for ourselves after such a scare. Makes me glad that we moved here."

Charlene noticed a bowl of Halloween candy that had the Snickers dark chocolate variety and helped herself to a mini-bar. Chocolate was a known serotonin lifter. "How many trick-or-treaters did you get?"

"Quite a few that live in this building," her mom said. "They were so cute. We turned the light off at ten even though we had this half bag of candy left. Two and a half bags, so we know that we'll need three for next year, and Dad was right to buy more supplies. Then we watched the streaming of the city's festivities last night, which was why we were up for the shocking news at midnight."

"We recognized Kevin right away," her dad said. "We sometimes stop at Brews and Broomsticks for burgers."

"Why weren't you and Avery downtown with your guests?" Mom took four mugs from a cupboard and put them next to the electric kettle.

"We were at first," Charlene said, "but we'd left early to help Isabella and Rico with the *ofrenda*." She rolled up the empty wrapper and tossed it into the trash under the kitchen sink.

"The altar I told you about, Michael. And," her mom turned back to Charlene, "did it work?"

"No," Charlene said. "We didn't contact Marisol. She might not be dead, or the prayers and offerings might not have been a strong enough temptation. We are trying again tonight, which is the primo evening for when the veil is the thinnest."

"We think that Rico is trying to trick Isabella into believing that he can feel Marisol's presence," Avery said. She had removed her canvas army jacket and folded it over the kitchen chair.

"Did you feel anything?" Mom's brows rose as she leaned toward Charlene. "Like a spirit?"

"Not Marisol, no," Charlene said firmly. She wasn't about to tell her parents about Jack, not after Sam's reaction. She also took off her lightweight coat, putting it on top of her purse on the couch.

Avery didn't mention Jack either as she helped herself to a Snickers.

"Detective Jimenez is working on Cindy Sherman's case. I'm sure she'll have it solved in no time." Charlene paced to the window. It would be nice to have such an expansive view. She could see the bay and the wharf. The boats in the harbor. Yes, she could make out the ocean from her roof with the telescope, but it wasn't the same.

Was that Persephone, and Jonas? Charlene squinted against the glare off the water.

"Spot a dolphin or something?" Her dad gave her a lightweight pair of binoculars. "I love how everything is always in motion. These might help."

"Thanks, Dad." Charlene put them to her eyes and adjusted them to bring the two figures into focus. Pink hair—not such a giveaway these days, but the trim body shape was similar. Purple headband. "Avery—is that Persephone?"

"Yeah, it is," Avery said with assurance. "Talking with a guy. Wasn't he with Rico last night at the Captain's Wheel?"

"Jonas McCarthy. Isabella's honorary uncle from New Orleans." Charlene adjusted the binoculars. "They're arguing."

She remembered how Persephone had seemed surprised that Jonas was in town yesterday. They must have known each other back in the day, or maybe they still did.

"Can you make out what they're saying?" Charlene asked. It was impossible to zoom closer. Didn't help that Jonas had his back to them.

Avery was using an app on her phone to bring them into sharper view. "Persephone is yelling something. I think a name? *B* . . . or maybe *P*?"

"Could it be Brian Preston? He's that weasel, Mom,

who followed Persephone to the coffee shop." Charlene shook her head. "Come on, Jonas, turn around so I can see you. Thatta boy. Something about Marisol's clients . . ." Jonas again moved so she couldn't see him.

"Was Brian a client of Marisol's?" Avery asked.

"I don't know. Isabella accused him of stalking Marisol. She'd been shocked to learn they'd hooked up a few times. Kass said Brian transferred his attentions to Persephone after Marisol disappeared." Charlene had seen him come out of the mail center behind Persephone's business. Dang it. She'd meant to tell Sam about the possible owl on his key ring.

"Attentions?" Her dad looked adorable in his cardigan button-up sweater and glasses.

"Stalkery behavior," Avery said.

"Well, that's not all right." Dad frowned.

"The security guard who smacked on the window to get Persephone's attention? She wanted to give you the love note from your secret admirer. Let me see those binoculars," her mom said. "He was creepy with a capital *C*."

"Not a love note, and it wasn't a secret." Charlene handed her the binoculars.

Her mom zeroed in on the harbor. "Huh. Yep, I remember Persephone. The guy she's arguing with has been in town since Thursday. Sturdy blue boat, red captain's wheel. Not sleek like some of the yachts around here."

Charlene stepped back from the window and tilted

her head at her mother. "How can you be sure it's the same man?"

"His bushy beard. Looks like an old-fashioned sea captain." Her mother handed her back the binoculars. "The red wheel on his boat is also unique. Most boats have their name visible, but his doesn't have one."

"Captain Jonas is here in Salem to deliver items to Isabella. I guess he used to be in business with Marisol, Isabella, and Rico when they owned the Santa Muerte shop." Charlene watched as Persephone pushed Jonas on his massive chest and then stomped away. "Jonas knew the girls from when they all lived in New Orleans and their mother was still alive."

"I don't suppose we can just ask Persephone what they were arguing about?" Avery asked.

"We could give it a try, but I doubt she'd answer." Charlene laughed. "*Hey Persephone, we were watching from my parents' window and noticed you had a blow out with the captain. What about?*." She gave her dad the binoculars. "Takes snooping to a new level I'm not ready to admit to."

"What if they're both involved somehow with Marisol's disappearance?" Avery asked. "They were completely upset about something, and we can't assume it was Brian."

"The problem with snooping is not being able to ask direct questions." Her dad put the binoculars on the kitchen table. "It drives your mother crazy."

"What do we know about Persephone?" Mom poured hot water into all four mugs as Dad set down a basket of assorted teas. "She came to the shop to deliver the note from your secret admirer—the one she wishes she could have—but she just guides his life."

"What secret admirer?" Avery asked her mother. "Does Sam know?"

"Not a secret. Benjamin passed me by Friday evening as he left Persephone's building, which has a mail center. Brian must use it too. Persephone denied that the guard was a client when I mentioned I'd seen him exit the premises, thinking to warn her."

"Benjamin Fiske, the dude on all the benches? He's cute," Avery said.

"And rich," her mother said. "But Charlene's heart belongs to Sam."

"I'd love to change the subject," Charlene said.

Her mom leaned toward her, head at a tilt. "Is everything okay?"

Charlene couldn't lie with Mom so close. "No, it's not." She returned to the window.

Avery exhaled and picked up her mug, watching Jonas on his nameless boat, shoulder to shoulder with Charlene. She murmured, "You should tell them what happened and see what they think."

"They don't need to know." Charlene stared at the horizon, mug in hand, tears welling up in her eyes and blurring her vision.

"Charlene," Avery said. "You are not alone in this."

"Honey?" her dad asked.

The tears spilled from her eyes, something Charlene hadn't wanted to deal with. She blinked and dabbed her face with the sleeve of her shirt.

She turned so her back was to the window. "If I was to tell you that my bed-and-breakfast was haunted, would you believe me?"

Her parents exchanged a look.

"We'd have questions," her dad said. "Is it?"

"Yes," Charlene said. "It is."

"Are you in danger?" Her mother straightened to her full height from the kitchen chair and took Dad's hand.

"No." Charlene shook her head. "Not even a little bit."

"How do you know?" Dad's tone went into scholar mode.

"I can see him. His name is Jack Strathmore. He was murdered and is tied somehow to the property."

"Oh." She plonked back down, still holding Dad's hand. "I never had the gift of intuition but my mother used to know who was calling before the phone even rang."

Charlene glanced at Avery, who nodded with encouragement.

"So, you both believe me?"

"Of course." Her dad looked at Avery. "Do you?"

Avery nodded. "I can also see Jack. It happened after my head injury. Silva does too."

"All right." Her dad removed his glasses and cleaned the lenses with a cloth napkin. "Very intriguing. So, what's the problem? Do you want to help him reach Heaven?"

"Jack says he is happy with us at the B-and-B," Charlene said. "Sam . . ."

Her mom put her fingers to her chin. "Oh. Black-and-white, show-me-the-proof Sam. You told him?"

"I did, because he asked, and then he didn't believe me. This morning, we had . . . a moment of reckoning, I guess, because Isabella is trying to reach her sister, if her sister is dead, tonight. The veil between dimensions is supposedly at its thinnest then. Sam pulled me aside and asked me point-blank—I reminded him that I'd told him the mansion was haunted years ago."

Charlene pushed from the glass pane and dropped onto the kitchen chair, sliding her mug toward the middle of the table. Avery was at her side in an instant, her hand on Charlene's shoulder.

"He said I wasn't the woman he thought I was." Tears, ugly and hot, streamed down her cheeks.

"Honey!" her mother said. Her dad rounded the table and hugged her from the other side.

"Sam didn't mean it," her dad said. "He loves you."

"Not enough to find a compromise over something like this," Charlene sniffed. "He needs proof of Jack. It's not enough that I said Jack is there, and Avery too."

The four of them hugged and cried.

At the end of the cryfest, Charlene didn't feel alone, and though it still hurt, she knew she was cared for.

"You love Sam, Charlene, so here is my advice that you didn't ask for," her mother said. "Give him time to come around. Sam loves you too. For a man who has built his life around black-and-white, it must have been a shock to the core that there is gray."

Charlene and Avery left the condo. "Have I told you how grateful I am to have you in my life, Avery Shriver?"

She got behind the wheel of the Pilot and started the car.

"We're family, Charlene." Avery belted up and squinted to the main road. "Is that Brian, following Persephone? What a creep! I don't think she's aware he's there."

Persephone was walking away from the wharf, with no sign of Jonas. Brian rode an electric bicycle, circling on the street to keep Persephone in view. Charlene left the parking lot and passed Brian on his bike, honking as she drove. He didn't respond. She pulled the car to the side of the road to halt Persephone.

"Persephone," she called.

The pink-haired witch had her earbuds in and couldn't hear her and was completely oblivious to Brian behind her.

The security guard passed her and gave her the middle finger.

"Hey!" Avery said.

"What should we do?" Charlene asked.

"He's not breaking the law, yet," Avery said.

Charlene hardly felt better when Brian passed Persephone, ogling her as he did, completely aware of his audience. At least he was gone.

"I think he might have an owl charm on his key ring," Charlene said. "I noticed it when he followed Isabella into Kass's shop, thinking she was Marisol."

"Marisol's missing bracelet charm?" Avery hummed. "Criminals sometimes keep trophies."

"The fact that Marisol and Brian hooked up clouds the issue, doesn't it?"

"I don't see Brian's appeal." Avery sent Charlene a cajoling smile. "Should we get ice cream? I have school on Wednesday, so only a few more days for junk food."

"Cod and Capers? I can tempt you with a healthy lunch. I will miss you when you're gone."

"And the restaurant offers a view of Jonas and his boat. That's interesting, don't you think, that it doesn't have a name? Probably illegal," Avery said. "I'll Google it."

"Terrific points. Lunch." Charlene parked in the lot and they entered. It was the odd time between lunch and dinner, and Sharon seated them by the window that had a terrific view of the water.

"How have you guys been? I saw on the news that one of your group knew Cindy Sherman. My kids had her as a teacher." Sharon's eyes were rimmed in a red that inadvertently matched the shade of her dyed hair. "She was very sweet."

"Darla was standing next to her," Avery said. "Charlene and I were at home with some other guests."

"I'm glad you guys are okay." Sharon exhaled and brought out a tablet to take their order. "What can I get you?"

"Shrimp fettuccine," Charlene said. "Avery?"

"Fish and chips."

"Drinks?"

"Iced tea for me," Avery said. "You want a glass of pinot grigio? You aren't on van duty today."

Charlene grinned at the unexpected bright spot. "Yes, please."

Sharon returned with their drinks and food. "Glad

you beat the rush—Benjamin always brings an entourage." She jerked her chin toward the handsome man on the bench ads, who'd winked at her. He saw her staring now and smiled.

Blushing, Charlene picked up her wine.

"He has that effect on me too," Sharon joked. "Makes me want to buy a boat I can't afford."

His table was filled with men all dressed in nice suits.

Avery peeked around Sharon and waved. "The cute old guy!"

Sharon laughed. "To be a teenager again."

They were midway through their meals when Avery used her phone app to focus on Jonas's blue boat. "Jonas is walking away from his vessel, Charlene. Headed in the opposite direction. We should go check the boat out at the harbor while he's gone."

"What?" That was a good idea masquerading as a bad one, or vice versa. Sam didn't like it when she set a poor example for Avery.

"What if there are clues on that boat that lead to Marisol?" Avery suggested.

"You are not giving up your career before you graduate college to find out," Charlene said firmly.

"I didn't say break the law." Avery smirked.

"What then?" Charlene ate the last shrimp on her plate.

"A stroll down the pier." Avery sipped her iced tea. "Maybe the name will be visible on the other side."

Charlene considered this possibility. "A walk after lunch helps with digestion. And if we find a name on the boat, we can set my mom's mind at ease. I blame her for my curious nature."

Avery read from her phone. "According to what I found online, a commercial rig must have a name, but pleasure crafts don't."

"Rico and Persephone both said Jonas supplied merchandise." Charlene finished her wine. "That would mean business, right?"

"We don't know if this was the same boat," Avery said.

"True." Charlene placed cash on the table for Sharon and stood up. The table where Benjamin and his associates had sat was empty. Still, she smoothed her hair from her face. "We have lots of questions, per usual. Jack is great at online answers."

"If we come across anything of interest, we can have Seth make a phone call to Detective Jimenez," Avery said. "We leave Sam out of it."

"Deal." Charlene covered her plate with her napkin, waving to Sharon as they left.

Charlene sucked in a breath as a gust buffeted them. The Pilot was fine in the lot while they stretched their legs on the pier.

Avery's canvas jacket was bulky, with lots of pockets. She pulled a knit cap from one of the recesses and put it over her short hair. Adorable.

Charlene zipped up her lightweight jacket, regretting the lack of a scarf for added warmth as the sky darkened.

"Brian following Persephone is shady," Avery said. "Sometimes stalker behavior can escalate to murder."

"Like Brian and Marisol?" Charlene asked. "Could he have killed her for breaking the relationship off? Rico said he wanted Marisol to stop messing around with Brian because he had to stop seeing Persephone. They argued about it the day she disappeared."

During a break in traffic, they stepped in sync across the street to the wharf.

"It would help to know for sure if Marisol is dead."

"Isabella believes so, in here," Charlene patted her chest.

"Yeah. I don't have a sibling, so I can't speak to that heart connection." Avery adjusted her cap in the stiff wind. "If I were Jimenez, I'd have Brian under observation. Jonas too. What had Persephone and him so heated? It's been two years since Marisol's disappearance. This argument was quite intense."

Charlene and Avery reached the harbor and strolled nonchalantly down the rock pier. Birds cawed and hardy tourists snapped pictures of the lighthouse in the autumn chill. The scent of brine added a musk to the air.

Jonas's boat could have been like any other boat with the exception of the red captain's wheel, which set it apart.

"No name on this side or the front or back." Charlene studied the craft closely and felt a bit of disappointment.

"What if it's on the other side of the boat?" Avery asked.

"I have an idea," Charlene said. "I have a selfie stick in the car. Maybe we can angle a phone . . ."

"Not a phone, but a mirror might work and be less expensive to replace if we dropped it," Avery said. "The plan has a high probability of failure."

"True."

"My arms are shorter than yours," Avery said.

"I'll do all the work, so you keep your nose, and name, clean." Charlene shook her head. "You know what? No. We are going home. This is a bad idea."

"It's not!" Avery said.

"It is. I am the adult in this situation, and I was caught up in the idea of helping Isabella. We are not police officers." Charlene tilted her head. "You want to be a detective."

"Charlene." Avery's cheeks turned pink in the cold.

"I can hear Sam now, yelling at me for being a bad example. I've disappointed him enough today," Charlene said. "Can't add this to it."

Avery grew angry. "I am an adult. I know the law. We have to help Isabella find out what happened to Marisol. Sam point-blank does not believe in something that we both know is true. That is a hard fact. He's not always right, Charlene."

Hard facts.

Charlene's phone dinged and she read a message from Sam. **We need to talk.**

She had a feeling she knew what about. He would officially want to break up with her and would do it face-to-face. A gentleman.

Charlene had to avoid that conversation until her guests went home. Until Avery returned to school. Then she could handle whatever came. She had her family.

"Sam?" Avery tipped her chin toward Charlene's phone.

Charlene nodded. "I'll talk to him later."

Now was not a good time. She'd need to be strong, and she wasn't just yet.

She would be, eventually. She'd learned that she was a survivor.

CHAPTER 17

Charlene snapped pictures of Jonah's watercraft to show Jack. Maybe he'd have some ideas regarding the name, or lack thereof, for the boat. "It's great that we have our own cyber assistant for these things. Who knows what will be important to the investigation?"

"I agree." Avery checked the time on her phone. "Should we head back to the B-and-B? Happy hour is in forty minutes."

"I'd love to get Kass's honest opinion of Persephone," Charlene said. "Was she jealous of Marisol? Did she steal Marisol's clients, or was it just lucky that she got them after Marisol disappeared? If we hurry, we'll have enough time to stop at the tea shop."

Charlene drove toward the parking garage that allowed easy access to the Pedestrian Mall.

Avery pointed out the window to her right. "There's Persephone, ugh, and Brian. He must have been on his way to work earlier. He's in his uniform now. And who is that with them?" The teenager pressed her nose to the window glass.

Brian was shouting at a small woman in a nun's habit with a fierce expression as she plastered REPENT signs on Persephone's front door and window, with SINNER interspersed.

Charlene rolled down her window to hear what was going on. "Stop it," Brian shouted. "I've called the police, Sister Abbott, you've left me no choice."

"Sinner! Devil worshipper!" Sister Abbott screamed at Persephone. No wonder tourists thought the manic nun was part of the theater surrounding Salem.

"You are crazy, lady." Persephone stood her ground. "Stay away from my business!"

Kass hurried down the block from her tea shop, her long strides skirting people with skull faces in white-and-black makeup for *Dia de los Muertos.* "Hey! What's going on?"

Brian seemed unsure of how to grab the livid nun as she slapped more posters on Persephone's building. "I will not abide by such debasement—I won't stand for it," Sister Abbott screeched. "Salem is a godly town."

"I feel like I should be videotaping this." Avery's eyes widened. "Who's in the right? Who is the criminal?"

"Do something, Brian!" Persephone shouted. "You are worthless, I swear."

The sirens of a police vehicle chirped as it came to a halt. Two officers got out of the car. The nun turned on them.

Sister Abbott thrust out her arm, her fingers pale. "You can't arrest me—arrest the Devil worshipper!"

"For the record, I do not worship the Devil." Persephone raised her hands and backed up. "I didn't do anything. I came home and saw this lunatic debasing my place of business. And Brian Preston is useless. Can't you take away his uniform?"

"He doesn't work for the police," the male officer said. "Take it up with the museum."

"Sister Abbott, this is the second time we've had to talk with you today," a young female officer replied in a strained voice. "I hate to do this, but you are coming with us to the station until you calm down."

Charlene had to hand it to the officers who respectfully did their job. It hurt her to see the nun struggle against the restraints, but she'd left the police no choice.

"I'm not afraid of a jail cell!" the sister shouted as she was escorted in. The male officer quickly shut the door.

"I will press charges, Sister," Persephone promised.

"She believes that her way is the true way," the female officer said with an apologetic shrug.

"I don't debase the church, do I?" Persephone crossed her arms.

"No, ma'am," the male patrolman said.

The officers left. Kass helped Persephone take down the posters. Brian tried to help, but Persephone told him to back off.

It had all happened so fast. "Should we stay?" Charlene asked, not turning off her car. She wanted to help Kass, and Persephone. She wouldn't be able to ask Kass about Persephone in front of the witch.

"Let's just go home," Avery said. "We should be there right at four. Um, did that really happen just now?"

"Seems so ridiculous."

"What if Sam has a religious belief that prevents him from being open to ghosts?" Avery suggested.

"I don't know . . . we've never talked about church or religion. I don't really go, unless Mom and Dad ask. Christmas and Easter kind of thing."

"What do you believe?" Avery asked. "If you don't mind telling me."

"Not a problem," Charlene said. "I believe in a higher power. I think there is more than this existence. I don't have the answers."

Avery nodded. "Same. There were times when I was little, before Mom allowed me to live at Felicity House by giving up custody, that I prayed. It always made me feel better. I can't explain it, but my heart warmed and I knew I would be okay."

"That's really nice." Charlene drove up Crown Pointe Road, her angst easing at the elegant black-and-ivory Charlene's Bed and Breakfast sign.

She'd created a place to host travelers from all over the world, with a multitude of beliefs. She'd learned in the last few years that life, and death, were out of her control. To live in the moment. It hadn't happened overnight.

To expect Sam to accept such a huge reality check in a day wasn't reasonable. Charlene had to be fair. She loved him, so she would give him space and hope that he'd come around as her mother had suggested. Her heart settled.

She parked between Minnie's silver Hyundai and Avery's car, realizing Isabella's car was gone. "Isabella and Rico are out. I worry about Isabella."

"You mean, what if Rico is a killer?" Avery asked astutely. "People aren't always what they seem."

"That's it." Charlene turned off the engine and they exited the SUV.

Avery shut the passenger door and pocketed her phone. "I really like Isabella. She's so gentle and genuinely kind. Her sister had a harder edge in the picture that Rico painted."

"You're right," Charlene said.

They climbed the steps and Avery punched in the code, then opened the door. "Honey, we're home!" Avery sang out.

Silva glanced their way from the gallery railing, giving her tail a flick.

The place felt empty. "Where is everyone?" Charlene asked.

Minnie came out of the downstairs laundry room with a gasp. "Oh, you startled me! How are your parents?" She tightened her grip on a stack of six fluffy white towels.

"Wonderful. They enjoyed the cookies. That was a good idea to decorate the sugar skulls," Charlene said. "People can be so creative!"

"Got it from my daughter, who did it at her work for a team building exercise." Minnie grinned over the towels. "Can't take the credit, but it was fun."

"Juleen deserved to win that ten-dollar gift card," Avery said. "It was so artistic. I bet she might even have beat Rico."

"Isabella and Rico asked about a card table for the living room, so I had Will drop one off from our house that you can borrow," Minnie said.

"Thanks. We're going to try the altar down here where we have more room for Kass and Persephone and whoever else Isabella can recruit. The more magical people the better. Do you know anybody?" Charlene asked.

"Just the same ones you do," Minnie said. "Isabella asked if I had any powers, but I don't. Our friends are already committed to other events, like the Day of the Dead parade. I am staying up for it, and taking the grands, so call me if Marisol comes through. I'll worry until I hear from you."

"I'll keep you in the loop," Charlene promised. "Where did Isabella go, do you know?"

"Sam called for them to come to the station," Minnie said. "On the house phone, so I assumed it was for business."

"Is that right?" Charlene and Avery exchanged a look. Maybe Sam's request to talk had to do with Marisol.

That's what she deserved for thinking she was on Sam's mind after such a dressing down.

A cool wave of air snapped her from her thoughts. "Can you and Avery come to your suite?" Jack hovered in the hall.

Charlene smiled at Minnie, who said, "I've got the towels in from those who wanted fresh linens. I'm running the carpet sweeper upstairs. Already dusted."

"Do you need help?" Avery asked.

"No. I've got my music to listen to, and it goes by fast. You guys are always on when you're here, so let me help." Minnie brought the folded towels up the stairs, her back straight, her shoulders strong.

Avery and Charlene went to the suite, depositing jackets and purses on Charlene's love seat. Charlene closed and locked the door.

"How's it going?" Jack asked.

"We saw Sister Elizabeth Abbott get arrested and put in the back of a cop car," Avery said with a straight face.

Jack arched a brow. "You're kidding?"

"Nope," Charlene said.

"And when we were at Charlene's parents' apartment, we saw Persephone and Jonas the boat captain arguing. Charlene refused to let me try to read the other side of his boat—"

"Why would you need to?" Jack interrupted.

"To see if Jonas McCarthy's boat is registered. If he had a legit business bringing merchandise in from, well, wherever he brought it from, it should have a name and identifying numbers. It had none of those things," Avery said.

"But it also might be a pleasure vehicle," Charlene warned. "I took pictures so that you can check it out, Jack."

Avery screwed up her nose and giggled. "Pleasure vehicle!"

"You know what I mean." Charlene nudged the teenager, a smile on her lips.

"Jack, have they made any headway on Cindy Sherman's killer?" Avery asked.

"No," Jack said. "I've been keeping the news on just in case they share something. I've also been watching documentaries on how to call the dead, using the laptop."

"Oh! Smart idea," Charlene said. "What did you find?"

Jack shrugged. "The usual speculation but nothing concrete."

"We could make a mint, Charlene," Avery said. "One teensy-tiny manual on the paranormal world and any money concerns would be gone."

"Are we not going to talk about Sam and what he said on the porch?" Jack, with a whirl of air, spun Charlene around. "I did my best to make him see me. I failed."

"You did not fail and there is nothing more to say." Charlene lowered her gaze and leaned against the love seat.

"Sam will realize what happened and change his mind, you know that, right?" Jack brushed Charlene's hot cheek.

Charlene met Jack's gaze. "I'd like to believe he will come around, so I'm not going to be a jerk about what he said or how he said it." It would remain etched in her mind forever, but she would give it time.

Jack smoothed her hair back from her face. "You couldn't."

"Well?" Avery gestured to the laptop, taking the heat off Charlene. "What are we missing to draw in Marisol across dimensions, if she is indeed deceased?" She plunked down in Jack's armchair and crossed her arms.

"Isabella and Rico are on the right track," Jack said. "One of the things they didn't have was Marisol's favorite music. It's something to try. Tonight at midnight is the optimum time to locate her. Candles, music, and chanting prayers to guide her way."

"I wonder what kind of music?" Avery asked. "Rico had us humming last night, but singing is not my strongest attribute."

"Mine either." Charlene's phone rumbled with a text message from Brandy, warning her to be careful. "It's Brandy." She scanned Brandy's text. Brandy had a bad feeling about tonight. The veil would be the thinnest. She wished she could help but couldn't get out of her plans. Serenity will be around for an hour, but that's all she can spare.

Charlene showed the message to Jack and Avery.

"That's sincere concern for the outcome," Avery said. "Not like Persephone, who will be here tonight because of peer pressure from Kass and Serenity, and probably to tweak Rico's nose. I don't think she's as powerful as Marisol, or the other witches we know."

"I agree. I wish we knew what prompted Jonas and Persephone to argue at the wharf today. We thought we made out a *B*." Charlene shot off a text to Brandy that they were being cautious. What else could she say to keep her friend's fears at bay?

"Or possibly something about Marisol's clients. Since we were snooping, we can't ask Persephone or Jonas directly." Avery rubbed the spider tattoo on her nape.

"We wanted to chat with Kass and find out if Persephone was jealous of Marisol." Charlene put down her phone. "Could Persephone have stolen her clients?"

"And?" Jack prompted.

"We never got to ask," Avery said.

"*If* Marisol is dead, that would be a strong motive,"

Jack said. "From everything we've learned, the Santa Muerte shop was very lucrative."

"Money and passion," Avery said. "Rico was a dog and sleeping around. What are the chances that he'll stay faithful to Isabella?"

Charlene's mind circled Persephone. Could the witch have killed Marisol to get not only Rico but Marisol's clients?

It made twisted sense, and Charlene really hoped that Marisol and the expensive statue were safely tucked away in the Bahamas. What if Marisol feared for her life, and that was why she'd disappeared?

She had to talk to Isabella. Whose idea had it been to leave Salem? She'd bet it was Rico's.

Minnie knocked on the door at four sharp. "It's time," she called.

"I'll keep researching," Jack said. "Did you send the pictures of Jonas's boat to the cloud so I can see them on your laptop?"

Charlene pressed a button on her phone photo app. "Done. Thanks, Jack!"

Avery opened the door to the kitchen, and Charlene followed the teen out. Pumpkin, nutmeg, and cinnamon scented the air.

"I've got spiced apple cider," Minnie said. "Avery, if you can grab it?"

"Yep!" The teen easily lifted the caldron of hot cider and took it to the living room. It was cool to use the caldron three times this Halloween.

Charlene grabbed savory roast beef sliders with melted cheese, while Minnie balanced a tray of bony hot dog fingers and ketchup with a dish of bite-size twice-mashed potatoes that resembled eyeballs. "This looks scarily delicious."

"The ketchup has some hot sauce added, for extra kick," Minnie chortled. "I'm glad that we are celebrating *Dia de los Muertos*. It lets me celebrate Halloween for an extra day. I'm really going to miss my skeleton leggings."

Charlene, laughing, entered the living room. Avery had placed the cider on the sideboard, next to the plates, napkins, and silverware.

Isabella and Rico had returned from the police station. Their mood was subdued. She'd have to talk to them later, but for now, her job was to mingle.

"Hello, everyone. How's it going?"

Patrick was fresh from the shower, his brown hair damp and curling over his ears. "We slept until three. Not as young as we used to be, right, Leo? We'd get a couple of hours of sleep a night and party for a week straight."

Leo bumped his knuckles to Patrick's. "Truth! I'm ready to do it again. Any word on what happened to that schoolteacher?"

"Not yet," Charlene said.

"Last night was crazy," Leo said. "Let's hope that the midnight parade for the Day of the Dead doesn't add to the body count."

"Dude!" Spence dipped his head toward his wife, but Darla seemed to be in a better place than this morning.

"I'm fine," Darla said. "Dotty's advice was spot on— it wasn't our fault. I'll pour these emotions into my drumming later." She looked at Charlene. "I'm serious, though, about not going home until we know who is responsible."

Charlene clasped Darla's hand. "We will figure something out. The B-and-B is booked except for the small rooms Leo and Patrick are in for the next week, but you can move into one of those. They aren't as spacious as the suite you're in. They have bunk beds."

"We can pretend we're on tour," Spence assured his wife. He told the group, "When you're traveling on a budget, sometimes you have limited options of where you crash. Especially in Europe. We've slept on many a futon or lumpy couch."

"That sounds really fun," Juleen said.

"Sometimes the floor. We are ready to level up," Darla countered, using her fingers as pretend drumsticks to do a drum roll.

Patrick and Leo both chose local ales for their drinks, Rico had tequila, Isabella white wine, Dotty and Timothy had spiced cider. Marty had a red wine and Juleen, pink. Charlene loved a full house. Cindy Sherman's death and Marisol's disappearance, and her disagreement with Sam, kept her from total happiness.

"Are we supposed to dress up for the parade tonight?" Leo asked.

Silence greeted this question.

"Has anyone been to a Day of the Dead parade before?" Avery asked.

"Smart question," Jack said.

"I have. In Mexico City." Rico pulled his phone from his back pocket and showed it around. The paradegoers who dressed up were like skeletons or ghosts with white faces, black eyes, and bright clothes. Lots of flowers. "It's a celebration of those who have gone before us. My parents have both passed on."

"How long have you been in the United States?" Dotty asked.

"We came over when I was two, so practically all my life." Rico accepted the phone from Juleen, who'd had it last.

"I think we should paint our faces," Juleen said.

Isabella sipped her wine and set it down, smiling. "I can do all of ours because I have the makeup kit upstairs. It will be like decorating Minnie's sugar cookies this morning. I'm sorry we missed that."

"I'll help you, if you want," Juleen offered. "How fun!"

"Don't forget about the music," Jack said as Charlene surveyed her guests, chatting over food and drink. "You and Isabella both have long brown hair. Maybe you should add flowers to yours like she has . . . it's pretty."

Charlene stepped away from the guests to answer Jack in a low voice, holding the cup of cider to her mouth. "You're sweet, but I'm not feeling that festive. We have an *ofrenda* to create once everyone leaves for downtown."

"What's the driving arrangements for tonight?" Dotty asked. "Should we call for cabs?"

Turning her back to Jack, Charlene said, "I will gladly drop you off downtown." It was why she was sticking to cider instead of wine. "But you'll need to find your own way home. As you know, we're helping Isabella and Rico this evening at midnight."

Dotty nodded. "With the altar to try to reach Isabella's sister, Marisol. She explained a little about Santa Muerte, the folk saint that they worship."

"Dotty and I don't really go to church. We like to think that nature is our church—we feel very much at peace when we are in the woods, or by the ocean," Timothy said.

"Being open-minded is key," Isabella said.

"I agree," Juleen said.

Rico sipped his tequila—he seemed pensive and on edge. Was he worried about Marisol coming through? Or worried that she wouldn't? He had a lot at stake.

"I saw Jonas today, at the wharf," Charlene said to Rico and Isabella as Dotty and Timothy went for seconds on mashed potato eyeballs.

"That's where he keeps his boat," Isabella said. "Where were you?"

"Avery and I were at my parents' condo. Jonas was with Persephone. They were arguing," Charlene said.

Isabella's brow furrowed. "I wonder over what?"

Charlene couldn't explain that she'd been spying with binoculars. That she'd *maybe* made out something that started with a *B*. Had Brian acted out of passion when Marisol broke it off? Had Persephone been using Rico to hurt Marisol? "Do you remember how Marisol was behaving over that weekend she disappeared?"

"What do you mean?" Rico asked.

"Well, was she afraid, or concerned?" Charlene mulled the theory of Marisol under attack by Persephone to keep Rico through her mind.

"My sister was a very strong witch." Isabella's tone was confused. "She had no reason to be afraid of anyone." She turned to Rico. "Did you notice anything different about her behavior?"

"No." Charlene didn't believe Rico, who didn't say more. Could he have hurt Marisol? Murdered her? But then why would he stick around Isabella?

Sometimes killers like to hang around the scene of their crime.

Charlene sighed. "I had a thought about tonight's ceremony. Maybe we should add Marisol's favorite music?"

"Splendid idea!" Isabella said.

"What did she like to listen to?" Charlene asked.

"EDM. Electronic dance music," Rico said. "We can try it. We bought more candles, too, to light her way."

"Brighter is good," Jack said. "Our guests have lousy taste in music. Punk rock, EDM. What happened to classical piano?"

Charlene bit her lip to keep from laughing.

Juleen bounded over and tapped Isabella's shoulder. "Can we do the face painting now? It's almost five."

"Sure!" Isabella said. "Rico, want to come up with me?"

"No. I'm going to refresh my drink." Rico stalked over to the bar and helped himself to the silver tequila.

"Can you at least pick out some lively music?" Isabella asked with exasperation.

"I can," Avery offered. "Spotify—Mexican Cantina for a party vibe?"

"Terrific," Isabella said. "I'll be right back."

People snacked and refilled their drinks. Isabella returned in fifteen minutes with a cardboard box of goodies.

"Let's set up by the window," Isabella suggested.

Charlene unfolded the card table that Will had loaned them so Isabella and Rico could set up the altar for Marisol.

Until then, it would work as a makeup table.

"I'll do Juleen first," Isabella said. "And then, because you did win the sugar cookie competition, you can jump in so we can move it along, time-wise."

The festive music added to the party atmosphere. Within ten minutes Isabella had created a white canvas on Juleen's face, with black around the eyes and brows. She used pinks and reds to accent and the result was quite stunning.

"The final touch—a setting spray so it won't smudge." Isabella sprayed a light mist over her handiwork.

Juleen looked into the giant mirror above the mantel and clapped with delight. "I never want to take it off."

"You'll break out," Isabella warned with a pleased smile.

"Tell us about Santa Muerte," Juleen said.

"All right. My sister and I were raised by our mother, in New Orleans, with the worship of Santa Muerte. Santa Muerte rose from folklore obscurity to prominence when *one* woman asked her husband to build a shrine on their front porch to honor the Bony Lady, or the Death Goddess. She's known by many names." Isabella applied the white base to Dotty's face as she spoke, in a storyteller's cadence.

"Sounds spooky," Dotty said.

"Santa Muerte is a fierce protector," Isabella shared. "If you respect her, she will lift you up in love and light. She is a guardian after death to Heaven."

"But if you don't believe or are disrespectful?" Leo asked. He was getting his face painted by Juleen.

"Santa Muerte has been known to exact vengeance," Isabella admitted. "But only to those who have crossed her. If you love her, she will love you in return. We had an altar dedicated to her in our shop when we lived in Salem. We were very successful."

"She will grant miracles," Rico said. "You must honor her." He set his drink on the mantel and whipped off his shirt to show them a full tattoo of Santa Muerte on his back, in addition to the skull on his inner forearm. Roses adorned her crown and trailed across his shoulders. A scythe, a globe, and an owl were clear to make out.

"What do those symbols mean?" Spence asked, coming in for a closer look at the work of art on Rico's back.

"That looks like the Grim Reaper, man," Patrick said. His face was now painted too.

"In a way she is. She will protect you after death through the underworld," Rico said. "If you cross her, you're going down to Hell. You do good, she escorts you to Heaven and makes sure no demons get you."

Patrick shuddered. "She's as terrifying as a demon."

"What's the globe for?" Leo asked.

"It signifies her ability to astral travel, which is why she is a favorite with psychics and mediums. Brujas," Rico said. He shrugged his shirt back on.

"Cool tats," Marty said.

"I drew them myself and had a friend fill in the ink. Come see me in New York if you want work done," Rico said.

"No tattoos for me, but I'd love my makeup done," Minnie said. "Do you mind? My grands will think I'm so cool."

"Come over here," Juleen said, patting the space next to her.

Avery let Isabella do her makeup as well, but Charlene declined, as did Rico.

Isabella had Juleen do hers and, when it was done, deemed it perfect. It was getting closer to seven.

"Reaching my sister tonight is so important," Isabella said. "Otherwise, I would totally be at the parade with you to honor my ancestors. My mother and grandmother were powerful psychics, and they taught my sister and me to always respect those who have gone before."

"We will miss you and Rico," Juleen said. "But I understand."

"I want you to have fun tonight at the parade," Isabella said. She reached into the cardboard box she'd brought down and gave each of the guests a cloth pouch. "Put this in your pocket. It has amethyst to protect against psychic negativity and hematite to ground you in this realm." She handed them to Avery and Charlene and gifted some extras to Minnie for her grandkids. "Just be careful to guard against bad mojo. I believe in love and light, and that is my protection, but I also have my crystals." She pulled a necklace from under her peasant blouse to show them her personal crystal protection. "If anybody feels like they need help in the morning, I can cleanse your auras. I did it for my sister on a weekly basis. Some of her clients were very dark and dangerous."

"Thank you!" Minnie dropped the pouches into her apron pocket.

"You all look amazing," Charlene said. "Can I get your pictures for the blog?"

"Yes!" they chorused in agreement. Though the mood remained festive, by seven, the guys were getting antsy.

"I want to walk," Leo said.

"Me too," Patrick seconded.

"Who needs a ride?" Minnie asked. "I can take four in my car, and that way Charlene, you don't have to drive the van."

"I don't mind," Charlene said. But it would be nice to stay home.

"Spence and I will walk," Darla said. "We can meet you four downtown by Kass's place. I bet we beat you there!"

"I'm feeling restless too," Spence said. "We are usually on the go at top speed, right, babe?"

"Yeah," Darla said.

"You're sure?" Juleen asked.

"Positive! Like I said, I bet we beat you." Darla's grin was eerie because of the skull makeup.

"See you there," Dotty said. "Timothy and I will gladly accept the ride. Charlene, what a wonderful vacation. You said we'd all be besties for five days, and you weren't kidding."

Minnie transferred the crystal pouches to her purse from her apron.

"Text me," Minnie reminded Charlene as Timothy, Dotty, Juleen, and Marty bundled into their coats. "Even if nothing happens. I want to know either way."

"I promise." Charlene walked them out to the porch. It was already dark but still in the forties and not rainy. She waved, thinking her parking area looked like a car lot with Avery's vehicle, Isabella's car, the Pilot, and the rental van.

"That was nice of Isabella to paint their faces," Jack said, manifesting his body next to her on the porch.

Charlene gasped. "And here I thought you were a cold breeze," she teased. How hadn't Sam felt that? "You're right. She's a sweetheart. I really hope Rico is worthy of her."

They went inside to the foyer. Silva meowed from the gallery railing she liked to survey things from, safely out of the way of guests.

"Music on or off?" Avery asked.

"I like it," Isabella said.

Rico danced a few steps and tugged Isabella's hair. "It reminds me of Mexico. It could be so full of life, but there was a dark side too."

"Minnie was so sweet to loan us this card table. Rico and I went shopping and bought incense and Santa Muerte candles." Isabella moved the makeup back to the cardboard box and covered the card table with a black cloth she'd had inside it. This didn't have any symbols on it, like the owl fabric from the day before.

The *ofrenda* had the picture of Marisol and Isabella as teens, and the drawing of the Santa Muerte statue. The tarot card of the lovers. The key, the bracelet

Isabella had made for her sister, with the missing owl charm.

"Is it possible that Marisol gave Brian the owl charm?" Charlene couldn't fathom the beautiful witch and the creepy guard, but it had been a thing.

Isabella picked up the bracelet. "What do you mean?"

"Like a token because they were lovers. I might have seen a circle with an owl like this on Brian's key chain that day he followed you into Kass's tea shop." Charlene shrugged. "I can't be sure."

"I can't either." Isabella briefly closed her eyes. "I never imagined Brian with my sister."

"It wasn't personal," Rico said. "Passion."

"Stop it, Rico." Isabella adjusted the items on the table, ignoring her boyfriend.

Charlene liked the scent of incense from a silver owl holder. She saw a globe, a scythe, scales of justice, an owl. The pendant, a figurine. Tequila from Mexico. Louisiana grits. Pink hibiscus. Cigarettes.

"There has to be a hundred candles around this room," Charlene said in midprep.

"We want Marisol to come to us, if she can." Isabella sighed and glanced at Charlene. "I know you keep reminding me that she might be alive somewhere . . . I hope so, but I don't believe it."

"Minnie said that you'd gone to speak with Sam today. How did that go?" Charlene asked. There'd been too many distractions to chat privately before now.

"Detective Holden wanted us to identify some Jane Doe pictures." Isabella pressed her hand to her stomach, her painted face even paler. "They weren't Marisol. The shoulders had no owl tattoo. It was difficult to look at the dead women."

"It was vile," Rico chimed in with a shudder. "We should have drinks. Tequila. The good stuff Jonas brought from Mexico. I got a bottle especially for us tonight." He looked at Charlene. "You only have the gold tequila left."

"I don't really care for tequila unless it's in a margarita," Charlene said.

"You have to have a drink, Charlene," Isabella said. "It's fine for Avery not to partake . . . unless she wants to?"

"No, thanks. I'll use some orange juice." Avery poured a small amount into a paper cup.

Rico passed a shot glass of silver liquid to Charlene and to Isabella.

"To Marisol," Isabella said.

"To Marisol," Charlene, Avery, Rico, and Jack said.

After clinking glasses they drank, and tears came to Charlene's eyes at the strength of the liquid spirits.

Jack chuckled. Avery patted Charlene's shoulder as she wheezed in a breath.

"It's my sister's favorite brand," Isabella said.

"I can't believe it's only nine thirty," Charlene said. "How shall we pass the time until midnight?"

"Let's talk about Marisol," Rico said. "Share our memories of her." He pulled a deck of cards from his pocket. "And we could play poker. She liked to play— she was a risky cardplayer."

Avery rose in a fluid motion and dragged the coffee table between the sofa and the two armchairs. She positioned one so that the back was to the mantel and the shrine. "Sounds like fun." She turned off the cantina music on her phone. "Let me know when you're ready for the EDM."

"I will. Marisol loved to dance," Isabella said. "And she liked her music loud—the louder the better."

"Not conducive to cards," Charlene said.

Rico and Isabella shared the sofa. Avery took the armchair she'd just moved next to Charlene's chair.

"Should I light the fire?" Charlene asked.

"I don't think so. What if she comes in that way?" Rico said with a frown. Candles covered the mantel and tables all over the room.

"That's ridiculous," Jack said.

"We don't have to," Avery said, covering her mouth with her hand to hide a smile at Jack's comment.

"Be careful not to touch your face," Charlene warned. "You don't want to smudge your makeup."

"It will be hard," Avery said with a frown. "Thanks for the reminder."

Rico shuffled. "Shall we use real money?"

Isabella shrugged. Charlene shook her head. "I barely know the rules."

"I'm just learning in college," Avery admitted. "We use pretzel sticks."

Rico snorted.

"I rarely had time for poker in college," Jack said.

"How about we use the Halloween candy?" Charlene suggested. She got up and searched the pantry for the bags of treats. She returned with M&M's, Skittles, all black licorice jelly beans, SweeTARTS, and fruit snacks. Isabella laughed with approval.

Avery snagged the jelly beans, Isabella chose the

M&M's, and Rico the SweeTARTS, leaving Charlene to choose Skittles or fruit snacks. The Skittles won.

Rico dealt out the hand. "Five-card stud. Basic rules are I will deal you each five cards. You can choose to trade in up to five cards. We bet on what we are holding, or you can pass. No matter what, the next round will be in play."

The game would be a nice way to pass the time, allowing Charlene to direct the conversation back to Jonas without it being so obvious. She waited until they'd played the first round and Rico got up for more of the Mexican tequila.

Charlene nodded at the bottle of tequila. "Does Jonas sail his boat from Mexico to Salem?"

"Why do you ask?" Rico handed Charlene a shot.

"I'll sip, thanks." If Charlene had another one, she'd breathe fire through her nostrils. "Well, you'd mentioned that he'd brought Marisol's favorites, but he was also bringing things from New Orleans. I am awful with geography. Is that all on the coast?"

Avery reached for the fruit snacks to open and eat. She was down to only ten jelly beans from twenty.

Rico gave Isabella another brimming shot glass. "To Marisol." They clicked and drank.

Avery opened her phone and pulled up a map, showing it to Charlene. "It seems pretty straightforward. Land would be faster."

"Not for Jonas." Rico filled his and Isabella's shot glasses again. It was now after ten.

"He's a brilliant captain," Isabella said fondly. She made a half circle with her finger. "New Orleans and

Mexico City are very close on the Gulf of Mexico—imagine a crescent shape. Marisol and I, and Mom, too, loved to ride on the boat with him. He'd call us mermaids when we swam."

Rico sat down again to shuffle and deal the cards. "Who's in?"

Charlene put down a Skittle, and Avery put in one jelly bean. Isabella placed an M&M in the center.

"And coming around the Florida Keys to the Atlantic Coast would be very simple," Jack deduced. "One of my regrets from when I was alive was not learning how to sail."

"Benjamin Fiske could've sold you a boat," Avery said.

"We don't need a boat," Rico replied. His brow arched. "Good thing you aren't drinking. You can't handle your jelly beans."

"Gotcha, Avery," Jack chuckled. "The man has commercials to go along with his park benches, showcasing his yacht sales' prowess. Since he's good-looking, the news reporters give him free advertising. It's shameful what they do for ratings. Though I think the live streaming on Halloween was a good idea."

Isabella's phone hummed with a notification at quarter till eleven. She read it and scowled. "Persephone is bailing for tonight. No reason, either. Rude."

"Dios," Rico said. "We will be short a witch. She's doing it to get back at me, I bet. And Kass?"

"Kass should be here at eleven thirty, same as Serenity. Serenity is very strong and worth a thousand Persephones. She can only be here for an hour, though."

Isabella hugged her waist and eyed the ceiling. "This is so hard, but I won't give up."

"We will just have to try," Charlene said. She folded her cards. "I'm out of candy."

"Me too," Avery said, popping her jelly beans in her mouth. "Want me to start the music?"

"Yes, please," Isabella said.

By eleven thirty, the music was rocking the house. The cards were back in Rico's pocket. Serenity had arrived, as had Kass. Charlene had asked Jack not to be visible so for all she knew he was there but hiding.

At midnight, the six of them held hands and entreated Marisol's spirit to come forward.

"My sweet sister," Isabella crooned. "Come to me!"

"Marisol Perez," Serenity said, her eyes closed as she poured her power into the name summoning.

"Marisol Perez," Kass said, echoing the intensity of the name. Charlene and Avery did the same.

"Marisol Perez," Charlene said, feeling the power of the name surge through her, connected to these people.

"Marisol Perez," Avery said in a strong commanding voice.

"Marisol Perez," Rico sang.

They spent an hour entreating Marisol to come, but at one in the morning it was clear that Marisol wasn't there.

"Why can't I reach my sister?" Isabella sobbed.

Serenity and Kass embraced her.

Rico made a fist. "I feel her! I feel her!"

"Do you?" Serenity asked, clearly not believing him.

Jack arrived. "Nobody is here. Rico is lying."

"Rico, be honest," Charlene said.

"I feel her—but now she's gone." Rico glared at Avery and Charlene, Kass, Serenity, and Isabella. "Your negativity chased her away."

"Or," Avery said, "she might be alive. If she's not answering our SOS, that's the outcome I am hoping for."

CHAPTER 18

"Avery, I pray that my sister is alive, but I know she is no longer with us," Isabella said. "I can't explain how I know, only that I do. I would wager my life on it."

"Let's not go that far." Charlene was a planner, and she wondered what would happen to Isabella after tonight, and the next night, if there was no closure regarding Marisol's disappearance.

Serenity checked her watch. "I've got to go, Bella," she said. "It's already one and I promised Nana that I'd only be gone an hour." She hugged Isabella and waved to the rest of them in the room, who remained in prayer mode. The electronic music pounded from Avery's phone. "Text me in the morning!"

Kass made the mistake of checking the time, and Rico pounced. "You have other things to do as well? You weren't much help, Kass. Just go."

"Rico!" Isabella exclaimed. She peered at Kass with

watery eyes. "I'm sorry. This just hasn't worked out at all the way I thought it would. I thought Marisol would want to come through and set my heart at ease."

"I can stay," Kass offered, her words sincere.

"No. Just go," Rico said. "We don't need you anyway. Right, Bella?"

"Not true, Rico." Isabella placed her hand on Kass's shoulder. "But it's probably best if you leave. I'll walk you out. He will only get more obnoxious, and you don't deserve that."

"Neither do you," Kass said pointedly.

Isabella blinked rapidly. "Drive home safe. Let's talk tomorrow. If Marisol doesn't come through tonight, I have to try again tomorrow. And . . . I don't have another plan if this fails."

Charlene patted Kass's wrist when they crossed the living room to the foyer. "What do you think of Persephone?"

Kass shrugged. "It's crappy that she didn't show up."

Rico bumped into something in the living room.

"Maybe hide the tequila?" Jack suggested. Charlene turned to see Avery nod. She'd quit counting how many shots he'd had to drink.

Kass left with a baleful scowl at Rico that he didn't see as he was rearranging the items on the *ofrenda*, placing the lover's card more visibly on the display.

Charlene locked the door and returned to the living room. Kass was an excellent friend to have, and she hoped that Isabella would maintain her ties in Salem when she returned to New York.

It was now quarter past one. Charlene stifled a yawn. She dared Rico to try to kick her out of her own house.

"Why were you so rude to Kass?" Isabella demanded of Rico. He sat on the couch and Isabella stood next to the card table. "She's a powerful witch and you treated her terribly. How am I supposed to pull Marisol through when I am the weakest link?"

"We don't need anybody else. She was already here. I felt Marisol," Rico repeated, waving his hand. "She gave us her blessing. She wants us to be happy."

"He's lying," Jack said. "No other spirits have been here."

"I don't have time for games, Rico," Isabella cried. "You really felt her? I'm not as sure that we're doing the right thing. Why else would she ignore me?"

"You doubt my love?" Rico attempted to straighten from his slouch on the sofa but slipped. Liquid sloshed from his tumbler. "How dare you! After all I've done for you."

Charlene made a note of where it fell on the carpet to clean later.

"What has he done?" Jack wondered. "From what I can see, he's a sponge living off of what Isabella and Marisol earned."

Isabella lowered her crossed arms to her sides, studying Rico with disappointment. "I . . . I just want her to tell me it's okay."

"You are a grown woman, Isabella, not a child." Rico got up and stumbled to the bar. He poured more tequila into his cup, and Charlene wasn't surprised to see that the bottle was almost empty.

"You are cruel." Isabella stared at Rico, who glared right back.

Avery cleared her throat and wandered to the *ofrenda*. "I love the picture of you and your sister. How old were you here?"

Isabella gave up the staring contest with a belligerent Rico and joined Avery by the square table. She picked up the photo with a smile. "We were thirteen and fifteen. Our mother was still alive. Our world hadn't collapsed yet. I think Jonas and Mom dated occasionally. He brought us the peasant tops we are wearing from Mexico."

Charlene smiled at the sweet memory. "You've known Jonas a long time, then."

"He is family," Isabella said. "I am not interested in opening another Santa Muerte shop, though. I like my quiet life in New York, working as a barista. No pressure."

Avery picked up the brass key. "What does this go to?"

Isabella opened her palm and Avery dropped it into her hand. "Marisol had this with her jewelry. The costume jewelry, not the real stuff. I don't think it's important, but I really don't know."

"It could be a safe-deposit key," Jack suggested.

"Have you checked the banks to see if it could be to something?" Charlene asked. "Like that mail center near Persephone's business? It would have been close to your old shop too. It might have answers."

"No." Isabella scrunched her nose. "I didn't think about it like that."

Rico slurped his drink. "You are not practical, like Marisol."

"I managed our business account," Isabella protested. "We had money to live on. Our needs were not extravagant."

"In order for us to declare Marisol dead without a body, she needs to have been missing for five years." Rico leaned against the armchair and started to slip, but he righted himself without spilling any more.

"How do you know that?" The sharp look Isabella gave Rico went right over his very intoxicated head.

"I, I had some questions. When we liquidated the merchandise from the shop I wondered about the legalities." Rico peered up from his drink. "Why are you mad? It was research. There was no ill intent."

Jack burst out laughing.

"Ask whose idea it was to get married," Jack suggested. "If Rico is married to Isabella, he's entitled to half of whatever inheritance comes in or the statue, if found, which is probably worth serious money if it's solid gold."

Charlene narrowed her eyes at Rico, wishing bad people had a danger sign imprinted on their foreheads.

"I'd like to believe you," Isabella said. "I need to know you love me and that you are on my side. Our side."

"I do." Rico kissed her, and what a few days ago might have swept Isabella into giggles now had the young woman unaffected.

"Do you know what this key goes to?" Isabella asked Rico.

"Nope."

"Don't be upset, Charlene and Avery," Jack warned. "It's an interesting phenomenon, but the essence of the in-between dimensions, the *veil* referred to by psychics and mediums and witches, is thin. Tapping into it is like being surrounded by eerie shadows. I've been calling for Marisol."

Avery frowned at Jack in concern, while Charlene felt a wave of fear for Jack. He had to be careful. They didn't know anything about that other dimension except that at this time of year it was thinner to allow the spirits through.

Maybe.

Charlene wanted to scold him, but she couldn't do it here and he knew it, which was probably why he'd brought it up.

Jack chuckled. "I love you too, Charlene and Avery. Relax. I'm being careful. If I can help Isabella find peace, that would bring me joy. She's a very genuine person."

Charlene was often guilty of just wanting to help, so she couldn't berate Jack without being a hypocrite.

Be careful, she mouthed.

"The incense burned out. Should we get another stick?" Avery asked.

Rico sank into the armchair, the tequila semibalanced on his knee. "G'd dea."

"There are more in the box," Isabella said, gesturing toward the supplies by the sideboard. "Thank you. I'm going to be on my knees praying for guidance from Santa Muerte." The young woman dropped before the *ofrenda* and bowed her head. Her long dark hair draped loose over her shoulders.

Avery replenished the incense and then joined Isabella, so Charlene did too, the three ladies with their heads bowed.

Rico sprawled in the armchair.

Marisol Perez.

Marisol Perez.

Marisol Perez.

Marisol Perez.

Marisol Perez.

Charlene was so into just thinking Marisol's name over and over that when she felt a tickle on her ankle, she squealed, her heart thumping.

"It's just Silva," Jack assured her.

The cat rubbed up against her leg again, purring loudly.

Avery's shoulders shook as she tried to hold in her laughter, but even Isabella, once she saw who had caused the commotion, sat back with giggles.

"Silva!" Isabella patted the cat.

Rico stood and bent to scoop Silva up. "I'll toss her outside, so she doesn't ruin your concentration. This is our best chance to reach Marisol. Not a time for jokes."

Isabella stopped him with her hand over Rico's and a shake of her head. "Silva is fine." She bowed her head and tears fell onto Silva's fur.

"Dios!" Rico backed away with his palms up. He went for the tequila.

"He has got to pass out eventually," Jack surmised. "He's got one hell of a tolerance as it is."

Isabella stroked Silva's fur. Charlene knew from her own petting sessions with the cat how much it could help ease emotional pain. "I don't know what I'm doing wrong to reach Marisol. Unless she is ignoring my plea because of me and Rico. What if she doesn't approve?"

Avery patted her shoulder. "She could be alive."

"I don't have the psychic abilities Marisol did, but I know in my heart she no longer is with us." Isabella glanced at Avery and then Charlene, before focusing on Silva.

"If you know your sister is dead, then why won't you marry me?" Rico demanded with drunk authority.

"I want her blessing," Isabella stated. "That hasn't changed."

A knock sounded on the door. Charlene checked the time on her watch.

"One thirty in the morning. It could be our guests returning from the parade."

Jack disappeared and reappeared by the time Charlene straightened from her prayer position.

Handy.

"It's Persephone," Jack said.

Avery narrowed her eyes and stood. She helped Isabella rise as the young lady was tipsy. Silva jumped from Isabella's arms to the couch, avoiding Rico.

Charlene strode to the door, with Avery at her heels.

"Why would she be here?" Avery murmured.

"We are about to find out." Charlene opened the door. "Hello, Persephone," she said.

"How did you know it was me?" Persephone asked in alarm.

Charlene gestured to the security cameras on the porch.

The pink-haired witch relaxed. "Oh, these days everyone has those doorbell cams. I should get one for my business. Catch Sister Abbott in the act. I noticed you two in your car, watching what happened earlier. Weirdos."

"Is she in jail?" Avery asked.

"I couldn't care less." Persephone tilted her head, her arms crossed. "Can I come in?"

Charlene waited, not liking being insulted in her home and especially not at one thirty in the morning. "Why are you here?"

"To talk to Isabella."

Isabella and Rico left the living room, arm in arm. They reached the foyer.

"Do you want to talk to Persephone?" Charlene searched Isabella's expression for clues—if Bella wasn't willing to talk, then Persephone could go right back home.

"Okay." Isabella didn't make any other welcoming move.

Charlene stepped back and allowed the witch in.

"Thanks," Persephone drawled. "I've had warmer welcomes. Let me guess—Marisol didn't show up?"

Avery shut the door behind her, locking it. The teen was holding up very well considering the late hour and the drama. She eyed Persephone with a look that warned the young woman to be on her best behavior.

"No. We've been trying to contact Marisol. It didn't work, probably because you bailed. Serenity and Kass were both here to help." Isabella tightened her hold on Rico's arm. "You have some nerve coming here now."

"Settle down, Isabella." Persephone raised her palm. "I have a message from Marisol."

Charlene heard Avery gasp. Persephone had powers, though not as strong as Marisol's, so it was possible the witch was telling the truth.

"I'm listening," Isabella said.

Though this should have been joyful news, her demeanor exuded sorrow.

"What's wrong?" Avery asked. She bypassed Persephone to stand next to Charlene and Jack.

"Right?" Rico stepped away from Isabella with only a slight stumble. "You've gotten a message from her, which is what you wanted. What *we* wanted."

"Can we go somewhere comfortable?" Persephone asked.

"The living room," Isabella decided. "My feelings are complicated."

They entered the spacious room. Persephone perused the seating choices and selected the armchair by the fireplace. "Cool room. Love the mirror." Her gaze passed over Jack but snagged, as if she wasn't sure what she'd seen.

Charlene gestured for Jack to scoot before Persephone noticed him.

He scowled but disappeared. "I'm here," he said, though they couldn't see him. "Don't trust her."

Charlene nodded.

"Would you like something to drink?" Charlene asked, cursing her hostess gene.

"Yes. Water." Persephone curled her fingers over the

edges of the armrests. "Psychic messages always make me thirsty."

"It was the same for Marisol," Isabella said. "If you're tired, I can do a crystal cleansing for you tomorrow."

Persephone accepted the can of water from Charlene.

"Thank you, Charlene, and I will take you up on that, Isabella, since I had to come all this way in the middle of the night," Persephone complained. "Crystal healing isn't something I'm adept at."

"Comfortable?" Rico's question was filled with sarcasm as he drained the bottle of tequila into his tumbler. "What the hell did Marisol say?"

Persephone straightened and looked down her nose at Rico. "Are you drunk?"

"*Sí,* so?" Rico shrugged. "We've been drinking to Marisol."

Isabella gave a little pout. "We've been drinking, true, but it is Marisol's favorite tequila."

Charlene had had one shot and sipped the other for two hours. She enjoyed wine as her beverage of choice. The occasional margarita was also good, but she'd never been one to sip spirits.

Having heard Charlene's story about her husband Jared being killed by a drunk driver made it more personal to Avery. The fact that she wanted to be a detective meant she was often the designated driver when out with her friends.

Persephone got up and studied the *ofrenda* meant to beckon Marisol, her gaze hesitating on the key. Charlene had been watching for her reaction to the items on display.

"Why would my sister reach out to you and not to me?" Isabella's voice was thick with emotion, and suddenly Charlene understood why Isabella had been so sad. She'd wanted to connect and had been rebuffed.

"You don't have as much psychic power as I do," Persephone said. It was a brag, though also true.

Charlene was glad that Isabella didn't take offense at the bold statement.

"I feel a masculine energy here," Persephone said.

Jack.

"Sorry," Jack said—his body not visible.

Avery rolled her eyes.

"There was a doctor who was killed here," Rico said. "Could he be blocking our Marisol from coming in?"

Persephone waved a diffident hand. "The ways of the spirit world are rarely clear. I don't feel it as strongly now."

She scanned the room and kept her back to the mantel.

"She's got that right," Jack said.

Avery clenched her jaw, her move when annoyed. Jack had better behave or he'd be in for a lecture later.

"Why didn't you show up today to help me here as I asked?" Isabella asked.

"Something came up," Persephone said vaguely.

Charlene wondered if it had to do with Jonas. She couldn't get the image of Jonas and Persephone arguing out of her mind.

"And a promise you made to me," Isabella continued, "wasn't a priority. You could just have been honest if you didn't want to help."

"I had every intention of being here!"

"Sure," Rico drawled.

"I felt as if I would get more answers at my own place, tapping into my own power," Persephone said.

That made sense.

"You've always been one to drag out a moment," Rico complained. "Theater!"

Persephone bristled. "You know nothing about psychic gifts, Rico—you don't have any talent in the realm between."

"Rico's gifts are his art," Isabella said, coming to his defense.

"A human gift. Come, Isabella, you know crystal work, and Marisol's powers were on the next level. Sketching is not the same."

"Gifts from our mother," Isabella said. "I can't claim them as something I've earned."

"Don't let Rico drag you down to his mundane level," Persephone warned. "Santa Muerte is a goddess who will take as well as give."

Rico nodded. "Truth!"

"You dare lecture me about Santa Muerte?" Isabella scooted to the edge of the couch. "Marisol and I introduced her to you and others in Salem."

Persephone ignored Isabella. "What did the Death Goddess take from you, Rico?"

"The gold statue we had in the shop that was our protector," Rico answered at once. "Poof!"

"Don't you mean my sister?" Isabella said, angry that he'd put the gold before Marisol again.

"We need that Santa Muerte icon back," Rico said. "Our business has failed. We are out of money. It doesn't just grow on trees."

"Out of money?" Persephone spoke in a pleased voice. "Marisol claimed to never need to worry about cash. Guess she was wrong."

"She is dead," Isabella said.

Persephone tilted her head. "Yes. It seems that is true."

Rico said, "You have a message to give us, or was that just a ruse to crash our party?"

"I was invited, idiot." Persephone stood and walked to the mantel, where she centered herself and closed her eyes, arms to the side, like she was doing a yoga pose.

"Patience, Rico," Isabella warned as he stepped toward Persephone with rage on his face that made Charlene fear for the pink-haired witch.

Persephone kept her eyes closed and murmured, "Marisol came to me with a warning of danger."

"What danger? Where is the statue?" Rico asked.

After opening her eyes, Persephone focused on Isabella with an eerie half stare. "Marisol says it's time for you to return to New York. Stop asking questions about her death."

Isabella brought her hands to her heart. "New York? She knows we've moved?"

"Marisol is a spirit, she knows all." Persephone waved her hand between Rico and Isabella. "*All.* She's not pleased. It's probably why she came to me and not you, because you are hooking up with her boyfriend." Her nose twitched. "Don't blame her."

Isabella burst into tears.

"I want to talk to Marisol, to explain our side," Rico said. "Let's go to your place immediately."

"No," Persephone said.

"No?" Isabella repeated, mouth agape.

"Marisol has gone back to the energy she is once more," Persephone said. Her mouth twisted and she closed her eyes, keeping them at half-mast. Charlene got the feeling that she was looking at the items on the *ofrenda*. Did she know about the key?

"Interesting," Jack said. "The essence is a strange substance."

Charlene feared for Jack, dabbling in the unknown dimension, but focused on Persephone's words.

"Is there more to the message? It had to be important," Avery said. "For Marisol to come to you, Persephone."

"Good point! Marisol didn't like you," Rico said. "She thought you were weak."

"Rico!" Isabella cried. "You will make things worse."

"It's true." Rico's eyes narrowed. "Prove that it was Marisol. She would have mentioned the statue."

"You are the only one who cares about that statue," Isabella said.

"It's unfortunate," Persephone said, "but Marisol didn't bring it up." She gave the table a longer perusal, not letting her gaze settle on the key, which meant she was very interested in the brass object.

"Could you ask her?" Rico pleaded.

"I've had it with you," Persephone said. "Isabella, Marisol's warning is to get out of Salem and stop asking questions about her death. . . ."

"Yes?" Isabella clasped her hands together, tears shining on her cheeks, the makeup from the skeleton smudged.

"Before *you* are killed next. You won't get so lucky a second time."

Isabella's knees buckled and Charlene leaped forward to catch her and bring her to the couch. Her lids were closed, her body loose.

"I'll call Sam," Avery said.

CHAPTER 19

Charlene patted Isabella's wrists; the makeup on her face had rivulets from tears on her cheeks. She didn't rouse from her faint. Avery sat next to Charlene on the sofa and smoothed Isabella's long dark hair.

"I had to leave a message for Detective Holden. I told him about Persephone's warning that Isabella would be next to be killed if she didn't stop investigating Marisol's death." Avery's eyes were sad, her makeup also smudged.

"*Lucky a second time?* What does that mean?" Charlene murmured.

Jack hovered around them. "What if—and this could be a stretch—but what if Cindy was killed because the shooter thought Cindy was Isabella?"

"Rico, is there any chance that you know Cindy Sherman, the schoolteacher who was shot?" Charlene asked.

"No." Rico stood and leaned over the couch, staring at Isabella. "Wake up, *mi amor.*"

Isabella moaned, and Charlene shifted so that Isabella's head was on her lap. "Avery, will you bring her a glass of water?"

Persephone returned to the armchair, her hands to her temples as if she was tuning in to the other side.

"Cindy, the schoolteacher on the news?" Persephone studied Isabella. "The long brunette hair, the oval face, and the big brown eyes. I suppose you're right. I thought the warning was to keep you from asking questions over Marisol's death. I didn't put it together with Cindy Sherman."

Her cheeks paled.

Isabella sat up when Avery returned with a full glass and handed her the water. She sipped and attempted to gather her composure.

Rico had discovered the gold tequila in Charlene's bar cabinet and was drinking straight from the bottle. "Somebody wants to kill Isabella? No. Why? She's the sweetest person I know."

"Marisol *was* killed." Isabella's eyes grew dazed. "Persephone, is there anything more you can tell me? I don't know anything that would be a threat to anyone."

"Unless you are getting close to who killed your sister," Charlene said softly.

Avery read a message on her phone. "Detective Holden is on his way and asks that nobody leave. He has some questions."

Persephone clenched her fingers over the armrests as if she wanted to leave but didn't. "Marisol was murdered. You have to stop asking questions, Isabella. It's not safe for you."

"Who killed Marisol?" Rico asked.

"Why?" Isabella questioned and slumped against Charlene. Rico drank and stared at the *ofrenda*, searching for who-knew-what.

"I don't have answers," Persephone said.

"The key is gone." Rico faced Persephone. "Hand it over!"

Persephone didn't try to deny that she'd taken it and gave it to Rico, who placed it on the table again.

"Thief! What does this belong to?" Rico asked.

Persephone shrugged.

"Why did you take it?" Isabella asked. "You are the worst. You must have an idea."

"I felt compelled to take it." Persephone showed no signs of remorse. "When I am under the influence of the paranormal, I don't question my impulses."

"That's still stealing," Avery said.

Sam arrived in record time and knocked on the door as if he'd been minutes away. The station was only ten minutes, but he'd been closer.

"Welcome." Charlene studied Sam's dear face, looking for acceptance or understanding. She'd hated disappointing him. "Isabella is on the couch, and Persephone is in the armchair. She tried to take one of Marisol's altar items, a key, but claims not to know why."

Sam gave a brief nod, his jaw hard. "It was smart to call me about the threat against Isabella's life. Why Avery and not you?"

"I was helping Isabella to the couch. She fainted at the warning from Marisol."

"I see." Sam passed her and strode into the living room.

"He's still upset," Jack said.

"He will need to get past it," Charlene murmured. She wasn't looking forward to nights without Sam, to being *just friends* again.

Those were thoughts for later. She returned to the living room.

"Hi. I'm Detective Sam Holden." Sam held his tablet and didn't offer to shake Persephone's hand.

"Persephone Lowell." The witch stayed seated. "Psychic. Medium."

"Right." Sam shifted and took up a spot before the fireplace so he could survey the room and its occupants. "Tell me about the message warning Isabella that she was in danger."

"She said that Isabella would be next if she didn't stop asking questions," Avery said.

Sam turned so that he was speaking directly to Persephone. "Did you know Marisol Perez?"

"Yes," Persephone said.

"In what context? Were you friends?"

Persephone shifted on the chair. "Not exactly. We were both tarot readers and mediums, with our businesses on the same street."

"Mediums?" Sam asked.

"A medium is someone who can commune with the dead," Persephone explained, "or decipher messages from those who have passed on."

"And you are saying for certain that Marisol Perez is deceased?" Sam asked. Outwardly, his composure remained cool and collected, but Charlene knew him well enough to see that this intrigued him.

"Yes," Persephone said with assurance.

Sam leaned in, a tiger about to pounce. "How?"

"I don't know," Persephone said.

"How did you receive this message?" Sam tapped his pen to the tablet. "Explain it in simple terms so I can understand."

Persephone touched her temple. "I opened my mind and called for Marisol's spirit to come to me."

Sam pointed to the *ofrenda* for Marisol. "Why didn't you join Isabella and the others here tonight to help?"

"She was going to," Rico said. "And backed out. We needed her. Kass came, and Serenity, as promised. We needed strong witches."

Sam made a note on the tablet and turned back to Persephone with an arched brow that spoke volumes in the silence.

"I was at my place of business, resting after the Day of the Dead parade, when I felt an urgent need to try to reach out to Marisol, on Isabella's behalf," Persephone said. "Who knows the ways of the spirits?"

Sam kept a neutral expression. "Tell me again about the warning. Be precise, please."

Persephone cleared her throat. "It was for Isabella to return to New York and stop asking questions about Marisol's death or she would be killed next. That she wouldn't get so lucky a second time."

"Was the message in reference to Marisol's death or Cindy Sherman's?" Sam asked. "Are the two connected?"

"I don't know." Persephone raised her palm. "And before you ask, I'll tell you the same thing I told Isabella and Rico—there is no more to the message than that. I can't ask for details because there are none."

Sam pocketed his tablet. "I need more than a message from the dead to act."

"Figures," Rico slurred.

"But I'll tell you what I'll do," Sam said.

Charlene, Avery, and Isabella all straightened, alert.

"What?" Persephone scooted to the edge of her chair.

"I'll check the cameras on the corner of your business to see who has been coming and going, to give you that threatening warning," Sam said.

Persephone's eyes widened.

"A spirit won't be on the camera," Isabella said.

"A human will be. I hope for your sake, Ms. Lowell, that I can find the person responsible for the death threat to Isabella Perez. Otherwise, you are a person of interest in the deaths of Marisol Perez and Cindy Sherman."

Persephone sank back in the chair. "*What?*"

"None of you should leave town without letting me know." Sam turned to make eye contact with Persephone, Rico, and Isabella. "I'd hate to have to drag you to the station for questioning. We are busy and you might need to cool your heels for up to twenty-four hours."

Sam left the living room without looking at Charlene, who tagged along with him. "You seem extra angry, Sam."

"I'm furious." Sam stopped in midfoyer and braced his shoulders, finally looking at Charlene. His eyes were molten brown without a hint of mirth or warmth. "The woman I love believes in ghosts and could be in danger from a foe that I can't see."

"You still love me?" Her eyes welled.

Sam pulled her close and slammed his mouth to hers in a kiss that answered that question for her.

She gasped for breath when it was over.

"Please be careful, Charlene."

With that, Sam left.

Her heart eased in her chest. They would figure it out. It wouldn't be easy, but she believed they would find a way to compromise. Tears of relief blurred her vision, but she batted them back.

Jack ruffled her hair. "Sam's got a temper," he teased. "But he came around."

"He will, I know that now." Charlene and Jack shared a smile of understanding. She whirled at the sound of something crashing in the living room.

"I hate you, Rico," Persephone yelled.

Charlene and Jack returned to the drama unfolding in the living room.

Rico drank even more tequila. "You're not as good as Marisol and that just eats you up."

"What did I miss?" Charlene asked Avery.

The teen shoved Rico away from the table and the candles before he tipped it over and caught it on fire.

"Rico wants to go to Persephone's for precise answers, which she can't give, so he's resorted to name calling. Bruja I got," Avery said. "And I don't want to know the rest."

Isabella stayed on the couch, Silva in her lap. "Could you please stop arguing? I need answers. Who murdered Marisol?"

"I gave you what I know." Persephone stood and crossed her arms, putting the chair between herself and Rico. "Calm down, Rico. You've always been a lousy drunk. How does Isabella put up with you?"

"Persephone, I just don't understand why anybody would want to harm Marisol. . . . Can you please tell me what you remember of her from that time?"

Rico wagged his finger at Persephone.

To warn her?

Charlene watched the ex-couple closely.

Isabella already knew they'd been sleeping together, so what other secret could they have?

Could it have to do with Jonas? The circle of people they'd known had been relatively small. Salem wasn't a huge city.

Before Charlene could ask Persephone, Isabella stood, frustration on her face. Silva meowed but stayed on the couch.

"Marisol was kind, and talented, and beautiful."

Persephone threw her hands in the air. "Get real!"

"What?" Isabella asked.

"Take off those rose-colored glasses, girl," Persephone said.

"I don't understand."

"Marisol was greedy and manipulative," Persephone said. "How can you not see the truth? Love is blind; it must be, considering who you are with."

"My sister wasn't greedy! Our business was so good because of our allegiance to Santa Muerte."

Persephone shook her head. "Marisol was crooked. How do you think she made all that money? It had nothing to do with the Death Goddess but her skills at—"

"It's time for you to go." Rico pointed toward the door. "Out, or I'll call that detective back."

"I haven't done anything wrong," Persephone said.

Charlene couldn't help herself. "Why were you arguing with Jonas McCarthy today? We saw you this afternoon on the wharf."

"You and Jonas?" Isabella asked. "Is there nobody in my family you haven't tried to poach or corrupt?"

"It's not your business, but I'll tell you." Persephone shrugged. "I wanted to know if he'd cut me the same deal he had Marisol for merchandise."

"You want to open a Santa Muerte store?" Rico exploded. "You can't be Marisol. You can't compete."

"I don't understand." Isabella crossed the room and peered up at Persephone. "Tell me what's going on!"

"Should I?" Persephone smirked toward Rico. "I kind of like having you on a short leash."

"Go, Persephone." Rico walked around Isabella and tugged at Persephone's elbow.

"I'll leave because I want to, not because of you, Rico."

Persephone sauntered out of the living room to the foyer.

Her hair, short and pink, didn't have the sway of Isabella's or Marisol's. Or Cindy's, for that matter.

"If you still have questions, come find me tomorrow, Isabella," Persephone said. "Until then, be very, very careful."

Persephone left and Charlene locked the door. She was surprised that her guests hadn't returned yet. It was two in the morning.

She returned to the living room to see Avery sitting next to Isabella. The woman was shaking, but not with sadness. With anger.

"Tell me the truth, Rico," Isabella said. "If you don't, we are over."

Rico kicked the slate on the fireplace. "Really?"

"Really."

He pinched his thumb and forefinger together. "Maybe Marisol had a dark side to her."

"Do better than that," Isabella said.

"How do you think she got the money for the shop?" Rico asked. The question was serious, without an ounce of sarcasm.

"I don't know." Isabella curled a lock of her long hair around her finger. "Santa Muerte was our patron, so I assumed the abundance came from her benevolence."

Rico sipped his drink. "And the merchandise in the shop, well, it came from Mexico."

"So?"

"Maybe not *legally* from Mexico," Rico said.

"Jonas smuggled it in?" Isabella gasped.

"It was something Marisol trusted Jonas with because of growing up in New Orleans." Rico gestured with his glass, and tequila sloshed over the side.

"Did our mother know?" Isabella asked.

"No. It was after you'd moved to Salem," Rico explained. Considering how much he'd had to drink, Charlene was impressed that he was able to piece together a semicoherent conversation.

"Why didn't you clue me in? I feel so stupid." Isabella stared at Rico, then glanced down at her folded hands.

"Marisol wanted to protect you, Bella," Rico said in a low voice. "In case anything went wrong, legally."

Isabella digested the information, her nostrils flaring, her brow furrowed. "Could the smuggling be why Marisol was killed? Could Jonas . . . we need to talk to Jonas. I have been at an incredible disadvantage when asking anyone about Marisol. I'm the one in the dark."

Rico listed slightly to the left but straightened, concentrating on not spilling another drop of his drink. "Got it."

"Impressive," Jack said. "I hate to think how much Rico drinks on a daily basis to have built up such a tolerance. Alcohol changes the perception. We need to keep an eye on Isabella."

Isabella stood and paced the area behind the couch. "I'm a fool. What else don't I know? Why did Persephone want that key?"

Rico picked up the brass key and squinted at it. "Persephone is a skilled liar."

Isabella joined him by Marisol's altar. She took the key and studied it. "I think there might be a mark of some kind."

"Maybe we don't believe her about Marisol being dead." Rico too carefully sipped his drink. "Did Marisol ever get sudden messages out of the blue and run home to receive them?"

"Marisol's gifts were honed by our mother at an early age, so I don't know the answer to that." Isabella exchanged the key for the picture of them as teens.

Smiling sadly, she put it back. "She just knew things and used the cards for dramatic effect. For business."

"Marisol didn't need the paraphernalia?" Rico asked. "It was for show." He rocked to the side, cradling his tumbler. "She was much more powerful than Persephone."

Isabella blew out a breath. "We need answers. Tomorrow is our last night to reach Marisol for ourselves, because she is angry with us, for falling in love. I didn't expect that. I want to explain to her how it happened."

"*Mi amor! Te amo*. You can't let what Persephone said affect you. Besides, I think she was lying." Rico shook a finger. "I just don't know why."

"How come?" Charlene asked.

"I lived with her for a year before I met Marisol," Rico said. "I just . . . know. She's not being honest. Could be about Marisol coming through, or the key, or the message, or Jonas. Something is off."

Isabella grabbed Rico by the shoulders and forced him to look her in the eye. Tequila spilled down his shirt. "Could Persephone have killed my sister? She's gained clients since Marisol is gone."

"No." Rico slumped but straightened, then listed to the other side. "I don't think so."

"Somebody did." Determination took over the sadness and shock of what she'd learned about Marisol. "Where are my car keys? We need to find Jonas and ask him."

"You should stay here, Isabella," Charlene said.

"You received the warning of danger. She's right."

Rico realized his tumbler was empty and set it on the card table but missed. Jack's essence saved it from hitting the slate on the fireplace and breaking.

"In the morning, then. I have a list of calls to make, starting with Jonas. I'll clean the key and try to make headway there." Isabella picked up the charm bracelet. "Could Marisol have given Brian the charm from her bracelet? Maybe she didn't even know it was missing. Though she wasn't careless with her totems, and the owl is the symbol for her psychic connection."

"We need to ask Brian about it," Rico said. "We can call him too." He patted his pocket. "Where's my phone?"

"In the morning, Rico." Isabella rolled her eyes.

"Who was in her circle here in Salem?" Avery asked.

"Me, Rico, Jonas, her clients, Kass . . . Brian." Isabella snapped her fingers. "If Brian took the charm, maybe he also has the gold statue. What if he went from stalking to murder because Marisol broke things off that day? I never saw her after July fourth."

"Which means that Brian might be holding on to a statue worth a million dollars," Rico said.

"Let's find out if his lifestyle changed at all," Avery said. "Does he have a new car or house?"

"I'll do that. It won't take long." Jack disappeared. Charlene appreciated his cyberskills, which were much faster than hers.

"I'll start a list." Charlene opened the note app on her phone. "Brian. Maybe instead of asking who was in Marisol's circle, we should be asking who her enemies might be?"

"Brian would still be on the list." Isabella hugged her middle. "Who else?"

"Persephone," Rico said. "I'm glad the detective is checking out her story. She's jealous for so many reasons."

"Yes, I can see her motivation," Avery said.

"You sound like a police officer," Rico scoffed.

"I'm studying to be a detective," Avery said proudly.

"You will be wonderful at it," Isabella said. "I'll make you a protective talisman with black tourmaline, amethyst, and bloodstone. Gladiators used to wear that for strength and courage in battle."

"Thank you!" Avery replied warmly.

"Pay attention, Bella." Rico attempted to snap his fingers but missed.

"Don't be rude," Isabella said. "You have been keeping secrets from me all this time. Do you know what this key is for, or why Persephone would want it?"

"I already told you that I didn't. I was surprised Marisol had it in her jewelry box," Rico said. "Wouldn't be a shock if she had money stashed somewhere."

"Why?"

"Marisol had her ways for getting what she wanted, no matter the cost. Could be she didn't want you to know," Rico said. "She was blessed in business, thanks to Santa Muerte."

"And her own gifts," Isabella said.

And the smuggling, Charlene thought.

"Yes." Rico realized he didn't have his tumbler and looked around for it, giving up when he didn't find it

because Jack had tucked it under the card table. He
stood. "I'm leaving."

"No, you aren't," Isabella said. "Where do you want
to go?"

"You're stranded here, so I need to find Jonas, and
then Persephone." Rico's eyes narrowed. "It can't wait
till morning. What if they killed Marisol together?"

CHAPTER 20

"Jonas and Persephone?" Charlene thought it might explain why they'd argued so vehemently. Rico pulled Isabella's car keys from his front pocket.

"I'm going. Stay here or not," Rico said, stumbling over the sofa leg.

Avery snagged the keys when he loosened his grip. "Probably not a good idea."

"Bella can drive," Rico said, not arguing his case.

"I've been drinking, too, so no. We have to wait for tomorrow." Isabella pulled her cell phone off the side table near the sofa. "Let's call Jonas now." She dialed. It rang and rang.

"I'm going!" Rico snuck the keys back from Avery. "It's been two years since Marisol left us," he sobbed.

Charlene leaped between him and the foyer. "I'll drive you. But let's calm down and make a plan. Where do you want to go?"

"The wharf," Rico huffed. "Isabella should stay here.

In case, you know, Jonas did it. Killed Marisol and tried to kill you, *mi amor*."

"Jonas wouldn't!" Isabella said. "Besides, I'm going with you. I need answers. How could I have been so blind? Don't even think about arguing with me."

Charlene held out her palm. "If Rico gives me the keys, I won't argue."

Rico handed them to Charlene, who then gave them to Avery. "Hang on to these, would you, please?"

"Sure. Should I come too?" Avery asked.

"No, stay here and help . . ." Charlene nodded to Jack, "find out if Brian came into a sum of money two years ago."

"Be careful," Jack said.

"Keep your phone on," Avery said. "You have your mace?"

"In the car," Charlene promised. This was not her first foray into questionable activity. "Wait here." She hurried to her suite and grabbed her jacket and purse. She returned to the foyer as Rico helped Isabella with her coat. He declined the need for a jacket, sweating.

That would be the copious amounts of tequila, she thought.

Getting into her Pilot, Charlene turned on the engine. She wasn't happy playing chauffeur to a drunken Rico, but she couldn't let him drive, or Isabella. Sam wouldn't be happy, but it was a personal choice not to let anyone drive intoxicated. The tequila she'd had hours ago had long since worn off.

And, she admitted, she wanted answers too.

Rico claimed Persephone was lying about something.

Jonas being a smuggler was a validation of their concerns. It made sense that his boat didn't have a name or serial numbers if he used it to smuggle Santa Muerte merchandise from Mexico to Salem. Who knew where else, or what else?

Did that make him a killer? Persephone had said that she and Jonas were arguing about opening a Santa Muerte shop together. If only Charlene knew who was telling the truth.

Isabella climbed into the front seat after helping Rico into the back, where he sprawled low. Maybe he'd pass out and they could go home sooner rather than later.

Who was right? Isabella, that Jonas was family? Or Rico, that Jonas might be in cahoots with Persephone to kill Marisol?

"Do you know how to get to the wharf?" Isabella asked. "I can pull it up on maps if you need directions."

"That's okay, Isabella. I know where the wharf is. My parents have a condo nearby, which is how we saw Persephone and Jonas arguing." Charlene waited for Isabella to buckle up before backing out of her driveway.

Rico flipped forward, resting his head on the console between them. "I want to go to the cemetery where that lady was shot."

"Why?" Isabella asked.

"To see where a shooter might hide," Rico said. "Jonas is a crack shot. Did you know that?"

"No," Isabella said. "I didn't know a lot of things."

"We were trying to protect you." Rico didn't sound like he was sorry for the lies, but the fact that he could lie so easily would bother Charlene if she were Isabella.

Isabella stared out the window in the dark.

"Do you think Persephone made up the message from Marisol?" Charlene asked.

"She was lying, but I don't know about what part," Rico said. "We should confront her right after Jonas." He punched his fist to his open palm with a smack.

"Let's just check in with Jonas at his boat. No promises. I can't be driving around all night," Charlene said.

Rico had to get tired eventually and they could return to the B&B, where he'd probably pass out.

Isabella wiped silent tears from her cheeks. Her skin was shiny beneath the makeup she'd scrubbed off. She wanted answers and she was getting them, but not in the way she'd expected.

To find out that the sibling you adored had feet of clay sucked.

Where were Charlene's guests? It was after two in the morning. Using Bluetooth, she dialed Kevin, the one person she knew would still be awake, as he usually closed the bar he managed.

"Charlene! What's up?" Rock music blasted in the background.

"Hey! I was wondering if the party downtown was still going on?"

"No, but if you're checking on your crew, they're here dancing with the live band I hired. Spence has pipes with serious range," Kevin said with admiration. "Darla can drum as well as Cindy Blackman—Cindy toured with Lenny Kravitz."

"I want to party." Rico tried to straighten up, but his elbow slipped off the console and he sprawled on the back seat instead.

"I'm glad they're having so much fun. I won't worry about them, then." Charlene loosened her grip on the steering wheel. "We're still up at the B-and-B."

"Why's that?" Kevin asked.

"I'll tell you later. Gotta run!" Charlene ended the call.

"Let's go!" Rico said. He was suffering FOMO—fear of missing out.

Isabella turned to shake her finger at him in disapproval. "You've had enough to drink."

"You aren't my mother or my *wife*. Until we get married you can't tell me what to do," Rico replied with belligerence.

"That is sure something to take into consideration." Isabella glanced at Charlene and sighed. "My mind is spinning like a hurricane."

"I completely understand." Charlene reached the main street by the bay, passing her parents' condo to arrive at the water. The bench with Benjamin Fiske's smiling face was occupied by a pigeon beneath the clouded night sky.

"Shall I park?" Charlene asked. She peered through the windshield but didn't see the blue vessel with the red captain's wheel. "Jonas's boat isn't in the slip anymore. I don't think it's there."

"What?" Isabella said in disbelief. "You have got to be mistaken."

Rico snored in the back seat.

Charlene stifled her laugh as she turned off the engine.

"Let's be sure he didn't just move it." Isabella opened her door to step out into the night.

Charlene and Isabella used the flashlight app on their phones to light the way; the streetlamps weren't great. Where the nameless boat had been moored was now a vacant spot, the chop of the waves smacking against the wooden pier.

"I'll call Jonas," Isabella said. She dialed and held the phone to her ear.

"Still no answer?"

"This isn't good!" Isabella lowered her phone. "I can't believe this. Jonas. He was part of our family."

Fifteen minutes had passed. "I'm sorry, Isabella." Charlene headed back toward the car. She climbed in, waiting for Isabella to join her. Rico turned onto his side.

"Should we seat belt him?" Charlene asked.

"Don't bother. Let's go straight to the B-and-B," Isabella said. "We can call Persephone later. Honestly, the conversation might be better face-to-face. I can't stomach it right now. Is there nobody I can trust?"

Charlene sent a text to Avery that they were on their way.

She'd just turned around a curving section of road when high beams from a truck flashed into her rearview, blinding her.

"Hey!"

The Pilot was rammed from behind and she struggled to control the car. Her mouth dried with panic. "Isabella?"

The truck connected with her bumper even harder. The SUV skidded on gravel for what seemed like forever and then careened into a ditch. Isabella's head smacked the window and Charlene's hair fell forward as her body strained against the seat belt. Why hadn't the airbags deployed? She could hear her rear tire spin as the nose of her SUV was pointed down, elevating the back.

The menacing truck stayed behind her. Rico, awake and furious, exited the rear passenger seat, waving his fist while cursing in Spanish.

The truck revved menacingly and then sped off.

Charlene lost sight of both the speeding truck and Rico. She put the SUV in Park and turned off the engine. Isabella's eyes were wide with shock as she gripped the console with one hand and the handle on the ceiling with the other.

"Isabella! You're hurt. Let's go to the hospital."

"No, take me to your house." Isabella lightly touched the mark on her forehead. "It's just a scratch. That was a deliberate action to run us off the road. Let's go."

"Should we," Charlene's voice quivered, and she cleared her throat. "Should we search for Rico?"

"His temper gets him into trouble. No, let him walk it off and sober up by the time he gets to the B-and-B."

That sounded like a good plan.

Charlene rummaged in her glove box and found some napkins and gave them to Isabella to put pressure on the wound.

"Are *you* all right?" Isabella asked.

"Yes." Her hands were shaking, but she'd be fine.

"Who do you think did that?" Isabella asked.

"Let's talk when we get home." Charlene's nerves were jarred, but the trusty Pilot reversed out of the ditch and she was able to drive to the mansion. The front axle seemed wonky, but she'd take it to the mechanic tomorrow. No, she reminded herself, seeing the time. Two thirty a.m. Later today.

She didn't text but concentrated on the short drive in case the truck showed up for another round.

Why?

Persephone's message from Marisol, if that was to be believed, had said to stop searching for answers and return to New York before she was killed next.

Charlene parked next to Avery's car and hopped out to help Isabella from the vehicle. Her eyes were dazed, but it could be the emotion of everything in addition to hitting her head on the passenger window.

Jack would know how to help with the injury.

Should she call Sam? Or text him?

Once inside the foyer Charlene shouted, "Avery?"

Jack appeared.

"Coming," Avery said, having been in Charlene's suite.

"What happened?" Jack studied the cut on Isabella's forehead.

Avery turned on the kitchen light, and Charlene brought Isabella to the dining room table. The teen had taken the time to wash off the Day of the Dead makeup.

"We were run off the road."

"Accident?" Avery asked.

"On purpose," Charlene said. "It had to be to scare Isabella."

"Did you call anyone?" Avery asked.

"Not yet." Charlene went into the downstairs bathroom, running a washcloth under the tap. She then grabbed antiseptic cream and a selection of bandages and brought her supplies to the table.

"Where is Rico?" Avery asked.

"He jumped out of the car, the idiot," Isabella said, "and chased the person in the truck who rammed us."

"Have you called Sam?" Avery asked.

"No, I was too shaky to talk and drive." Charlene held out her hands, which still trembled.

"I'll do it," Avery said. She pulled her phone from her pocket and texted Sam.

Charlene's phone rang and she answered. "Hello! You're on speaker. I'm okay. I think. I'll tell you more in a second, once I settle down. It just happened moments ago."

"Why did you leave the house?" Sam said in a too calm voice.

They all straightened up around the dining table at his tone.

Charlene took a deep breath. "I realize that leaving wasn't ideal, but it was better than having Rico drive after he'd been drinking, which I couldn't let him do. You know that about me."

Sam exhaled. "I do. All right. Go through what happened again."

"Isabella has discovered more about her sister's business with Jonas McCarthy."

"Boat captain?" Sam asked.

"Yes," Charlene confirmed. "Rico had questions for him and wondered if he could have killed Marisol, possibly with Persephone's assistance. We wondered if

Cindy was shot by accident, if the killer thought Cindy was Isabella, as they both have long dark hair."

"Mistaken identity," Sam said.

"It's possible, right? Everyone loved Cindy, according to the news reports," Charlene said. "Avery and I saw Persephone and Jonas arguing at the wharf today, and when we were just down there, Jonas's boat was gone. He'd been living on it."

"All right." Sam's exhale rustled through the speaker.

"What if Jonas and Persephone were working together to kill Marisol, like Rico suggested?"

"Charlene!"

"Persephone was very jealous of my sister, Detective," Isabella said.

"Do you want a bandage?" Avery asked.

"Hold up!" Sam growled. "You're bleeding? Do you need an ambulance?"

"No, Sam," Charlene said, trying for patience. "Isabella has a small cut."

"No stitches needed," Jack proclaimed.

"I'm fine." The wound had stopped bleeding. "Persephone channeled a message from Marisol that my life could be next if I didn't stop asking questions," Isabella said.

"I'm checking on that. Street cameras show a man forcing his way into Persephone's shop about thirty minutes before she left to give you the urgent message."

"Who?" Charlene asked.

"A client of Persephone's named Benjamin Fiske," Sam said.

"Benjamin Fiske." Isabella tapped the table. "He used

to be a client of my sister's too. Persephone got extra business with Marisol dead—it's why we think she might be involved. Benjamin is a millionaire, and he had Marisol on speed dial."

"I've tried calling Persephone, but she's not answering and she's not home," Sam said. "Charlene, please tell me that your door is locked."

"It is!" Charlene said.

"Benjamin, the one who asked Persephone about you?" Avery said.

Charlene scowled at Avery. The last thing she needed was Sam thinking she might be interested in another man.

"When was this?" Sam asked.

"The other day—Benjamim was leaving either Persephone's or that mail center in the building at the same time I'd walked Dotty to get her tarot reading." Charlene thought of the man's friendly wink. "It's not a big deal."

"I have some things I'm still checking on. If you step out that front door, text me and let me know, all right? Considering you aren't listening to my request that you stay home. We've had lunatics up the wazoo today because of the Day of the Dead parade."

"Sorry, Sam," Charlene said contritely. Where did that leave them if neither was willing to change?

"Ah. Me too. I'm just tired. Please. Stay home." Sam ended the call.

"What if it was Persephone who ran us off the road?" Isabella queried. "If Sam said she wasn't home or answering her phone?"

"Let me text Kass to give her a heads-up on what's

going on." Charlene sent the text and then poured herself a big glass of ice water and drank half of it down.

Kass texted back that she and Persephone were together for the last forty minutes on the beach to gather moon magic.

"Darn it!" Charlene said. "Kass is with Persephone." She forwarded that to Sam. "She wouldn't lie."

"It was worth a try," Avery said.

Charlene sat at the table.

"I'm sorry," Isabella said. "I've brought trouble to your house."

"You haven't. At least not intentionally." Charlene looked at Avery and Jack. "What about Brian?"

"We didn't find any big money purchases, but he does have a truck that he finances," Avery said. "Were you able to get the make of the one that hit you?"

"No. They had on the bright lights, which blinded us. Me."

"It was intentional," Jack said.

"It was on purpose, to scare me," Isabella said, unknowingly echoing Jack's sentiment.

"That could be," Avery said. "They drove off?"

"Yes, and Rico ran after them," Isabella said.

"The rest of our guests are partying at Kevin's still," Charlene said. "The bar will stay open until people want to go home."

"Maybe that's where Rico went?" Isabella suggested. She tried to call him, and a phone rang from the living room.

Avery jumped up and brought the phone back to the kitchen table. "It was in the sofa cushions. I love the idea of partying all night in theory, but my eyes are closing." The teen had had a very long day.

"Go lay down, hon. Should I go get them?" The idea of getting up from the chair seemed daunting.

"If you leave this house, Sam will lock you up and toss the key," Avery warned. "I'll have some tea. Anybody else?"

Isabella raised her hand. "Yes, please." She stood and peered toward the foyer. "I'm starting to get worried about Rico."

"I hate to ask this," Charlene said, "but how much do you know about Rico's past? Or his relationship with Marisol?"

"Could he have killed her?" Avery asked. "Oh, that was harsh. Sorry. It's late."

"She brings up a good point," Jack said.

Avery handed out steaming mugs and a ceramic container of assorted tea bags.

Charlene finished her cool water, quenching her thirst.

Isabella made her tea, going with a soothing chamomile and lemon. She stirred in some honey. "Rico was living with Persephone before we moved to Salem. We were here for ten years. Marisol was a stunning nineteen when we arrived. Persephone didn't have a chance to hold on to her man."

Isabella stirred the honey with a spoon and stared into the mug.

"She was lovely," Jack agreed.

"Marisol didn't mean to collect men, she just did. She had that sex appeal that collected them like flies to honey." Isabella lifted the spoon with melted honey. "That caused her not to have many female friends. I was different. I was her sister. Her family. We had each other's backs."

Charlene decided to make her own cup of tea. "And Rico . . ."

"Could Rico have killed Marisol in a fit of passionate rage?" Isabella shrugged. "Before tonight, I would have said no way."

Jack disappeared and reappeared. "Rico is here. I think she should ask him point-blank if he killed Marisol."

CHAPTER 21

R ico tried the lock twice but must have forgotten the code.

"Coming!" Charlene quickly opened the door and Rico stumbled into the foyer. He had a bloody nose and bruised knuckles.

Avery, Isabella, and Jack all hovered around him.

"Where have you been?" Isabella cried. She gently moved hair from his cheek, stuck by blood. "Oh, babe."

Avery's eyes widened and she shut the door, locking it, after scanning the dark night. "Did you walk all that way?"

Rico groaned.

"He should probably sit down," Jack suggested.

"Let's have a seat," Charlene chose the staircase because it could be cleaned and was closer. She guided Rico to the steps, where he plonked down.

Avery went to the bathroom for another washcloth and small towel.

One of the things they didn't mention in the guest

services business was the amount of towels needed. People were messy.

"Here you go," Avery said, handing the cloth to Rico.

"Let me get that," Isabella crooned as she gently patted Rico's skin. "Who did this?"

"Jonas." Rico grunted.

Isabella stepped back. "Jonas was in the truck?"

"No, no. I lost that guy. But I was right by the Captain's Wheel, and so was Jonas." Rico lifted his knuckles.

"Why did you fight?" Avery asked.

"I asked him if he killed Marisol," Rico slurred. "Demanded the truth about Per, Perse, Persephone too—if they were arguing because of Marisol."

"Rico probably didn't kill Marisol if he's starting brawls to find out who did it," Jack observed.

Isabella crossed her arms and peered into Rico's eyes. "Did you kill Marisol? Was it an accident, from a moment of passion?"

"I would never have hurt her." Rico sounded drunkenly righteous. "No. I did," he hiccupped. "Not."

"I think he's telling the truth," Jack said.

"What about Jonas?" Avery returned to the original subject once Isabella gave a satisfied nod.

"I . . . I may have owed Jonas some money." Rico's eyes started to close.

Isabella pinched his wrist. "Stay awake, Rico. This is important. What for?"

"Santa Muerte merchandise for the shop that was smuggled from Mexico, the last shipment wasn't paid for . . . we couldn't tell you about."

"The smuggled merchandise," Isabella repeated. "All right. Why wasn't it paid for? We had plenty of money."

"I may have had something with Jonas on the side." His eyes closed.

Isabella gave him another pinch and Rico widened his eyes. "Like what? Rico!"

"We need that statue," Rico said. "It will take care of all the money worries."

Isabella fumed. "You wanted to leave Salem in a hurry to stiff Jonas?"

"If we find the statue all will be well again. You'll help me, won't ya, *amor*?"

A single tear escaped down Isabella's cheek. "You didn't really feel her here earlier, did you, Rico?"

"No. I didn't." Rico averted his gaze, showing the first instance of shame.

"Which brings us back to the possibility that she could be alive and have the statue somewhere," Avery said.

"I need it!" Rico said.

"You've been using me this whole time, for money." Isabella swatted Rico's chest with the towel. "For a place to live and hide out from Jonas McCarthy."

Charlene's phone dinged, and she read a series of messages from Sam. "Jonas was at the Captain's Wheel, as Rico said. He didn't drive me off the road. Brian was at his post on security cam for the last hour. Sam told Jimenez about the owl charm."

"Who ran us off the road?" Isabella sank down next to Rico, in shock rather than emotion or support.

"Not Persephone, not Brian, not Jonas," Avery said.

"What did you see when you jumped out of the SUV?" Charlene asked. "The lights were so bright."

"I was so mad." Rico clenched his fist. "I was going to find him and make him pay—tricked-out black truck with a silver boat hitch. Chrome trim. Had a fancy boat sticker kind of thing on the back window."

"Could you see anything on the license plate?" Avery asked.

"No numbers." Rico tilted to his right. "Looked like Salem, with the red against the white."

Hmm. Charlene asked, "Did it have lights or anything around it?"

Rico shook his head and started to slide into Isabella. She shoved him back. Not so loving as when they'd first arrived.

"Can you tell us anything else?" Charlene asked.

"He had on a hat," Rico said.

"Cowboy hat? Knit cap?" Charlene patted the top of her head. "Beanie?"

"Like a boat captain's hat."

"Let me send these details to Sam. Everyone around Salem who has a boat owns a truck to go with it," Charlene complained.

"What should we do?" Isabella's entire body exuded misery.

"I don't know," Charlene said. "This is a lot to take in."

Isabella pushed away from Rico, and crossed to the living room, returning with her sister's picture. "Marisol wanted to protect me. I love her, no matter what, and I will search for her. I hope she's drinking Mai Tais somewhere, I really do, but I just don't think she's still with us. You hear how protective she was of me, don't you?"

Avery nodded.

"I'll help you." Rico's eyes settled at half-mast. His butt remained glued to the stairs.

Isabella took a seat on the step next to him but with space between them.

A cool tendril like an invisible finger traced across Charlene's nape. Isabella must have felt it too.

"What's that?" Avery called in alarm.

"I'm here," Jack assured them. He manifested his body, complete with a stylish black suit.

A knock pounded on the door.

Charlene answered it and was relieved to see her wonderful Sam. The only hint of his long hours was the tiniest drooping of his mustache. He wore jeans, boots, and a regulation SPD all-weather jacket over his holstered gun.

"Sam!"

Sam hugged her to him and then tipped her back just enough to study her face with concern. "You're all right."

"I am." Charlene never wanted to let him go.

"Is there a reason you are hanging out in the foyer?" Sam put her at his side, his arm around her waist.

"It's . . . we are all very tired but can't pull the plug on such an eventful evening," Charlene said. Her heart was lighter now that Sam was here.

He loved her, and she loved him. The rest was semantics.

"I can't stay." Sam faced Isabella and withdrew his arm from Charlene. "I wanted to deliver the news in person." He pulled a printed photo from his interior jacket pocket.

The pocket had a ring-box shape inside it, too, not that Charlene was noticing. Her spirits soared that their future held hope.

"What is it?" Bella's lower lip quivered.

Rico straightened, as if sensing the importance of the moment.

"Is this Marisol Perez?" Sam asked.

Isabella took the picture from Sam and gasped. He'd kindly only brought the face. It was Marisol.

Rico slumped over, as if he might be sick.

Isabella ignored him. She compared it to the picture Rico had drawn. Identical.

"Yes. That is my sister." Isabella slowly inhaled, steadying herself. "Where was she found?"

Rico rubbed Isabella's shoulder.

"One of the alerts we'd sent out paid off. This Jane Doe was a match for Marisol Perez. Her body is in Boston. The autopsy determined that she was hit over the head with a heavy object. This is a homicide. I'm very, very sorry that nobody took this more seriously at the time she went missing." Sam rocked back on his bootheels. "It's been two years."

Isabella nodded, clearly numb and speechless.

"Persephone Lowell called me—at your suggestion, Charlene—and I confronted her with the street camera footage. She confirmed that Benjamin Fiske threatened her if she didn't give that message to you, Isabella." Sam's gaze sharpened. "Benjamin Fiske was questioned in several cases where women with long brunette hair have gone missing."

Charlene touched her hair, her body chilled. "Does he drive a truck?"

"The arrogant SOB drives the latest, with decked-out chrome," Sam confirmed.

"Oh no!" Isabella cried.

"Persephone said that Marisol had warned her of him, but she thought Marisol was just protecting her well-paying client. It seems that Benjamin might have killed before. We have an APB out for his arrest." Sam's jaw tightened. "I promise we will put a stop to his murderous ways."

"Benjamin gave Charlene his phone number," Avery said.

"The luxury boat salesman has a million commercials," Jack said. "His face is everywhere. Hiding in plain sight?"

"How did he know where I was? Most people are in bed at this hour." Charlene shivered. "He must be watching me, or us, somehow." She gestured to Isabella.

"Is Persephone okay?" Isabella twisted her hair up off her neck.

"Persephone was at the beach when we spoke with her. She believes she is in danger from Benjamin Fiske. She's staying with a friend until we find him." Sam smoothed his mustache. "She'd wanted Jonas McCarthy to help her set up shop in Louisiana with the Santa Muerte merchandise that had created such a lucrative if illegal income here in Salem. He refused, and that's the argument that Charlene and Avery saw."

Charlene was relieved that Sam knew the whole story. Jonas and Persephone wouldn't be going into business—at least not in Salem.

"Is Charlene in danger?" Avery caressed Charlene's long dark hair.

"Of course not. I'm fine!" Charlene said. Love blazed from turquoise eyes and golden brown.

"I will protect you," Jack said.

"I will protect you," Sam said.

CHAPTER 22

Charlene didn't need two protectors, but she felt their love and knew she had to be the luckiest woman in the world.

A touch tickled her nape again and she shivered. Avery and Isabella turned to each other and then looked at Charlene.

"Do you feel that?" Isabella asked. "Rico?"

"No—what?" Rico propped his elbow on his bent knee.

"It's like fingers trailing over my skin," Avery said.

"Exactly!" Isabella seconded.

"Jack?" Charlene asked. "Is that you?"

"No." Jack shimmered, his black suit turning gray before brightening. "I felt it earlier, before Sam came."

"Who are you talking to, Charlene?" Isabella asked.

"Jack Strathmore."

Isabella's mouth gaped. "The doctor who was murdered?"

"Yes," Charlene said.

Sam's chest puffed out and he exuded strength and confidence that he would handle whatever happened. "Jack is here?"

"Yes." Charlene kept her hand on Sam's arm to be reassuring.

Sam scanned the foyer with purpose. "Where?"

Charlene nodded at Jack, who was trying to make himself even brighter for Sam to see him. "Behind Avery."

"Jack really is haunting this place?" Isabella grinned. "Marisol was right."

"She was very powerful," Rico said, subdued.

"There is a loving essence and emotion with us right now," Jack said. "Marisol? Is it you?"

Jack disappeared.

"Jack?" Avery and Charlene shouted in unison. What if he was lost in the veil, never to return?

"I really hate this," Sam said, scanning the ceiling and area as if he could force himself to see Jack just by willpower.

A second later Jack returned with a bodiless spirit in swirls of golds, pinks, and purples. The room was so cold that even Sam could see his breath. "What's happening?"

Charlene gripped his hand, offering an anchor in the confusion. "It's okay. Jack brought Marisol through the veil."

"The colors are her?" Isabella jumped up. "Sister?" Her eager gaze perused the foyer. "I can't hear anything."

"She hasn't spoken yet. I think Jack is trying to help her," Avery said.

Sam squeezed Charlene's hand and let out a calming breath. Frost glittered on his mustache.

There was no explanation for what was happening now. They weren't outside on the porch to explain the cold. Charlene remembered what it felt like to have your senses skewed and promised herself that she'd be patient.

Marisol's voice came through like an off-station channel. Jack gave her a boost of his energy and it worked; suddenly her voice strengthened.

"I'm here, Isabella, I'm here," Marisol said in a very echoing tone. "I'm so sorry I really messed things up."

Avery repeated Marisol's words for Sam, Isabella, and Rico, who still couldn't hear Marisol, but the colors pulsed emotion.

"It's okay." Isabella sobbed with joy and relief.

"Ask about the statue. And the key," Rico interjected.

Marisol could hear him just fine. "What key?"

Rico left the foyer, suddenly very, very awake. He returned with the item in his palm from the *ofrenda* on the card table.

"It's to the safety-deposit box by Persephone's house. I tried to keep you safe, Bella. I'm so sorry. There are letters inside to folks I've blackmailed."

"I forgive you, Marisol—I just don't understand." Isabella placed her hands over her heart.

"Bad people, my clients; I knew their crimes. I got greedy and demanded payment for their silence."

Sam stiffened as Avery repeated Marisol's words. "Benjamin Fiske was her client? Did she blackmail him?"

"I remember Benjamin," Marisol said. Her voice thinned, as if she was afraid.

"Who killed you?" Rico interjected.

"I don't really know," Marisol said.

"It was the same for me; you don't remember those last fuzzy hours," Jack said.

"I remember being with . . . someone . . . on a boat. Benjamin always had boats, and he would take women out and kill them, then drop them out to sea. I wasn't hurting anybody by making him pay us extra," Marisol said.

"Could Benjamin be your killer?" Charlene asked softly.

"He had our Santa Muerte on the boat. . . ." Marisol's voice trailed off.

Avery repeated the words, her eyes wide as Silva's golden orbs.

"The statue is solid gold. You were hit on the back of the head." Isabella sobbed. "Detective Holden will find him. And make him pay."

"I will," Sam said.

Charlene didn't understand the sound echoing around the foyer. Suddenly there were holes in her front door and the doorknob shot out, as did the hinges.

Sam pushed Charlene out of the line of fire and drew his weapon as Benjamin Fiske kicked back the door.

Benjamin had a pistol in his steady hand. He shot at the wide staircase where Isabella sat with Rico. Rico screamed as blood poured from his ear. He tugged

Isabella up the stairs to the gallery, putting her over his shoulder to hide behind the railing. Silva darted down the hall of the second floor.

"I'm calling the police," Isabella shouted. "Go away, murderer!"

Benjamin barreled inside, using the door as a shield. He looked up at the gallery, but Isabella was hiding.

Avery!

Charlene jumped toward the teen as more bullets fired. Her arm stung.

"Coward is hiding behind the door," Jack said.

Charlene tightened her grip on Avery as something warm trickled down her arm.

"Charlene, you're bleeding!" Jack said in alarm. With manic energy, Jack whirled like a tornado, whipping the door away from Benjamin and out to the front yard.

Charlene didn't feel a thing. She wanted Avery to be safe. She peered over her shoulder, worried for Sam.

Benjamin pointed his gun at Sam, but he had already fired, hitting Benjamin between the eyes.

Sam clutched his chest. Blood oozed between his fingers and his mouth widened in shock.

Benjamin landed to his side, dead.

Only then did Sam slowly allow himself to drop to his knees. Charlene crawled to Sam and clasped his hand. Sam's lids were at half-mast and he bled profusely from his chest. "You okay?" he drawled.

"Yes!"

Sam shuddered and took a wheezing breath, his

hand in hers limp, as was his body. He sprawled out on the floor of the foyer. "Sam! Sam, stay with me." Charlene looked for Jack, who had manifested completely. "Jack, help me save Sam's life. What do I do?"

Jack's body disappeared, cold air rushing around Sam's still figure. Sam wasn't breathing. It was like her stomach and lungs and heart knotted together, and she tipped sideways but fought against the oncoming faint. She had to be present.

Sam needed her. Charlene clutched Sam's suit jacket, drenched in blood. "Don't let him die, Jack."

"You can help him, Jack, like you helped me and Bella," Marisol said. "You're a doctor. Be a doctor now."

"What are you saying?" Jack shouted. His body flickered there and gone with his distraught emotions.

"Get inside of him and save him. Mend the hole from the inside," Marisol said. "You know how to do it. Only you can fix it."

Avery, sobbing, crawled over to Sam's other side. "I don't know what to do," the teenager said. "How can I help?"

"Apply pressure." Charlene couldn't see through her tears. She jumped up and grabbed towels from the laundry room and raced back, pressing against the mess that was Sam's chest.

"When you were injured Jack said to keep pressure on the bleeding. Not to let up." Charlene wasn't sure if the situation was the same at all.

Jack was gone.

A minute had passed—a minute in which every second felt like an hour.

Sam suddenly inhaled and his eyes—turquoise blue in Sam's beloved face—stared at her. Jack's eyes.

"He's done it!" Charlene said. Hope filled her. They had a chance. "Jack is inside Sam."

"How did you know to suggest it, Marisol?" Avery asked.

"Santa Muerte whispered it to me," Marisol said. "She is the granter of miracles. She is especially protective of the police."

"Is my sister still here?" Isabella and Rico crept down the stairs, hand in hand. Isabella had her cell phone in her other hand.

Jack/Sam passed out again, but Sam's chest rose and fell raggedly.

"You called the ambulance?" Charlene choked the words from her throat.

"I did," Isabella said.

"*Sí.* They should be here any minute." Rico scowled down at the corpse of Benjamin Fiske. "Right between the eyes."

Sirens sounded. The cool autumn air revived her. Charlene leaned down to press her lips to Sam's. "I love you. Do you hear me? You can't make me love you and then leave me. I couldn't bear it."

Sam didn't rouse again, but he was breathing. Not smoothly, but breathing. She couldn't stop crying. She'd just thought how lucky she was, and now she felt cursed. She kept the pressure on the towels over his chest.

"Please tell Bella that she can do so much better for herself than Rico. He is a weak man. She deserves someone strong—as strong as her," Marisol continued in an eerie voice with no body. "She simply needs to believe in herself. I'd left the copies of the blackmail letters in the safety-deposit box as insurance for our future, but she's doing fine on her own. If she wants to be a barista, that's fine, but she shouldn't be afraid of our magic. Her light will always trump the darkness."

Avery repeated the message to Isabella. Rico's mouth twisted at her words.

"I will destroy the blackmail letters," Isabella promised. "And honor Santa Muerte's gift by embracing mine. I'm scared of the darkness."

"You, Bella, are the brightest light. It's time to shine."

The ambulance arrived and Sam/Jack was loaded onto the stretcher. "I'm trying," Jack's voice whispered from Sam's mouth.

Charlene kissed Jack/Sam's lips and squeezed his hand. "I know. Thank you."

"Ma'am," the medic said in a gentle voice. "Let go so we can get him into the ambulance."

"I'll be at the hospital as soon as possible," Charlene informed the empathetic EMT.

"Drive safely, ma'am. I suggest you wait. Once we arrive, he'll be in surgery."

It wasn't looking good for Sam.

Avery stood next to Charlene, slipping her arm around her waist. "We'll drive together. Please, save Detective Holden. He saved our lives tonight. He's important to so many people."

The ambulance left the property, and suddenly the very pale ghost of Jack manifested by them. He collapsed, clutching his heart, though there was no blood or obvious injury. Avery joined him, wanting to touch and soothe him, but Jack was like ice. It was frigid in the foyer. Silva returned to her gallery perch and observed with wide golden eyes.

The police arrived to ask questions. Detective Jimenez had little to say to Charlene. One of the other officers realized that Rico had been shot, and so had Charlene. "Let's call another ambulance."

"We don't need one," Charlene insisted. "Avery can drive us. We're going there anyway."

"Fine." The officer eyed her blood-soaked sweater. "Please go soon."

"All right." She needed to talk to Jack before she left, so she turned her back to the police and joined Avery, Jack, Marisol, and Rico, who'd moved inside the dining room for privacy. She shut the door. "What happened, Jack? It was a miracle. Thank you."

"I was able to knit the artery from the inside, as Marisol suggested," Jack said. He hadn't manifested his body but remained a very ghosty shadow of himself. "I feel very woozy."

Avery and Charlene stood on either side of him, wanting to help but unable to touch him.

A shining light appeared in the dining room with two portals to Heaven.

"I don't understand," Jack said.

Marisol beamed and was able to manifest her body in all its beauty. Lovely brown eyes, long chestnut hair.

Isabella cried with pure joy. "Mari!"

"Love is love, my sister. My regret for my actions is sincere, as is my love for you. Jack's act of service and love gave him another chance. We must go. Jack, will you join me in Heaven?"

Jack was bathed in golden light. "Charlene? Avery?"

"Go, Jack. You deserve this." Charlene wiped tears that seemed to be in gush mode from her eyes. Lose her best friend? He'd saved Sam—or tried to, and that counted for so much. "Thank you. Thank you for healing me when I first came here, and thank you for healing Sam."

"Be free, Jack." Avery's chin tilted as she dashed her knuckles over her cheeks. "Thank you for all you've done for me. For opening my eyes in many ways."

"I will miss our family," Jack said. His voice weakened, but then strengthened. "I love you both."

"I love you!" Charlene said.

This phrase was echoed by Avery. "Will you visit, if you can?"

After a long second his voice resonated, "I'll be the blue jay in the oak tree."

With a whirl of light through the ceiling, Marisol and Jack were gone.

Charlene fell against the dining room table, in shock at the events that had just transpired. Was Jack really gone? Would Sam survive the trip to the hospital?

"Not yet, Charlene," Avery whispered in her ear. "You can fall apart tomorrow. Let's go get you stitched up and check on Sam."

The ladies took a wide berth around the deceased Benjamin Fiske. The police had suspected him of murder, but the wily yacht salesman had evaded arrest. And now he would never be punished on this earth for his crimes.

Isabella and Rico traipsed after them. It was three in the morning. "The witching hour," Isabella said. "My sister came through at the witching hour. Something to remember."

"Someday I might just write that manual," Avery said.

Charlene panicked when she realized the Pilot was blocked by police vehicles, as was Isabella's and the rental van.

Avery dashed across the gravel and climbed into her smaller sedan, easily maneuvering around the others. She rolled down the window. "Hop in."

Charlene climbed in front, her biceps smarting. "The guests are not going to believe what happened here tonight."

"They're still partying strong," Avery said. "It's like that scene in *Hocus Pocus*, remember? Only they were bewitched."

"I want to sleep," Rico said, placing his hand on Isabella's knee in the back seat.

Isabella picked it up like it was a rat and moved it to his own leg.

"I'll text people from the hospital." Charlene prayed with all of her might that Sam was alive and that whatever Jack had done would be enough to keep him that way. "How are you, Rico?"

"I don't know where I was hit. I think my ear? It stings," Rico said. "I don't think Salem is good for me."

"About that," Isabella said. "I realize the timing could be better, but I am officially breaking up with you. You can keep the apartment in New York. I will stay in Salem."

Avery and Charlene glanced at each other with pleased smiles. That was an awesome outcome.

Charlene prayed the entire way to the hospital that Sam would live. Love was worth the risk. Third time had to be the charm. Sam.

CHAPTER 23

When they arrived at the hospital emergency room Avery had to circle twice because the place was so busy. "I'll drop you guys off here and park on the street. It won't take long."

"Are you sure?" Charlene saw dots before her eyes and suddenly her arm really hurt.

"Positive." Avery turned to Isabella in the back. "Will you help Charlene into the ER? I don't think she's feeling good."

"Of course," Isabella agreed.

"What about me?" Rico whined.

"What about you?" Isabella exited the back of the still-running car and went around to Charlene's side. She opened the door.

To Charlene's surprise, she listed slightly and almost slipped from the car to the asphalt. Isabella caught her under the arm.

Charlene yelped.

"Rico! Get on Charlene's other side."

Rico did as Isabella instructed.

"Don't forget her purse," Avery shouted, as if her voice was muffled in cotton. Or maybe that was Charlene's ears.

Isabella stepped back for it.

"I'll be there soon," Avery said. "She's probably in shock. She took a bullet that would have hit me, in the arm."

Isabella slammed the door closed and steadied Charlene, who leaned against Rico. They were nose to nose.

This close she could see a divot from the lobe of his ear. Probably from when Benjamin had sprayed her foyer with bullets. Before Sam had saved them all.

Slowly, the three of them entered the ER. It was packed with people still in full Day of the Dead make-up. Lots of people who suffered their wounds in silence, though a few groaned.

A nurse took notice of Charlene just as her knees buckled. She came around the check-in desk with an office chair. "Here you go."

"Thank you."

"We are out of wheelchairs up front. Probably all in the back. Let's get you checked in." The nurse had a friendly smile. "What's your name?"

"Charlene Morris. How is Detective Sam Holden?"

The nurse's gaze sharpened. "I'm afraid I can't share his condition."

Charlene blinked tears from her eyes, her hand trembling. "We are a couple," she said. "I have his family's information, if you need it. But it's probably all on file. He was shot protecting us. Did he make it?"

"I really wish I could tell you, but I can't." The nurse glanced around and lowered her voice. "He's here and in surgery." She put her finger to her lips. "Now, let's get you looked at, all right?"

Charlene could only nod her thanks.

Avery burst into the ER entrance, homing in on Charlene. "Hey! Dang, this place is packed. How's Sam?"

"We don't know yet. He's here, though, in good hands. Jack always believed the surgeons here were top-notch."

"You are?" the nurse asked the teen.

"Avery Shriver. Have you had a chance to examine Charlene's arm?"

"Not yet."

"She was shot," Avery said.

"Oh! Well, that does put you up on the list of priorities," the nurse said in a chiding tone. "You might have mentioned that before asking about the detective."

"I love him," Charlene said.

The nurse smiled. "Crazy the things we do in the name of love." She stood. "I'll locate a wheelchair and find you a room."

"What about me?" Rico gestured to his ear. "I was shot too."

"Same incident?" the nurse asked.

"Si," Rico replied.

The nurse examined Rico and then gestured to the bloody towel at Charlene's side. "She's still bleeding. Give me twenty minutes?"

"That's fine." Rico frowned at Isabella. "Will you at least sit with me?"

Isabella's mouth twisted, but she agreed. "Okay."

The ex-couple took the clipboard with the insurance paperwork to vacant chairs. Avery and Charlene were wheeled back to a cubicle separated by cloth curtains. Avery filled out the insurance forms because Charlene couldn't write. Shot in her right arm.

"You saved me," Avery said softly. "Legit threw your body over mine. I can never thank you enough."

"I didn't think about it—I love you." Charlene bowed her head. "And Sam did the same for us."

A harried doctor entered the curtained partition. "Knock, knock." He entered and nodded at Charlene and then at Avery, who placed the clipboard on the small side table. "Insurance is a bitch." He nodded at the bloody towels around Charlene's arm. "Let's have a peek, shall we?"

It hurt worse than any pain Charlene had ever had before as the doctor poked around her arm. "Ouch!"

"I think the bullet is still in there. It's going to need surgery. Is this your daughter?"

"Yes," Avery said, understanding that claiming family was the only way she'd get to stay with Charlene. It wasn't their first time.

"All right. Let's get your mom set up in a room and scheduled for surgery. What a night this has been. What happened?"

"I was shot at my bed-and-breakfast. Detective Sam Holden saved our lives from a killer. Is he okay?"

"I can't tell you that, of course—but I will look into what happened." The doctor's smile conveyed professional neutrality that didn't tell them squat.

"I liked the nurse better," Charlene murmured.

Within moments a nurse's aide arrived to give Charlene an IV for the pain. Avery stayed at her side. Suddenly it was too much. If Sam died, what would she do?

Charlene woke up the next day, patting her bed for Silva. Her hand was attached to tubes. Where was she? This was no garlic-induced nightmare. The memories crashed around her, and she recalled Jack saving Sam and going to Heaven. She gasped as it all came back.

"Charlene?" Avery was at her side in an instant.

"Hey." Charlene swallowed, her mouth dry. "Did you stay with me?"

"The nice nurse let me sleep in the chair. The other nurse is not so lenient and will only allow two visitors at a time. Your mom just left to get coffee. Your dad is in the waiting room. We've been taking turns."

Charlene couldn't fathom a simple shot to the arm being so important.

"The bullet nicked a vein. You were bleeding profusely." Avery's gaze conveyed relief. "The doctor acted in time, though."

"How's Sam?"

"They won't tell us." Avery's pale face grew shadowed. "I may or may not have snuck over to the ICU where he is right now. He's hooked up to a bunch of machines."

"Alive?" Tears stung her eyes again, damn it. When would they stop?

Avery cleared her throat. "He hasn't woken up yet." She raised her hand. "I did some Google research. Sleep is the best way to let his body heal. I talked to Detective Jimenez when she visited, but she was her usual noncommunicative self. I'll chat up my other friends at the station to find out more. Officer Bernard has a big heart."

Sam was alive, if not awake. That was better than dead. "Be careful. You don't want to risk your career over something like this. But thank you, Avery."

Just then, her mom entered the hospital room. Her strides were brisk as she brought in a tray of coffee that smelled like pumpkin spice. She set it on the table and arrived at Charlene's side. Her glasses fogged with tears. "I've talked with June and Daniel, Sam's parents. We will pick them up from the airport to bring them here. Honey, they told me that Sam hasn't woken up from the anesthesia yet. The doctors are monitoring him carefully. He's a fighter, as we know."

She did know that. "I'm so glad you and Dad are friends with the Holdens. They won't tell me and Avery anything, but it's like you to find out the scoop."

Her mom patted Charlene's knee.

Charlene wanted out of the hospital bed. "When can I leave?"

Her mom passed Avery a coffee and took the top off a third one. "I thought you might like this smell, though I don't know when you will be released or be allowed to eat." Her voice quivered. "The doctor wants to talk to you."

Just then a knock sounded on her door. The doctor was there, with her dad. Dad looked older to her somehow, as if bowed by worry.

Avery took her coffee and stood in the shadows so as not to be booted from the room and the two-visitor-only rule.

"Charlene Morris? I'm Dr. Laughlin." He read the charts. "You are a fortunate woman. You could have lost your arm, but we managed to save it. Physical therapy should provide seventy-five percent range of motion."

"What?" She hadn't realized the severity of her injury.

"We'll keep you here another night and release you then, but only if you can promise that you'll have help at home."

"She does," Avery said.

"She will have even more," her parents agreed. Charlene, frightened for Sam but grateful for her family, nodded.

"I will follow directions to the letter." Charlene recalled her full house. "How are our guests?"

Avery edged from the shadows. "Minnie and Will are waiting for Detective Jimenez to give the all-clear so they can clean up the crime scene. Our guests were allowed to get their things. They send you their best wishes and understand why their stay was cut short by a day."

"We will need to send them a credit," Charlene said.

"On it." Avery held up her hand.

"Guests?" the doctor queried.

"We run a bed-and-breakfast. Charlene's, on Crown Pointe Road." Charlene's eyelids felt heavy.

"Doesn't that require a lot of physical activity?" the

doctor asked with suspicion. "I won't release you to your home without your promise to take it easy. I could suggest rehab."

Charlene widened her eyes. "I promise!"

"We will all help out," her mother said, Dad at her side. Charlene dozed off.

By the end of the day Charlene had practiced doodling her lists with her left hand. She was grateful for her phone and voice-to-text because she couldn't read her own handwriting.

Seth and Dani had stopped in with flowers. Avery had gone home for a nap. Brandy, Kass, and Isabella visited for short periods, and her parents were a constant.

Detective Jimenez showed up at six that evening. Her gray eyes lasered on Charlene as if to say that if Sam died, she would take out Charlene with pleasure and toss her in the ocean to feed the fishes.

"I have some questions about what happened the other night."

"Of course," Charlene said.

"Did you know Benjamin Fiske?"

"No."

"Persephone Lowell said he sent you his business card. Your mother gave it to us. His prints were on it. Not that it matters because the criminal is deceased. The prints match a tracker found on your Pilot."

"A tracker?"

"Yes. According to the notes on his phone, he planned to take you and Isabella that night when he rammed you. He was on the bench, watching. He'd never kidnapped two women before, and he was ready to up his game before he killed you both."

"When did he do that?" Charlene remembered that Benjamin had been at Cod and Capers that day. "How difficult was it to do?"

"They are the size of a quarter," Jimenez said. "There was one under the front bumper. He could have done it very simply."

"So, when Rico hopped out to chase his truck, he took off."

"Benajmin probably hadn't planned on a third party." The detective exhaled. "We will never know for sure."

"So, because he was thwarted then, he decided to come to my house? He knew where I was at all times."

"At least the location of your car. It's difficult when we don't get answers and now, with the perpetrator dead, we never will. The photos on his phone and what we found in his yacht are sickening." Jimenez tucked her thumb into her suit jacket pocket. "For a while we thought it might be Brian Preston behind the disappearance. He had an owl charm that Isabella said was missing from her sister's bracelet."

"I wondered about that! I'd seen it on Brian's key chain."

"He said that Marisol gave it to him." Again, the detective could only shrug.

"Did you find the statue of Santa Muerte?"

"We did. On the yacht. I've spoken to Isabella about it . . . she'll get it back once the investigation concludes. It was terrible that her missing person report was never filed." Jimenez stepped toward the door. "I've let your housekeeper know they can start cleaning your place."

With that, Jimenez was gone.

Though Charlene had been officially discharged, she spent every day at the hospital with her parents, Sam's parents, and Avery. The chaplain prayed with them for Sam's full recovery.

By the end of the week, when her sling itched and she longed for a shower where she could wash her own hair, she regretted her promise in front of witnesses. Daniel and June Holden were lovely people. They had Sydney, Sam's sister, on FaceTime. Charlene's parents drove her when Avery wasn't around.

Avery had talked to her teachers and was doing her schoolwork remotely for the next few days, but she had to be back in class the following Monday. Sam would want her to continue.

It was Charlene's turn to be in the visiting room. Only one person was allowed to be in it at night. She took Sam's hand in hers and thought with gratitude of all the sweet memories they shared. Her tears landed on their clasped fingers. "We've had good times, Sam Holden."

His fingers moved.

She lifted her gaze to his golden-brown eyes staring back at her. "We have had wonderful times."

"Sam!"

He gave her a weak smile beneath his mustache, which she'd helped groom over the last five days.

"I know I'm not dreaming. If I was dreaming, you'd be beside me in this bed." His eyes closed.

Charlene laughed. "That can be arranged if it will bring you back to full health."

His eyes opened, twinkling. "I love you, Charlene."

"I love you."

"Considering how our lives are constantly in upheaval, I'd better ask you right now—will you marry me?"

"Yes, Sam. Yes, I will."

"In that case, I will make a full recovery."

Sam passed out again, but Charlene knew everything was going to be okay. She raced into the hall to find the nurse, and Sam's father, who had decided to stay. Everyone took turns, believing that the love they shared for Sam would bring him through.

"Sam just woke up!"

The nurses grinned, as did Daniel. They all raced to the room, but Sam was sleeping peacefully.

At eight, Sam was wide awake and chatting as if nothing had ever happened.

"How's Avery? And Rover?" Sam asked.

"Your dog loves your mother's eggs," Daniel said.

"Let me call Avery. I know she'll want to see you for herself." Charlene left father and son talking in soft whispers.

Avery answered on the first ring and sobbed happy tears when Charlene shared that Sam was awake. She kept the proposal to herself, just in case it wasn't something Sam remembered doing.

When she entered the hospital room again Daniel

stood and gave her a giant hug. "I'm going to pick up June. We'll be back in an hour or so."

"Tell her hi." Charlene faced the hospital bed from the threshold.

"Shut the door, will you?"

"Sure."

"Come here, Charlene." Sam patted the bed at his side.

She lowered the railing and sat carefully.

Sam handed her the ring box. "I love you. It's time that we make this official."

"Sam! I wasn't sure if you were delusional the last time you asked."

He opened the box, his shoulders shaking with laughter. "Only you would think that. I don't know what happened to me that night at the house."

Charlene's stomach clenched.

"I have so many questions—but at the end of the day, none of that matters. I want to spend my life with you. If you will have the fool who didn't just believe you."

Charlene was speechless—but not for long. "I love you too. Yes."

He slipped the ring on her finger. Charlene's heart filled with joy.

A knock sounded and Detective Jimenez poked her head in. She noticed Charlene sitting on the bed and the ring on Charlene's finger. She swallowed hard. "I can't stay. Just heard the good news that you were awake. Congratulations."

With that, the detective left. The woman loved Sam. There was no helping who you loved, for better or worse.

Charlene hoped that she would find another person to love. She was proof that you could have more than one.

"What was that?" Sam asked.

"Jimenez loves you," Charlene said.

"No way. I . . . really?" He shook his head.

"It's why she never really liked me in your life."

"Oh, damn." Sam sighed and smoothed his mustache. "This will make things awkward at work."

"It doesn't have to. Treat her the same as always. She's a good detective," Charlene said. "She located the Santa Muerte statue on Benjamin Fiske's yacht. He wanted to kidnap me and Isabella both to up his game—two victims instead of one. Thanks to you, he's never going to kill again."

Sam's jaw clenched. "I've got no regrets with how that played out." He noticed the sling on her arm. "You were shot too."

"And I'm fine. We get a happy ending, Sam. I'll take it."

"Isabella?"

"She broke up with Rico and is going to stay in Salem for a while. Kass has a spare room and can always use help with her tea."

"Now what?" Sam asked, smoothing her hair from her cheek.

"We heal. My arm is going to take physical therapy, and I don't think you're going to be released for duty any time soon."

Sam gave a low growl.

"But your parents are here to help. Sydney and Jim want to come for Thanksgiving."

"My house is not my own. I should have gotten us that midweek vacation place with the hot tub."

Charlene laughed, just grateful to have Sam alive. "No complaining about being loved."

The door opened and Avery rushed in. She saw the diamond and squealed. "Yay! It's about time, Sam."

"I better hurry between catastrophes," Sam said.

"I just talked to the nurses and they don't think you are going to be released for at least a week." Avery pulled up a chair. "How's your appetite? Minnie is making your favorites."

"I will never say no to Minnie's food."

Daniel and June arrived with flowers and champagne. Daniel had known that Sam was going to propose.

Her parents showed up, too, having heard the news, and they celebrated Sam and Charlene's engagement in the hospital room, as a family.

CHAPTER 24

June

Charlene Morris sat before the vanity mirror in her
bathroom, applying her mascara for the second
time. She kept getting emotional, which ruined the
makeup. She wore her gold earrings from Jared, which
showed to perfection with her hair swept up off her
nape. For a wedding present Sam had given her a gold
heart-shaped locket with their pictures inside of it. On
her ring finger was the giant diamond he'd finally pro-
posed to her with immediately after waking in the hospital.

Over six months had passed since Sam was shot and
saved by Jack. Jack had literally knitted him together
from the inside—and this unselfishness had given Jack
another opportunity for Heaven that he'd accepted.

She missed her ghost every single day. Silva and
Avery missed him too. It was as if a tiny piece of her
heart had gone with Jack that night. He'd promised to

be the blue jay in the oak tree, but despite a gorgeous spring and now a lovely summer, there hadn't been a single blue jay sighting.

She imagined Jack in Heaven, getting interviewed by God and the other angels. They'd be welcoming to the man he'd been, both dead and alive. Nobody was perfect, and this journey was one of learning. And love. So much love.

Damn it! Her eyes welled again, and she dabbed the corners with a tissue.

A knock sounded from the bedroom door that separated her living area, Jack's armchair, and her bed.

"Charlene?" Avery's voice was soft and caring. She'd finished her second year with high grades and incredible remarks from her professors on her intelligence and maturity.

"In here!" Charlene tossed the wadded-up tissue to the vanity's top. "I'm a mess. Tell me a joke or something, would you?"

Avery, in a pale blue silk sundress, her short hair in a very grown-up twist, entered, pausing in the doorway of the bathroom.

The young lady immediately understood that Charlene was on the edge, though she might not completely understand why.

"A horse walks into a bar. The bartender says, *Why the long face?*"

The silly joke worked, and Charlene started to laugh. "I adore you, Avery Shriver."

She tapped a manicured nail to her chin. Avery, Charlene, and Charlene's mother had gone in for manis, pedis, and facials just yesterday. "And I, Charlene

Morris-soon-to-be Holden, love you. How does that feel?"

"Scary—but in a good way." Charlene sorted through the memories of what had been with Jared, and with Jack, and now could be with Sam because of it. "How did I get so lucky?"

Avery slipped her arm around Charlene and looked at their images in the vanity mirror. "I ask myself that all the time. I don't know if there is an answer, outside of our hearts."

"You are a wise woman. I'm glad that you're my maid of honor."

"Brenda was going to wrestle me for it until you asked her and your dad to walk you down the aisle."

Charlene chuckled.

The afternoon ceremony would take place at three, with a fancy dinner at Cod and Capers afterward.

The main topic of discussion, which hadn't been decided as of yet, was whether or not Sam would move to the B&B, or if Charlene would move to Sam's house.

Despite their love, it was a difficult compromise. Why did marriage need to be about one person giving up something for the other?

Sam, and Rover, stayed overnight here occasionally, but it wasn't as easy for Sam because Charlene didn't have a fenced yard.

Charlene didn't think that Silva would be all right in Sam's smaller house and, besides that, this place was also her business, and so she needed to be here most days anyway.

When she was away at Sam's, Minnie or Avery cared for Silva.

"What are you thinking?" Avery asked. She curved her hand over Charlene's shoulder.

"You don't want to know." Charlene glanced at Avery with concern.

"Yes, I do. It's obvious that something isn't settled. I'm here if you want to talk about it." Avery smiled. "You know that the advice you gave to Seth about talking with his mom and his changing degrees really helped."

"This feels more complicated." Charlene put her hand over her heart. "It probably isn't, but you're right. I need to talk to Sam." She stood. "Do you know where he is?"

Avery's gaze clouded. "Uh-oh."

Charlene hugged the young woman to her. "No need for that response. If worst comes to worst, maybe Sam and I will find a home that we both like together that fits our needs." She released Avery and stepped back. "Not that I plan on dying soon, but just so you know, I've left you the B-and-B in my will."

Avery stumbled, and Charlene caught her shoulder.

Head shaking, Avery swiped a tear from her cheek. "Why?"

"You are a daughter to me, and I know that Jack felt the same." Charlene's dratted eyes welled up again, and she carefully dabbed her lashes.

"The B-and-B, though?"

"I love you. Who else is going to get my things? It's not like Sam and I are having children. Good Lord! Can you imagine the hellions they'd be?" Charlene burst out laughing at the idea of cute toddlers with glorious mustaches.

"What about Sam?"

"He already knows my evil plan and is totally okay with it—you might not have noticed, but he also thinks of you as a daughter and protegée."

"I always thought I'd be . . . well . . . needing to find my own home."

"You still can!" Charlene assured her. "But you will also inherit this one. Maybe someday you and Seth can have babies. . . ."

Avery gave a delicate snort. "Don't rush us. We've discussed the fact that we don't want anybody else, but school comes first."

"I'm really happy for you guys." Charlene blew out a breath and checked the time. She still had an hour before three. "I'm going to talk to Sam."

"The bride and groom aren't supposed to see each other before the ceremony," Avery said.

She and Sam had slept together last night at his house, so they'd already broken the rules. It was the benefit of a second marriage and being well over forty. Charlene's stomach fluttered.

"It's fine. It really is." Suddenly her heart was lighter. It didn't matter about the house or the dog or cat; what mattered most was Sam.

"Meet you in the foyer?" Avery called as Charlene hurried out, her ivory lace gown, something she and her mother had found at Vintage Treasures and re-designed, brushing against the love seat.

Minnie, in the kitchen to prepare appetizers and hand out champagne after the nuptials and before the big dinner, stopped Charlene with a concerned expression.

"What is it, Minnie?"

"How are you faring?" Minnie had decided to let her hair go gray and cut the shag short. It actually made her look younger.

"I'm fine, thank you. Why do you ask?"

"I've noticed that you leave your suite door open more often now and hardly ever have the TV on." Minnie's silver brow crooked upward over her glasses. She wore a flowered apron over a light pink skirt and top.

Of course Minnie would notice. The elaborate ruse had been to keep her conversations with Jack a secret. "I guess I was feeling lonely when I first moved here," Charlene said. "Now I don't."

Minnie hugged Charlene carefully, mindful of the delicate lace dress. "It makes me very happy to hear that." She pulled a note from her apron pocket. "From Brandy. She's offered a getaway car if you change your mind."

"What?" Charlene swayed on her three-inch heels. "That's silly."

Minnie's lips twitched. "That's what I told her. Why on earth would you want to leave Sam?" Her wrinkled hand clasped Charlene's wrist and her housekeeper grew somber. "But if you did, Charlene, I would support you. I might tell you that you're making a giant mistake to give up those broad shoulders, but I would still do it."

Charlene's gaze grew cloudy with tears. "Minnie!"

"It's nothing against Sam, because he is a man of honor and integrity, but my loyalty is to you," Minnie said.

Charlene's heart ached. She'd never in her life had

friends like this. "I would support any decision you ever made as well."

"I know that." Minnie made a shooing motion. "Sam is in the living room, examining the mantel. Maybe he has some ideas for a different style of wood?"

"Thank you." Charlene walked past the kitchen table, but no silver paw reached out to snag her ivory shoes. Silva was probably in the living room with Sam.

Sam had learned that Avery had hit her head on the mantel and, through that injury to her head, been able to see Jack.

They had talked about Jack until Charlene couldn't give any more information. Avery had also answered questions, but it didn't provide proof.

It was enough for Charlene that Sam was alive and damn the proof. They'd agreed not to discuss it, and Jack hadn't been a topic of conversation since March-ish.

Her parents had believed her without proof. She didn't let Sam's obstinate nature get in the way of their loving union.

They didn't have to agree on everything. All the marriage professionals said so.

Charlene entered the living room, accepting Sam by the mantel instead of Jack. She recalled how desperate Jack had been to reach her, appearing in a turquoise blue smoking jacket. He'd opened her mind.

Sam's black suit had been made for him. The shoulders fit perfectly, the length of the slacks hitting the heels of his black boots. His brown hair had been recently styled, though he kept it short. He smelled like sandalwood and pine and just Sam.

She would recognize that scent anywhere.

He'd groomed his mustache so that it was silky and waved to his clean-shaven jaw.

Damn but he was a good-looking man. Her insides clenched as she recalled how they'd spent the night before. They were a match in the ways that mattered.

He saw her, and his eyes turned a warm golden brown, glinting with mischief.

"What are you doing here, bride-to-be?" Sam's drawl brought goose bumps.

Charlene reached his side and put her hand on his chest. She could feel his heart beat beneath the suit jacket.

"Sam . . . if you really want me to move into your place, I will." She glanced up into his compassionate gaze.

"I was thinking, Charlene." Sam touched the heart locket and the gold at her ears. It had been his idea to include them in their ceremony. Without Jared, she wouldn't be the woman she was right now. "Why do we have to choose?"

Her knees buckled and he caught her to his body.

"What do you mean?"

"Our marriage is our marriage. Who says that we have to change addresses?" Sam's fingers skimmed her locket, and her skin hummed, electric.

"I've been worried about that . . ."

"I know." Sam placed his hand over hers and brought it to his chest. "I can feel your concern. I want you to know that I will gladly move in here. We just need to build a fence so that Rover doesn't get loose."

Charlene nodded. "A perfect solution. I can spend three days a week at your place, and you can do the same here. We can alternate odd days." She looked into Sam's beloved face, her heart singing.

"Exactly!" Sam said. "I still need to travel for work, so it makes sense for you to be here on those days."

"I can take care of Rover at the B-and-B once we build the fence." Charlene felt like she might levitate with joy at any moment.

Sam swooped down to kiss her. His lips were firm and filled with heat that made her melt. Charlene responded and then groaned.

"What?" Sam brushed her cheek with his knuckles.

"Now I have to do my makeup again." Tears spilled down her cheeks, but she was so dang happy that she really didn't care.

On the lawn a hundred white chairs had been set out, white rose petals created a path so there were fifty on either side. Charlene was between her mother and her father. The music played and the three of them began to walk.

Sam waited by the oak tree. Avery, stunning, held a bouquet of peach roses and sage greens that was a simpler version of Charlene's. A priest from Mom's church held a book of prayers. Brandy, Serenity, and Evelyn were to the left, with Kass, Kevin, Amy, and Franco to the right. Friends of Sam from the department were there. Jimenez was absent. Rover was with Sydney and Seth held Silva.

It was three o'clock, and for some reason Charlene remembered that it was the Witching Hour. She glanced toward the oak tree as she reached Sam.

There, watching her from a leafy branch, was a turquoise-blue blue jay.